D1500153

THE ART OF LOSING

Rebecca Connell

THE ART OF LOSING

Newfoundland Area Public Library

Newfoundland, PA 18445 (570) 676-4518

Europa
editions

Europa Editions
116 East 16th Street
New York, N.Y. 10003
www.europaeditions.com
info@europaeditions.com

This book is a work of fiction. Any references to historical events,
real people, or real locales are used fictitiously.

Copyright © 2009 by Rebecca Connell
First Publication 2010 by Europa Editions

All rights reserved, including the right of reproduction
in whole or in part in any form.

Library of Congress Cataloging in Publication Data is available
ISBN 978-1-933372-78-5

Connell, Rebecca
The Art of Losing

Book design by Emanuele Ragnisco
www.mekkanografici.com

Cover illustration © Mk Lane

Prepress by Plan.ed – Rome

Printed in Canada

CONTENTS

THE ART OF LOSING

For my parents, Nigel and Elaine,
and my husband, Daniel Cormack—
thank you for all your love and support so far.

LOUISE
2007

U ntil I was ten, my father told me a bedtime story every night. I suppose that in the early days the stories covered the usual ground, but after my mother died they changed. His new stories were all about her. Sometimes he would attempt to disguise them a little, holding up a book as if he were reading from it, but I wasn't fooled. Other times he would simply sit at my bedside and pour out memories—his own, and those she had passed on to him. Often they made him cry, and I would comfort him.

I thought for many years that the stories were my father's way of keeping her alive for me; that he was anxious not only that I should not forget her but that I should learn even more about her than I would have done if she had lived. Now I don't believe those were his motives at all. It was simply that there were no other stories he could tell. When she died, it closed off all other avenues, and for many years circling around these old memories was a compulsion and not a choice.

The last story he ever told me started off innocuously enough. Out at a party together, my parents had begun talking to a woman who claimed to be clairvoyant, and my father, instantly fascinated, asked her to read their future. The woman spun a pretty tale: two children, plenty of travelling, long and happy lives. My mother seemed to accept her words readily enough, but when they left the party she exclaimed how ridiculous it had been. Still basking in the rosy glow of the predicted future, my father was a little hurt, and questioned her on how she could be so sure that everything the woman had foreseen would not come to pass. She stopped dead in the middle of the road to face him, and said, evenly and quietly, *Because I won't live past forty*. Irrational as they were, her words upset my father, and he demanded to know what she meant. She shrugged, and refused to elaborate. The next day, when he asked again, she claimed drunkenness and laughed the incident off, but in retrospect he believed that she was the one with the second sight—another attribute, albeit an unwanted one, to add to her extensive list.

When he finished this tale I was quiet, not knowing how or what I should reply. The point of the stories had always been that they were happy, but this one had left an unpleasant taste in my mouth and an eerie feeling sliding up and down my spine. My father was quiet, too, for a long while, staring down at the pink patterned coverlet. Although I can't remember his expression, I can guess at what it would have been: the familiar lost, uncomprehending blanket of despair that was his face's default setting after his wife's death. After what seemed like hours, he heaved himself to his feet and left the bedroom without a word. When the next night came I half dreaded the bedtime story, but there was none forthcoming. The explanation was that I was getting too old for such things. Even at that age I knew better. The truth was that I was too young for the stories he had left—the stories he really wanted to tell.

I exercise it rarely, this talent I have. Scurrying down darkening streets, shivering in my rain-slicked clothes, I allow my muscles to relax into a familiar rhythm. I'm a dancer remembering a long-forgotten dance, a gymnast whose body instinctively recalls the twists and turns set aside many years ago. I haven't played this game since school. Back then, I used to skulk behind an admired teacher as he made his way from classroom to car park, always keeping a few steps behind. As he unlocked his car and drove off I would be there watching, only yards away, my breath still shallow from the excitement of the pursuit. He never noticed me. I have this talent for following.

The man I am following now is just as oblivious. He thinks he is alone, but ever since he left the lecture hall, I've been with him. Down the high street, I slide through the crowd like mercury. His heavy burgundy coat glints wetly ahead like a jewel. As I keep my eyes on that coat now, I can't help but compare it to my own. I want to be wrapped up in his coat, engulfed in its warmth. It would swamp me; he must be six foot two, a clear eight inches above me. It would smell of—what? Cigarettes: I saw him light up as he left the hall, cupping his hand to shield the tiny flame from the wind. I'm getting too close. I hang back as his pace slows, counting my steps in my head.

Abruptly he stops, as if hearing his name called. I shrink back into the recesses of a doorway as he puts a hand to the back of his neck. He's forgotten something, perhaps—a book, an umbrella, a scarf. No. He's simply forgotten himself—passed his destination. He hurries back up the road and ducks into a brightly coloured café, swinging the door shut behind him. I wait a few moments, then sidle up to the café, leaning back against its wet orange wall. Through the rainwater that streaks the window-glass, I watch. He's settled into a table near the window, rummaging in his bag to withdraw a newspaper, turning the pages with the enjoyment of a ritualised routine. A minute later, a waitress brings him a cup, and I see his lips move in silent thanks. I watch him for five, ten minutes. His black hair is heavily threaded with silver; closer than I've been before, I can see fine lines exploding out across his face. I know that he must be fifty-five years old.

The letter he wrote almost twenty years ago is in my pocket. Its words are always with me. They run through my head when I talk, an almost-heard undercurrent bubbling just below consciousness. I tap them on an imaginary keyboard, my fingers digging privately into my palm. Close to my heart, I keep them folded up tightly in their faded paper everywhere I go. The name at the top of this letter is not mine, but I intend to borrow it for a while.

The lights in the café are so dizzily bright that when Lydia turns away they're still imprinted on the damp grey alleyway in front of her like the afterglow of a camera flash. She blinks, once, again, to jolt herself out of the cocoon he has wrapped her up in. It works. The cold returns and clamps her like a vise. Suddenly she's alone on the street with no idea where she is.

Lydia wakes without warning, dragged up sharply by the sudden dip of her elbow off the ledge. For a second she glances around bewildered, expecting to see the cool blue walls of the rented attic room encircling her. The dreamlike hour that has passed drips back into her mind: rising after too little sleep, riding down town to the faculty lecture hall in the November half-light, falling into her seat. When she arrived the hall was almost deserted. Now it's packed with students, huddled in little groups and chatting, their steady buzz of conversation punctuated by shrieks of laughter and groans of disbelief. A few are still snoozing, heads pillowed on the wooden ledges. Undisturbed, Lydia watches them all. The snatches of conversation she picks up are inane but compelling. She has never had this: the easy banter between friends, the talk of nights out unrestricted by parental guidelines or curfews.

She is leaning forward to listen more intently when she sees a boy sitting a few seats along the row, watching her. Dark hair swept over his face and stubble prickling his chin. Curious eyes that look hazel in the sunlit hall. He's looking at her insolently, half smiling, as if he's thinking, *I know what you're up to.* As she catches his eye, there's none of the embarrassed gaze-shifting she expects, only a slow deliberate wink. Flushing, she scowls at him and looks quickly away. A moment later she risks a swift glance back to check that he is properly subdued. He isn't. He's laughing, and when he catches her eye again he mouths something. She doesn't get it at first, and can't resist a puzzled frown. The boy leans farther towards her and mouths the phrase again, full lips moving soundlessly and exaggeratedly among the noise around them. *Forgive me*, they say.

She bites the bubble of laughter back into her throat as the lecturer walks down the aisle and takes the stage. He's wearing a long trench coat, his black hair swept back into peaks, highlighting the silver strands running through it. As he strides to the podium the students fall silent, settling expectantly back in their seats. He takes a moment to survey the room, holding his audience, then starts to speak. Although she knows that she must have heard his voice many times as a child, she has been unable to recapture it in her head, and yet it has a familiar quality; deep, powerful and harsh.

'Sensibility,' he says. 'It's a word that has become downgraded over the centuries. Now, it aligns itself with sentimentality, and that carries a pejorative ring—mawkish, oversensitive, weak.' He spits out the words one by one. 'But sensibility was once the encapsulation of the finest feelings of which man was capable. An acute sensitivity to emotion, significance, mortality, all the things that still surround us in modern society but which are more often forced underground than brought out into the open. This was a different time, a time where a man crying at the symbolism of a caged bird was accepted as part of the natural order of life. Such over-analysis, such keen awareness of pathos and significance in every living creature, be it man or fly, was actively celebrated—and satirised too, of course, as every great movement is—'

She is dragged away from his words by a muted commotion a little farther down the row. With horror she sees that the dark-haired boy is nudging his neighbour and passing a folded piece of paper, whispering in her ear and gesticulating. His friend puts up a show of resistance, rolling her eyes laughingly, but takes it and turns to her neighbour in turn. The paper makes its whispering way down the row until it reaches the girl sitting next to Lydia, who passes it on with a look of contempt. Lydia smiles at her apologetically—*we're on the same side*—but the other girl turns away and makes a great show of listening to the lecture. Hurriedly, Lydia unfolds the paper and smooths it out on the ledge. The note is written in uneven capitals, like those a child might use. YOU LOOK VERY SERIOUS, it says. I'VE NEVER SEEN ANYONE PAY SO MUCH ATTENTION TO A LECTURE. OR ARE YOU JUST IGNORING ME?

She puts the note to one side and tries to focus her attention back on the front of the stage, but she can't concentrate, the lecturer's words flowing over her in an incomprehensible torrent. Angrily, she snatches the paper up and writes quickly. *In case you hadn't noticed, everyone is concentrating, except you. Only someone very presumptuous would assume that a complete stranger should be looking at him rather than listening to the lecture. P.S. Your handwriting is terrible. I'm surprised they even let you in.* She refolds the paper and passes it to the unamused girl next to her, who shoots Lydia a look of scorn and pushes it to her left without looking at it. It's only five minutes before the paper boomerangs back. This time the girl lets out a long sigh and hands it to Lydia pointedly. She's right; this has gone far enough. Lydia determines to read the note and then crumple it into a ball and discard it, no matter what its contents.

WE USE COMPUTERS NOW, it reads. ANYWAY, THERE'S NO POINT ME CONCENTRATING. I HEAR ALL THIS AT HOME, THE LECTURER IS MY FATHER.

The last words hit her square in the chest. She looks back up at the figure at the lectern, tall and imposing, dressed in black. She can't connect this boy with him, or all she knows of him.

'The concept of an emotional journey is one we haven't lost,' the lecturer is saying now. 'But we've transfigured it into trite Hollywood movies, where a journey can be as simple as going from A to B with a ready-made message at the end of the rainbow. The ugly duckling transforms into a swan, and finds that in the end it's her inner beauty that has captured the high-school jock and that looks don't matter after all. Sterne's concept of a journey was very different. Here we learn more about the travelling than the arriving; false starts, irrelevant-seeming diversions, every emotion of the traveller dissected.' It seems to Lydia that his eyes are fixed on hers, blotting the rest of the hall out in a messy blur of light. 'Which is the more real? Which is the more true to life? Do we still understand the meaning of sensibility, or are our attempts at sensitivity, at love, little more than hollow flights of fancy?'

A sudden burst of nausea jolts her into action. She stumbles to her feet and pushes past the row of students, fighting her way towards the aisle. Heaving the oak door open, she lurches out into the cool dark hallway. She presses her head against the stone wall, so hard that she feels a jolt of pain pass through her. The sickness soon fades, but she knows she can't go back in there. She stands alone in the corridor, listening to the unmoved hum of the lecturer's voice behind the door, until a faint noise makes her swing round. The dark-haired boy is standing silhouetted at the end of the corridor, watching.

'I thought I should follow you,' he says simply, shuffling forward. 'I felt bad. Was it something I said?'

'No,' she mutters. 'I felt faint for a moment. I shouldn't have left. It's nothing.'

The boy moves closer. Up close he seems different, his initial cockiness replaced by a charming diffidence which makes it hard for her not to look at him. His eyes are fringed blackly with long lashes like a girl's, but there's something in the hard set of his jaw which she realises now does echo the lecturer's granite-carved face. 'Good,' he says. 'I thought it was me.' He breaks off and throws her a small smile. 'Presumptuous again,' he says.

'Sorry about that,' she says, hurriedly. 'I just couldn't understand why you were looking at me.'

'Really?' The boy looks her full in the eyes for a second, holding the gaze until she breaks it. 'I'm Adam,' he continues, extending his hand so that she has no choice but to take it. 'Just to get the introductions over with.'

'Lydia,' she says, and the name still feels strange on her tongue.

'Pleased to meet you.' Adam clears his throat. She knows this should be her opportunity to get away, to thank him for his concern and abandon the situation before it grows more complex, but she can't seem to rouse herself. 'What college are you at?' he asks now, smiling again and leaning back against the wall.

'Jesus,' she says automatically without considering her answer. She's picked a college she has never even seen, which she knows nothing about.

'Really?' Adam says eagerly. 'I'm at Lincoln. I'm surprised I haven't seen you on the street before, or in the Turl.' With difficulty she remembers that this is a pub which must presumably be near by. She shrugs. 'So what do you think of Sterne?' he asks, gesturing back towards the lecture hall.

This is too much of a minefield. 'Actually, I'm not doing English,' she says. 'I was just interested by the topic and thought I'd come along. I don't know much about it. I'm doing—' She pauses fractionally, trying to settle on a subject of which Adam might reasonably be expected to have little knowledge. 'Geology.'

'Wow,' he says. 'Interesting.' She forces a smile in response. 'So what are you doing tonight?'

'I don't know,' she says feebly. His rapid questions and

subject changes are starting to exhaust her. 'I have some work to do.'

'I'm going clubbing,' Adam volunteers. He names a place that she remembers passing a few nights back, and moving quickly away from as a gaggle of drunken students lurched out of its doors and started loudly heckling her. 'I might see you there?'

She nods. She wants to get away now. This isn't why she's here, and she doesn't want this boy to complicate things. She starts to edge away down the corridor.

'I'll see you,' she says vaguely.

'O.K.' He makes no attempt to follow her, and for a second she is perversely disappointed. She's almost at the door when he calls her back. She turns expectantly. He's smiling again, hands in his pockets, still lounging against the wall. Just as in the lecture hall, his lips move silently, exaggeratedly. *I was looking at you*, they say, *because I think you look amazing*. The unspoken words ring in her head. She turns and pushes her way outside, sharp winter air suddenly knocking the breath from her and making her light headed. Without knowing why, she breaks into a run.

When she is back in her bedroom it is still before eleven o'clock. She falls asleep again in the blink of an eye, and dreams of things that leave her lost and lonely when she wakes again and finds nothing but silence, silence and solitude and memories of people and places and things that feel so, so long ago that they seem to have happened to someone else—someone else entirely.

There are too many people in the club. After over an hour's wait in the queue, Lydia hands her rain-sodden coat over to the cloakroom, then heads for the dance-floor. She pushes her way into the centre of the crowd, letting the rhythm of the dancing carry her along, closing her eyes as music thumps and screeches above her. She wants to get a drink, but the bar seems so far away that she's not sure she'll ever reach it. Gasping for breath, she elbows a path through the mass of dancers, following the twisting gaps and breaks between groups as if she is tracing the tangles of a densely knotted necklace. When she eventually reaches the edge of the bar she grabs it tightly, looking back at what she has come from. Neon-lit heads bob in the air like beads of rain trembling on a washing line. She can't see the expressions on their faces, features blurred out in bursts of flashing red and green light. The music is changing now. Frenetic beats give way to slower, grittier rhythms, and the heads respond to it, bowing and swooping gravely back and forth.

She turns to the barman and motions him towards her. 'Water,' she shouts, but he seems not to hear her. She tries to shout louder, but her voice cracks and dries up. Instead she points at random at one of the bottles behind the bar. The barman nods and pours her a small glass of liquid that could be any colour, rippling over chunks of ice. She hands him a five-pound note and waits for change that never comes, taking a sip of the drink. It's vodka, pure and strong, hitting the back of her throat like fire. As she takes another gulp, she catches sight of herself in the long row of mirrors behind the bar. A strobe light sweeps across and dyes her dark brown hair a dazzling white blonde, and for a second she looks like someone else and what she sees makes her turn quickly away.

Ever since she reached the club she's been looking for Adam, somewhere in the back of her mind, but it's only now that she sees him. He's standing on a raised podium, a vantage point from which he is scanning the dance-floor. His dark hair curls around the collar of a bright white T-shirt, bare arms folded in front of him. He's not looking at her, but he's looking for someone, that much is clear. Before she can think about it, she leaves the bar and runs up the steps, weaving her way round the room. It takes her only a minute, but by the time she reaches him, he's not alone. Another boy and two girls have joined him and all four are laughing together: they've found him before he found them. The boy has white-blond hair cropped to the curve of his scalp, wiry shoulders under a black T-shirt. His arm is slung around one of the girls, a Latin-looking brunette in a short skirt and knee-high boots, rocking from foot to foot to the rhythm of the music. The other girl is closest to Adam. Lydia watches as she snakes her arm around his neck, having to raise herself on tiptoes to reach him. The girl is petite and blonde, hair feathered in a funky crop around her face, her black dress highlighting the paleness of her skin. She's snuggling in closer to Adam, hugging him to her; it's hard to tell whether the gesture is that of a lover or a friend.

At that moment he sees her. For a second his eyes look through her blankly. Then something snaps into focus. He breaks away from the group and walks towards her, his face serious.

'Lydia,' he says.

'Thought I'd pop by,' she says, and only then does he smile.

He takes her arm, and leads her back to the three waiting figures. Now that she's up close, she sees that the blonde girl is very beautiful; huge slanting eyes balanced on angular cheekbones, subtly pouting lips slashed with red. She beams and holds out her hand, but Lydia sees a swift head-to-toe glance of appraisal, sizing her up.

'This is Isobel,' Adam shouts into her ear. The girl nods and smiles again, saying something that Lydia doesn't catch. 'And this is Jack and Carla,' he continues, lumping them together with a wave of his hand. They are clearly a couple, the girl's hand now snaking into the boy's pocket to retrieve his wallet as he rolls his eyes and wriggles away.

'Hi,' she says, laughing and snatching the wallet. 'I was just about to go and get us some more drinks, d'you want anything?'

Lydia hesitates; she's not sure of the etiquette. They've barely been introduced, after all. 'I could give you some money—' she starts, but Carla dismisses her words with a flamboyant wave of the hand. 'Well, thanks,' she says. 'Vodka and lemonade, then.'

Carla disappears into the crowd, hips swaying confidently as she goes. Lydia sees Jack watching her out of the corner of his eye. 'Hello,' she says. 'I know Adam from lectures. He said he was going to come down here tonight, so I thought—' All too late she realises this sounds as if she has come deliberately in search of Adam, a fact she has barely acknowledged even to herself. Her cheeks flame up and she covers her embarrassment with a cough.

Jack's eyes flare briefly and wickedly. 'No worries.' Drawled, flattened vowels lend his voice a dry edge. He's only averagely good looking, but she can tell that his confident bearing would raise him a few notches on the scale with many women. He lights a cigarette now, narrowing his eyes above the smoke, and drags sharply on it. 'You known Adam for long, then?'

Adam cuts into the conversation, saving her. 'Ooh, a while,' he says teasingly.

'Yeah?' Jack says. They both laugh. Lydia looks from one to the other, not seeing the joke. By the looks of it, it's equally lost on Isobel, who looks briefly irritated before resting a hand on Adam's arm and leaning in farther towards her.

'So tell us about yourself,' she shouts invitingly above the music. Lydia smiles and shrugs. 'You know,' Isobel continues, 'name, college, what you're reading, where you're from, all that?'

Lydia fields questions until Carla returns with the drinks and Isobel is mercifully distracted. They find a small table on the far side of the club, but squeezing all five of them on to the narrow bench is a struggle, and Lydia finds herself pressed up tightly against Adam. At such close range, she can smell the tart citrus tang of his aftershave, and something deeper beneath, a mix of alcohol and cigarettes and sweat that makes her feel dizzy. His bare arm brushes her own, and all the hairs on her arm prickle in response. There's no way he can know, but for a second he looks at her in a way that makes her look hurriedly away. They barely exchange a word for the next hour. Banter flows back and forth between the two boys with practised ease, and Lydia gradually finds herself chipping in with the odd jibe along with the other girls. She's having fun, she realises with a shock as she tips back her fourth vodka. Laughter makes her hiccup on the last mouthful, and her eyes water and smart. Adam slaps her on the back, letting his hand rest there for a few moments longer than necessary, and she smiles her thanks.

'All right?' he asks, leaning in. She nods. 'Do you live in?' he half breathes, half shouts. It seems like a non sequitur, and an incomprehensible one at that. Her mind gropes around the strange unfinished sentence. 'Do you live in college?' he clarifies, seeing her lost face. 'Or out?'

'Oh!' she exclaims. 'No, I live out.'

'Whereabouts?' he asks intently, leaning in farther.

'Beechwood Road,' she says. The truth slips out easily; she's sick of the lies she has been telling all evening and it feels like a small relief.

'Really?' Adam says, his seriousness replaced by an amused smile. 'Which number? My mate Rob lives up there.'

'Nineteen,' she says. Again, it's the truth, but she feels uncertain about divulging it. Adam merely nods, draining his drink.

'How are you getting back?' he asks casually.

'I don't know. I'll get a taxi, I suppose,' she says. She hasn't thought this far ahead, but a glance at her watch reveals that it's almost 2 A.M. It doesn't seem to be the answer that Adam wants or expects; an irritated shadow passes over his face and he shrugs. Lydia is about to rephrase her answer into something more non-committal when there is a commotion at the other end of the table. Isobel is clambering up from her seat and standing on the table-top, spiky black heels sliding and gaining purchase on its shiny surface. She starts to dance, swaying seductively back and forth to the rhythm of the music, her short black dress snaking up and down her body and revealing tautly honed thighs. Her eyes are half closed, her red lips parted. Jack and Carla whoop in delight, whistling and slamming their hands down on the table-top. Before long a little crowd of men has collected around the table, encouraging Isobel on her self-appointed podium. She pouts her lips laughingly at them as she continues to dance.

Lydia is smiling, caught up in the moment, until she looks at Adam. He's staring up at Isobel, watching the black silk slithering over her body, the blonde hair forming a soft static halo around her as she shakes her head. The look on his face is rapt and lustful, and his gaze doesn't break until the song finishes and Isobel slips off the table to a chorus of cheers and wolf whistles. She crosses to behind where Adam and Lydia are sitting, puts her hands lightly on Adam's shoulders. He leans back, looking up at her, and she puts her mouth to his ear and speaks clearly, loud enough for Lydia to hear.

'Let's fuck.' The word jolts Lydia rigid and she stares down at the table-top, not knowing whether to laugh or cry. She doesn't hear Adam's reply, but she feels him shift away from her and get to his feet. When she next dares to look they have both gone. Abruptly she stands.

'Stay,' Jack calls over to her. 'They'll be five minutes, ten tops.' She can't bring herself to return his laugh or to say goodbye, pushing past the morass of people around them, heading for the cloakroom. The crumpled ticket is tucked inside her bra and as she fishes it out she feels her skin is burning hot and trembling. It's cold in the cloakroom queue, but she can feel the sweat dripping off her. She snatches her coat back and wraps herself up in it, stumbling out of the club into the drizzling rain. It seems she walks for hours before she sees the bright beam of a taxi blinking ahead. She runs for it and slips into the back seat. The driver is talking to her, but she can't make sense of his words. She can barely focus on the streets ahead as they zip through them, and when the cab pulls up in Beechwood Road she thrusts her last ten-pound note at the driver and slams the door without waiting for her change.

The noise wakes her hours later, a sharp, brittle sound like gravel hitting the windowpane. Head swimming, she sits up in bed and listens. A few moments later it comes again, stronger now. She hears him calling faintly below. 'Lydia.' A minute's pregnant silence, then a frustrated noise, halfway between a sigh and a shout. Finally something else grazing the windowpane before dropping down; a softer sound this time. She is out of bed now, shivering by the window, hand poised to draw the curtain back, but something stops her. She waits until she hears the footsteps crunching away and dying into silence before she peeks outside.

The street lamps that flank the house are still gleaming, illuminating the pavement. She sees the flowers scattered below the window. Long-stemmed roses, blood red, abandoned where they have fallen. Before she knows it she's running softly down the stairs in her thin T-shirt, pushing the door open, hurrying with bare feet over stone. She gathers the roses in her arms, their thorns grazing her fingers. Takes a deep breath, shakily inhales. In a moment she'll turn back inside, but for that instant, she's frozen in time, crouching motionless on the cold pavement, her head bowed as if in prayer.

Lydia waits at the orange café for five afternoons before the lecturer returns. Over those five days she's done little else. The waitresses recognise her now, and when the jangling door announces her arrival on the sixth day they both look up and smile. She orders her customary coffee, settles into her corner seat and opens up the same book that she has been bringing to the café all week. She's read through it twice already, but has taken in so little that she might as well be coming to it with fresh eyes. Her mind is elsewhere. She hasn't seen Adam since the night in the club, although a couple of times Sandra, her landlady, has reported a visitor searching for her while she has been out. He's an unwanted distraction, but nevertheless she can't stop thinking about him: his wicked dark eyes, the hair softly curling around his collar. Anyone else would put it down to lust, but she finds it hard to do even this. It isn't something she has ever experienced, and as a result it's hard for her to classify.

The sharp clatter of the bell raises her head. It's automatic by now, the hungry searching glance, constantly disappointed by a procession of scarf-wrapped students and nondescript families. This time she has to blink to make sure the lecturer is real. His outline shines against the bright winter sun and gives him the air of a mirage. He looks tired, distracted, and his clothes don't match, an old-looking red jumper slung like an afterthought under his black suit. He stands in the doorway for a moment as if announcing his arrival. There are two seats he could choose: one directly opposite Lydia, the other tucked away in the far corner of the café. He looks back and forth between them. She sees a mental coin being tossed in the instant before he turns towards her and settles into the seat, so close that she feels herself trembling. He takes a rolled newspaper out of his pocket, smooths it carefully out on to the table and scans the page blankly. So far he hasn't glanced at her, but she knows it's only a matter of time before he realises he's being watched. Sure enough, it is little more than a minute before awareness ripples the surface of his face. His head swings sharply towards her, and suddenly he's staring straight into her eyes.

For a second she thinks she sees a glimmer of recognition; something in her features calling up a memory so obscure and unidentifiable that it slips away almost instantly. In that instant his mouth has fallen slightly open, poised to identify her, but his lips abruptly close. A frown of incomprehension settles on his face. He's not a young man any more. He must be less used than he once was to students making eyes at him; perhaps he suspects an ulterior motive. She has thought about this moment many times, and with a shock she realises that she still hasn't decided which way to jump. Lydia the earnest scholar, keen to engage him in academic conversation. Lydia the breezy, talk-to-anyone novice student, looking for a friend and mentor. Lydia-Lolita, amateur seductress aiming at the depths of his vanity. As the options whir through her mind each seems more unthinkable than the last, but to her surprise the decision has been made for her. Her eyes are filling with tears.

He looks concerned, but she sees a faint irritation sifting beneath. 'Are you all right?' he asks in a low voice, glancing around as if he fears the waitresses will accuse him of attacking her. She doesn't reply, bowing her head as the tears start to fall. 'Come now,' he says, an edge of panic to his voice. 'This is . . . this is unnecessary, surely.'

What did she expect? A paragon of sensitivity? She battles a wild urge to laugh, sniffing instead and wiping an arm over her eyes. 'I'm sorry,' she whispers.

He clears his throat, scratching the back of his neck with long fingers. 'Is there anything I can get you?' he asks, looking around again. 'Another drink, or a cake or something? If you like cake.' She shakes her head. 'Well, then,' he says. He can make a polite excuse and leave, or he can ask the question he so clearly wants to avoid. 'Would you like to talk about it?' he asks. To his credit, not much of his obvious reluctance comes through in his voice, and for a second she almost warms towards him.

'I wouldn't know where to start,' she says, shrugging and smiling shakily. 'It's just . . . the sadness of things.'

He doesn't know how to respond to this. He inclines his head, perhaps respectfully. 'Life can be very hard,' he says eventually. To her shock she hears a raw edge of pain scraping his voice. He is frowning down at his paper, momentarily lost to her. She takes a moment to study him—the profile set into something close to cruelty, the strong Roman nose, lips hardened into a thin line. The sun pours a sharp radiance across his face, casting him in light. She knows what he is thinking of, and it makes her want to seize his hands roughly across the table and shout, *You see? You see what you have done?*

'I should go,' she says instead, not moving. He looks up at her again, nodding.

'Well, I hope you feel better soon,' he says. 'Take care, ah—' He pauses expectantly, waiting for her to fill in her name.

'Lydia,' she says, and watches him closely. This time the emotion spills across his face and he can't hold it back. She knows her reaction is crucial. She frowns as if puzzled. 'What's the matter? Are you all right?' she asks. He looks at her again, more intently this time.

'It's an unusual name,' he says. 'These days.'

'Is it?' she replies lightly. 'My mum always says it was my dad who chose it.'

'Does she,' he mumbles, retreating back into himself. Her words have dismissed any lurking suspicion that has pricked him. She can see he wants to be alone with his thoughts. As she moves towards the door she looks back and sees him fending these thoughts off, his shoulders hunched against them, his back rigid. She feels a surge of anger so great that she wants to hit something, so hard that she draws blood, but she simply turns and leaves, closing the door quietly behind her.

Back in my room I study my face in the mirror for traces of my mother. I've done this a thousand times but I never tire of it. When you lose someone, you take any small comfort that you can get, and it warms me to see any echo of a resemblance. We did not look alike, not really, but when I look closely I can see the line of her jaw beneath mine, the tinge of her eerily green eyes making its impression on my own. She's there inside me somewhere, but I don't want her there. I want her here, so badly I can taste it, the acid tang of need sickeningly fresh and surprising every time. The face in the mirror is blurring before me and suddenly it doesn't look like either of us. It doesn't look like anyone I know. I blink the tears away. I whisper my own name to myself, wanting to hear it as she used to say it. Louise. It's not the same, never the same.

I step back from the mirror, addressing myself in my head. You thought that this would be enough—to see him, to satisfy your curiosity. You were wrong. Nothing you can do will bring her back, but you have the right to know. This man murdered your mother. You need to understand why.

NICHOLAS
1983

I walked in to work across Waterloo Bridge every morning. I told myself that it saved me money, but in reality the walk was more about building a sense of occasion than anything else. It was something to do with height: the feeling that I was walking above the world and that the grey industrial sweeps of office buildings and the cloudy river beneath were somehow watching me and cheering me on. As I paced the bridge, I would often be hit by the sudden knowledge that the day was to be a momentous one, holding events that could alter the course of my life. It was one way—sometimes the only way—of getting me into the school and precipitating the same stultifying routine.

Strangely, I seemed to be able to fool myself with these false premonitions again and again. I thought they were harmless, but in retrospect they turned me into the boy who cried wolf. When the familiar sense came to me as I crossed the bridge on that bright morning of 17 May, I had no way of divining that, for once, the bubbling anticipation and queasy, faint foreboding sifting beneath my skin were genuine.

I had been working at the school for two and a half years, bumping along the middle ranks of the English department. Thirty-one, living alone in a box flat in Wimbledon, I had far too much time to convince myself that I was a misunderstood genius who was condemned to a life of a monotony as unremarkable as the recognition after my death would be ecstatic. I was writing poetry around this time: oblique fragments which aimed at Ted Hughes but fell anticlimactically short of the mark. I deliberately kept my flat in little better state than that of a hovel, telling myself as I drank cheap soup out of a grey chipped mug in front of my two-bar fire that I was the typical starving artist in his garret. At these times I conveniently forgot about the school, and my underpaid but decidedly middle-class position there. I hadn't had a girlfriend for three years. Not because I didn't want one, and not because I couldn't get one, but because the two states of wanting and attaining never seemed to coincide. I sometimes thought about becoming a monk. All in all I was ripe for a major life overhaul, and that is exactly what I got.

When I reached the school that morning I had twenty minutes before I was due to teach my first class at nine. It needed no preparation; the collection of oiks and devils that made up my fourth form were so laughably beyond reach that I had given up on them in all but name months ago. I toyed with the idea of going to the classroom early, sitting at my desk and staring at the whitewashed walls, but the restless mood generated by the walk was still on me. I prowled the campus instead. Sprawling and unstructured, a peculiar mix of original Gothic towers and tacked-on post-war concrete blocks, the school must have once been beautiful, I knew. Now it had the air of an institution gone to seed, an impression only reinforced by the grubby teenage louts crammed into its every crevice. I found myself turning towards one of the few unspoilt buildings remaining on the campus—the library, a converted church with honeyed, yellowing stone walls and candles that lit up its long arched windows when darkness fell. I often wandered its aisles when I was at a loose end, enjoying the temporary tranquillity, for few of the students ever ventured in except under sulky duress. That morning I hesitated before entering. I didn't feel like browsing, but I still had a quarter of an hour to kill. I pushed open the stone door and slipped into the silence inside.

I saw her almost at once. Sitting behind the check-out desk, she was slumped forward, reading a newspaper. Her face was shaded by her hand, but the curve of her blonde head, the long fingers splayed over her forehead and the narrowness of her sloping shoulders in their pink wool cardigan leapt out at me, as shockingly and unexpectedly as if she had jumped out of her seat and shouted at me across the library. *I know you*, I thought. It was an irrational thought, and I knew even as the words formed in my head that I had never seen this woman before, but that's what it felt like: seeing a much-missed friend again after a long absence. I had to stop myself from going straight up to the desk and telling her so. Instead I crossed softly to the rows of desks that flanked the library's darkest corner, and settled myself down to watch her. After a few minutes, she pushed the paper aside and looked up. Her face was finely sculpted, deli-cate yet sensual, dark brows and lashes framing large ethereal eyes. The way she looked, her ash-blonde hair falling primly over the pink cardigan, reminded me of a sixties fashion model, polished and restrained, but nursing a secret abandon. She was beautiful, but not really my type. I liked exotic girls, Mediter-ranean lips and curves, not wistful English roses who looked as if they should be clutching on to something at all times—a posy of flowers, a prayer book, a man's hand. And yet somehow, looking at her, I realised that the preferences I had thought I had were all muddled up and wrong, belonging to someone else.

I went over to the nearest bookshelf and picked a book at random, an obscure Henry James. Without giving myself time to think, I walked up to the check-out desk and slapped the book down, making her look up with a start.

'Have you read this?' I asked.

She glanced at the title, then back up at me. 'I haven't,' she answered. When she spoke, something seemed to light up inside her, animating her face and making her eyes shine. She was smiling quizzically. 'Should I have?'

'I don't know,' I said. 'I haven't read it either.'

'Oh.' There was a pause; she was clearly baffled. I couldn't blame her. As an opening gambit, it hadn't been one of my best—I was obviously out of practice.

I cleared my throat. 'My name's Nicholas Steiner. I work in the English department. When I asked if you'd read it, it was really just a way of saying hello.'

'I see,' she said. I couldn't read the expression on her face. 'Well, hello. Nice to meet you. I'm Lydia. I just started here this week.'

'Great,' I said inanely. The library walls suddenly felt oppressive and hot, closing in on me. 'So. I should probably go to my class, but . . . well, perhaps we could meet up later, go for lunch or something?'

She hesitated and brushed her hair back from her face, and in that instant I saw what I hadn't before: the pale gold ring on her slim finger. 'I said I'd meet my husband for lunch,' she said. 'He works in the chemistry department. You could always join us, if—'

I was already backing away. 'No, no, don't worry,' I said distantly. 'I just thought you might want someone to show you round.'

'Your book . . .' she began plaintively as I turned and strode away. I pretended not to hear and battled my way out of the stone doors, back out to the shrieking chaos of the campus. A dense tidal wave of pupils was surging across the square towards lessons, a contraflow to my own intended direction. Nine bells sounded out from the clock tower. I was going to be late.

It took me another week to work out who Lydia's husband was. I kept myself deliberately aloof from most of my colleagues, and I knew no one in the chemistry department whom I would have trusted to make discreet enquiries. On the face of it, few of the six chemists under sixty seemed like plausible candidates. Ranging from the prematurely aged Henry White, who spent his free periods huddled over textbooks and muttering in the corner of the staffroom, to the cocksure Terry Hudson, who was not long out of university and spent most of his time eyeing up the bustier sixth-formers, they were a singularly unappealing bunch. The front-runner was Simon Shaw, a good-looking, well-dressed man in his late twenties, who wore a wedding ring and who was conspicuous by his absence from the staff dining room at lunchtimes. Over the course of that week I imagined him with Lydia, laughing over their shared lunches elsewhere, enjoying a quiet evening in front of the TV, entwined together in bed . . . until I became convinced that the unpleasant images I was imagining were fact. Wanting to have my suspicion confirmed, I dropped Simon into conversation with one of the stalwarts of the school, Evelyn, who had been pushing sixty-five for the past five years and who was passionately fond of a gossip.

'I think I met Simon's wife the other day,' I said, gesticulating over towards where Simon was marking some papers in the corner of the staffroom.

Evelyn looked briefly shocked, then amused. 'Simon hasn't got a wife,' she said.

I was thrown off base by this. I assumed she was implying he was divorced. 'He still wears a wedding ring,' I pointed out.

Evelyn leant forward confidentially, her bright, ferrety eyes gleaming with the unexpected excitement of imparting knowledge. 'That's not a wedding ring,' she breathed significantly. 'It's more . . . well, how shall I put this? More of a *commitment* ring.' In case I hadn't picked up on the subtext, she clarified it for me. 'Simon's partner is a man,' she ended in an audible whisper, with a triumphant flourish.

The news jolted me more than might have been expected. It was 1983, and although the gay rights movement was in full

swing, there was still something of a 'not in my back yard' men-
tality clinging to me, however enlightened and progressive I
may have thought I was. Evelyn was watching me intently as I
struggled to keep the shock from my face.

'You didn't suspect?' she asked, a hint of glee in her voice.

'Really, I barely know the man,' I said brusquely. 'I simply
must have got him confused with somebody else.'

'I see,' she said, her tone implying that she did see, but not
in the way I was wanting her to. 'I believe they haven't been
together all that long,' she added. She obviously thought I had
secret designs on Simon Shaw and had invented a mythical
wife under some complex pretext. I battled down the rise of
discomfort that such a thought provoked in me. Let her think
it, if it kept her in staffroom gossip for a week.

'Excellent news,' I said sarcastically. 'I must just go and talk
to him now.' Somehow, the news that Simon was homosexual
freed something up in my mind, made it easier for me to
decide to ask him about Lydia. I went over to the corner table,
where his dark head was still bent over the pile of exercise
books, and sat down opposite him. He shot me a polite glance
of enquiry before returning to the books. We had done no
more than nod a brief hello occasionally around the campus,
after a hurried introduction on his first day several months ago.

'Sorry to disturb you,' I said briskly. He looked up again,
expectant now.

'Yes? Nicholas, isn't it?' he said. I wasn't given to stereo-
types, but I thought I caught the faintest whiff of something
about his manner, something that should have given me the
clue as to the true nature of that ring. He was smartly dressed,
as always, with a handkerchief tucked into his top pocket. I
noticed that his fingernails were very clean, very white and
finely shaped.

'Yes.' Now that I had begun, I didn't know how to go on.
Instinctively I felt that I couldn't pussyfoot around the topic

with this man. 'There's a woman,' I said bluntly. That got his attention. He put down his pen, a faint amused smile playing around the corners of his mouth. 'She works in the school library. She's married to someone in your department.'

Simon nodded. 'Martin Knight,' he said instantly.

I took a moment to digest the pill of information, which was even bitterer than I had imagined it would be. I had eliminated Martin from my suspicions early on, on the grounds that he was far too pedestrian a character to hold any allure for someone like Lydia. In his mid-forties, greying at the temples, with a face too forgettable to be termed ugly, he had few obvious attractions. Incomprehension was what I felt, and a petulant, steadily rising indignation.

'You're sure you know who I mean?' I said, just to make sure.

'Blonde hair,' Simon said eagerly. 'About thirty. And, of course, very beautiful.' He spoke with the detached relish of a professional connoisseur. I wondered whether he was trying to pretend that he himself had some interest in Lydia, to generate some sort of comradely atmosphere.

'That's her,' I agreed. 'Martin Knight. Well, no accounting for tastes.'

I had taken a risk, not knowing whether Simon and Martin were particular friends. From the smile that broke over his face I assumed that it had paid off, but he said nothing. The exercise books forgotten, he was leaning forward in his seat now, obviously awaiting my next move.

I didn't like to be toyed with. 'That's all I wanted to know,' I said, forcing a smile. There was no point in trying to backtrack or explain. 'I trust you won't mention this to Martin.'

'My lips are sealed,' Simon assured me. He hesitated, taking a furtive glance around the room before leaning farther in. His eyes fixed earnestly on mine. 'So,' he asked, with no little anticipation, 'are you in love with her?'

The directness of the question should not have surprised me—after all, I had been the one to break the norms of social convention between us—but for a second it made my breath catch in my throat. 'Yes,' I said, entirely without thinking, and saw his face blossom into delighted approval.

Later that day I made a half-hearted attempt to berate myself for my foolish declaration, but I didn't regret it. I tried to despise myself for falling in love on such scanty grounds; it didn't fit with who I thought I was, to be so ridiculously besotted over a look and a few awkward words. Try as I might, I couldn't make myself doubt my feelings, and the knowledge that I was not mistaken made me feel excited, righteous and determined all at the same time. I knew I could take her away from him. I did love her, I did want her, and in that moment, as thereafter, I made no apology for it. Not to anyone.

I struck up a casual friendship with Martin Knight. It wasn't difficult to do; he was the sort of person doomed to be overlooked and to blend into the background. The unexpected attention I showed him seemed to please him. I started off small—a cordial comment or two around the campus, an offer to borrow my newspaper in the staffroom—then progressed to lengthier conversation, commenting on current affairs or the steadily improving weather. Not forthcoming by nature, Martin nevertheless responded to these overtures with eagerness. Within a couple of weeks he was singling me out in the staffroom between lessons, giving me a brisk, confident wave in the knowledge that we were more than mere acquaintances. I don't know whether he ever stopped to consider why this unknown colleague, more than a decade his junior, had started to take an interest in him. With all that I came to know of him afterwards, I suspect that the question never arose in his mind. He had that peculiar yet surprisingly common combination, an acute academic brain coupled with a near-total lack of interest in human nature. He would wrestle with the finer points of molecular evolution with all the energy of a genuine truth-seeker, but when it came to emotion, he swallowed all that was told him without further question or argument.

As I got to know him better, I understood that he did have his qualities, however hidden they may have been on first inspection. He was cheerful and sanguine by nature, and spending time in his company was strangely reassuring. He had occasional flashes of quick, dry humour, invariably delivered with a sly look over the top of his glasses. He was automatically generous, often offering me things—a spare snack, a book to read in free periods. He didn't seem to feel the need to show off or to impress me with his knowledge as so many of my colleagues did. Attractive though these things were, though, none of them made me sit back and think, *Ah, so that's what she sees in him*. None of them seemed significant enough; there was nothing extraordinary about him, and I felt instinctively that Lydia deserved, wanted, something extraordinary.

I had decided early on not to mention Lydia until he did, but I didn't have long to wait. I think it took only two days of desultory chat before Martin dropped the phrase 'my wife' into the conversation. 'My wife always tells me I would make a terrible bachelor,' he said, in response to some casual remark of mine about living alone. As he said the words, his face was suffused pinkly with something between embarrassment and pleasure. Watching him shift self-consciously in his seat and stifle a smile, I realised that he worshipped her. The knowledge didn't soften me; on the contrary, it half angered me.

'Why's that?' I asked, biting back my annoyance.

'Well, I've never been very good at the domestic side of things,' he explained. 'Cooking, cleaning, tidying,' he added, as if this needed clarification. 'Lydia does all that.'

I adjusted my mental picture. I had assumed that she was

the sort of woman who sat back and was waited on. 'She must be very capable,' I said.

'Oh, very, very,' Martin agreed with enthusiasm. I waited for some elaboration, but after a pause he shifted the conversation back to my own living arrangements and Lydia was not mentioned again. Nor was I ever invited along to their private lunches, which seemed to take place every Monday and Wednesday. I noticed that he often came back from these lunches buoyant and brimming with bonhomie, his greying hair ruffled, and I envied him.

One morning we were walking across the campus together at the end of the school assembly, which I occasionally attended out of lack of anything else to do. I was holding forth about the latest Thatcher debacle, and I noticed that Martin's sporadic grunts of approval and murmurs of agreement had abruptly stopped. He was beaming, entirely distracted; I followed his gaze across the courtyard and saw that Lydia was approaching from the opposite direction. Clutching a bulging green carrier bag, books threatening to spill from its confines, she didn't see us at first. It was only when we were within speaking distance that Martin gave a curious whistle of greeting, obviously some private signal between the two of them. She looked up sharply and smiled as she saw him.

'Hello,' she said, and then her eyes flickered to me. Her expression changed in a second, but I caught the signals I wanted: surprise and dismay. In another heartbeat she was moving on gaily, rolling her eyes laughingly at the pile of books in her arms, and calling 'See you later!' back at Martin, but I wasn't fooled. She didn't want me around her husband. If I had ever had any doubts that that brief minute in the library had stayed with her as it had with me, they were instantly discarded, never to return.

I excused myself to Martin on the pretext that I had forgotten a textbook and hurried back in the direction in which

Lydia had gone. At the library, I saw her. She had stopped, leaning back against one of its yellowing stone walls and shifting the bag of books to sit more comfortably in her arms. I walked up behind her and put my hand on her shoulder.

I expected her to start, but she turned round with something close to resignation. 'Hello,' she said again. Her voice this time was softer, sadder. Her blonde hair was falling about her face, green eyes peeking up from under her fringe to meet mine.

'I'm sorry if I scared you,' I said, though it was obvious I hadn't.

She shook her head and made an effort to drag some normality between us. 'I didn't know you knew Martin,' she said cheerfully. The false brightness masked something closer to panic; I could see it in the aggrieved set of her mouth, the way she couldn't look me in the face for more than a second at a time. 'I assume you know he's my husband?'

'Yes. I only found out recently,' I lied. 'Not that it matters.'

She frowned, unsure of what I meant and whether to be offended.

'Well, I suppose not,' she said. 'After all, why should you care?'

'I do care,' I said. She gave a short exasperated laugh at this, hoisting the bag back into her arms and moving away from me.

'I don't know why we're having this conversation,' she said. 'Listen, I'm not stupid. I can see you're interested in me, but I'm afraid there's nothing I can do about that. I'm married, and even if I wasn't—' She stopped short, and I caught the first hint of another of her qualities that I would later come to know well; an inability to give voice to the harsh thoughts that formed so clearly in her head. 'It's embarrassing,' she contented herself with.

Silhouetted against the library, with the sun casting her in light, she was the most beautiful thing I had ever seen. 'Well,

I'm happy enough to be embarrassing,' I said. 'I like being underestimated.'

'Nicholas,' she said, and hearing her pronounce my name for the first time set off a strange erotic pang that felt as if it came from somewhere so deep inside I couldn't locate it. I expected her to follow it with some condemnation or other. I *think you should leave me alone. You're being ridiculous. I would never be interested in a man like you.* But she didn't. After a long silence, she just said my name again, softly and caressingly, as if rolling it around her mouth. She didn't seem to know what else to say.

After that day outside the library, it felt like only a matter of time before Lydia and I began an affair, and yet the next few weeks were the longest of my life. Every night that I spent alone in the flat I had once fancied an artistic utopia, surrounded by the paraphernalia of my suddenly unsatisfactory bachelor life, felt like an affront. At school I continued to spend time with Martin. Often I watched him and Lydia snatching a few moments together around campus, always laughing and joking between themselves, and I couldn't rid myself of the nasty, gloating sense that things would not always be this way. I didn't especially like it in myself, but at the same time I felt justified. I told myself that whatever it was between us was bigger than the English custom of stepping back politely at the sight of a wedding ring. Besides, it wasn't in my nature to forgo what I wanted—not when I genuinely wanted things so seldom, not when I could tell that she wanted the same thing, even if she didn't know it herself yet.

Over those few weeks I saw Lydia alone only twice. The first time, I sought her out, strolling casually into the library one morning to borrow a book. She greeted me brightly enough, tossing out some cheery query about how my week was going, but once again she couldn't look me in the eye. As she pushed the book across the desk towards me my hand brushed lightly across her fingertips. They curled back into her palm quickly, too quickly, at the touch, and I saw that the skin on her cheekbones was darkening, flushing into pink. The second time, I came out of a lesson to find her standing aimlessly in the corridor, staring at the mass of leaflets and flyers tacked on to the whitewashed wall. When she saw me, she feigned surprise. I didn't challenge her, even though I knew that she had no reason to be in the English block. She stood there awkwardly for a few moments, then declared that she had to go. Perhaps as a final gesture of defiance, she snatched a flyer from the wall as she went. It was the sort of gesture that from anyone else I would have found pathetic, but right then it made me smile. Looking after her as she hurried away across the courtyard, I knew that she had given me the nearest thing she could to a signal. It was time for me to test the water.

The next lunchtime, I excused myself from my lesson ten minutes early and went to the chemistry labs. I had reasoned that Lydia might well meet Martin there before their lunchtime dates, and my suspicion was right. She was sitting on a bench outside the lab, her bright blonde head bent over a book. When I saw her, my body went into overdrive, blood pulsing through me and adrenalin spiking my skin, making me feel light headed and delirious. My shadow fell across her as I approached, and she hurriedly tucked the book into her bag, but not before I had seen its title—the Henry James I had plucked from the library shelf on the morning of our first meeting.

'I hope you're going to write me a review of that book,' I said.

'I like Henry James,' she said defensively. 'I would have read it anyway.'

I laughed. 'Of course you would.'

She ignored me, glancing over her shoulder towards the

labs. 'I'm waiting for Martin,' she said. 'We're going to lunch.' I noticed that she had a basket by her feet, covered with a cloth.

'Having a picnic?' I asked.

'Not that it's any of your business,' she replied. 'But yes. We sometimes go to the park, when the weather's good. It's nice to be alone,' she added defiantly. 'To have some time just the two of us.'

I sat down next to her and took her hand in mine. It was hot, trembling in my grasp, but she didn't pull it away. Closer to her than I had been before, I could smell the scent of her perfume on her skin, a sweet, elusive smell that made me think of apricots and sunshine. Her green eyes were swimming with something that could have been excitement or tears, blinked away by long dark lashes that stood out dramatically against the paleness of her skin. Her pupils were fringed with a fine haze that graded from hazel through to almost gold. I wanted to kiss her, but something told me to wait. If I rushed things now, I could set us back days, and besides, I wanted to prolong the moment, now that I sensed it was so near.

'Don't wait for him,' I whispered. 'Come with me instead.'

At that moment the bell rang out sharply for the end of lessons. It galvanised Lydia, forcing her out of her seat as she wrenched her hand away from mine. She looked round wildly as the first students started to pour out of the lab behind us, shouting and pushing each other, swarming around us. I could have cheerfully murdered them all.

'O.K.,' I began, holding my hands up in surrender. She seized my arm, and I saw a new look on her face, a kind of fierce, almost angry desperation.

'Come on,' she said, looking me straight in the eyes. 'Quickly, before he comes.' The words hung between us in the air for an instant. I could see that she was half appalled at hearing them leave her lips; the betrayal tangible now, impossible to undo. In that instant I suddenly knew that all my certainty had been nothing more than bravado, and that deep down I had never expected this to happen. I couldn't speak. So fleetingly that I barely caught the echo of the impulse, I thought, *Stop this. Stop it now.*

She was hurrying away from the lab, almost running as she elbowed her way through the spreading crowd of students. I had to stride to keep her within sight, focusing my eyes on the slight but powerful set of her shoulders in their white shirt, her hair drawn up enticingly from the nape of her neck. She seemed to know exactly where she was going. I followed her through the exit at the back of the English block, leading out on to the backstreets that wound towards the river. She weaved through the streets, never looking back, making me feel like a stalker. I was excited now, willing to play her game. I had guessed by now where she was taking me. Sure enough, she took an abrupt right, and the church loomed in front of us. She unhooked the gate that led to the churchyard and slipped swiftly inside, leaving it off the latch for me. Still she didn't look back. She padded softly across the grass, slower now, taking her time to choose a spot. At last she came to a halt underneath a low cherry tree, masses of white and pink blossoms exploding across its thread-thin branches and casting a rose-tinged shadow on to the grass beneath. I came up behind her, put my arms around her waist and kissed the back of her neck, burying my face in the warm scented sweep of her hair. The touch seemed to flick a switch inside her. She twisted around in my arms and seized my face in her hands, brought her lips violently up against mine. I had thought she would be pliant, beseeching, easy to mould or overcome. Instead, as we kissed, I was shocked to feel the stirring of something strong and defiant, a will that could conquer my own. It was her whose fingers stealthily worked at the buttons of my shirt, her who took my hands and guided them, her who shook her head and pulled me towards her again roughly when I drew back and looked around. I began to speak—concerned someone might stumble upon us, someone might see—but she shook her head, staring at me, and suddenly it didn't seem important any more. We made love quickly, without ceremony. Her face was pale and transported, her head thrown back against the carpet of blossoms. It couldn't have lasted more than five minutes, but in those minutes everything changed. If any small cruel part of me had thought that once I had fucked her I could forget about her, it shrivelled and died.

Afterwards she was silent, turning away from me and lying on her side, her skirt still rucked up around her thighs. I ran my fingers through her pale gold hair, carefully unwinding its strands and releasing the scattered cherry blossoms that had tangled their way in among them. It was a few minutes before she rolled on to her stomach and looked up at me, eyes narrowing in the sun.

'I love you,' I said, because she seemed to expect me to say something, and because I meant it.

She looked more sad than rapturous, bowing her head towards the grass. 'I can see that,' she said. It should have sounded arrogant, but somehow it didn't. As would often come to be the case with her, I had a feeling that there was a subtext beneath her words which I couldn't catch, but which would always absolve her. 'I want you to know that this is the first time I've done this,' she continued.

'Do you love him?' I asked. I was prepared for either answer, or for the shaky middle ground of uncertainty. She nodded, and that was fine, because I didn't believe her. 'How long have you been married?'

She mumbled something I couldn't hear, so I asked her again. 'Six months,' she said, loudly and clearly this time, as if daring me to show any shock.

Despite myself, I *was* shocked. In my head I had built up an image of a marriage gone to seed. A teenage Lydia married far too young, a few happy years, then a growing sense of restlessness, the realisation of a decision too quickly and impulsively made. Not a cold-hearted newlywed casting round for some spice outside her life with her dull husband.

As soon as I had thought it, I knew I couldn't cast Lydia in that role. It would ruin everything. 'Tell me about it,' I said.

She sighed, scrambling to sit up and leaning her head back against the tree. 'I was working in a bookshop when I met him,' she said. 'He used to come in and browse the science section almost every day, or so he says, but I don't remember ever seeing him until he came up to me one day and asked me out. I was flattered, I suppose, even though he wasn't my usual type. There was still something about him.' She must have seen the incredulous frown that briefly split my forehead, because she rolled her eyes. 'Men like you never understand what a woman could see in someone like Martin,' she said. It felt like a rebuke, and I murmured an apology. 'But he is attractive, in his way. Anyway, we started seeing each other and it was only a few months later that he asked me to marry him. He was much older than me but that didn't seem to matter. I couldn't think of any good reason why I shouldn't marry him. He made me feel safe and loved. We married at the end of November last year. God, it was a horrible day—cold and pouring with rain. I remember shivering in my wedding dress outside the church. I couldn't think of anything except how cold I was.' She trailed off for a moment, recalling. 'Anyway, we were happy. We moved into a lovely little flat. This job came up a little while ago and I jumped at the chance, because I was tired of the bookshop, and it would mean we would see more of each other, and it seemed convenient.'

I was waiting for the end of the story: some catastrophic turnaround from the gentle domestic bliss that she had outlined. When it was evident that none was coming I cast my mind back over her words, trying to find some clue aside from the doom-laden storm of the wedding day, which hardly seemed a valid reason to embark on an affair.

'So why?' I asked finally, when I had found none.

Her face was vacant and puzzled. 'I don't know,' she said. 'I really don't.' Throughout her speech she had been confident and self-assured, hard even. Now she looked vulnerable, like a child seeking reassurance and comfort. I kissed her, stroking my hand across the curve of her cheek. She responded, but I could tell that her mind was elsewhere.

'We should get back,' she said. 'It's almost two. I'll go first, and then you can follow me in a few minutes.'

'O.K.' I watched her stand and smooth down her clothes. 'Will I see you soon?'

'Maybe,' she said. I must have looked hurt, because she bent down and gave me a brief, apologetic kiss on the forehead. 'I mean yes,' she said. 'But I have to think this through. I'll see you in a couple of days.'

She hurried through the churchyard, away from me, sunlight dappling her bare arms and legs, blonde hair glinting in a long rope down her back. I felt exhilarated and angry. I knew that she was wondering whether to give me the brush-off, and it irritated me that she could even consider it; it was so plainly impossible. I knew there was nothing I could do to hasten or influence her decision, and it gave me a sliding, nauseous feeling, as if I were playing a game of chance on which everything I had rode.

Later, in the staffroom, I saw Martin, dialling a number on the staff phone and waiting with an air of pinched concern. Relief broke over his face in waves when she picked up. 'I was worried,' I heard him say, and then, 'Where were you?' Whatever the lie was, it must have come smoothly, because when he turned away from the phone, he was smiling, a huge weight visibly lifted from his shoulders. In the weeks that followed, I was often ambushed by a brief photographic flash of his face as he had sat waiting at the phone. He had looked hunted, haunted, as if he were steeling himself against a blow from which he might never recover. I think he was imagining that she might be dead.

I could easily have sought Lydia out after our assignation in the churchyard, but I grimly resisted the temptation. I had never been involved with a married woman before, but already I was glimpsing the rules: she called the shots and she made the choices, because she undoubtedly had more to lose. It took three long days for her to make up her mind not to write the churchyard off as an insane aberration. On the fourth day, she turned up at the door of my flat after dark. At first I could barely believe she was there and thought I was hallucinating, that my wanting her so much had magically made an elusive image of her appear. She stood at the doorway in a long green dress and gold jewellery, dressed for the opera or a cocktail party. She was breathing heavily, as if she had been running.

'I got your address from the school files,' she said. 'I hope you don't mind. I was at a dinner party, and all of a sudden I knew I had to come and see you, so I said I was feeling ill and I was going home. I told Martin to stay, but he won't stay out late, so I probably don't have long.' She laughed nervously, giddily. 'I hope you don't mind,' she said again.

I unwrapped her like a present in front of the two-bar fire, glowing in the dark room and subtly illuminating her body. It was slower than the first time, more intimate. She whispered my name over and over again as we moved together, every whisper sending an almost painful reverberation straight to my heart. Afterwards she buried her face in my shoulder and I knew she was crying. I didn't ask her why, but I held her and stroked her hair as if I understood.

After that we started meeting whenever we could. Most of

our meetings were snatched half-hours around the school, at break times and before class. I often went to the library between lessons just to say a brief hello and have two minutes' worth of chat. The rest of the time I was on call, watching for notes in my pigeonhole written on the trademark yellow notepaper that she used. Some days there would be no note at all, and I knew that I wouldn't see her. Other days there would be a few scrawled words: *Can't get away. Missing you. Thinking of you.* And other days, less regularly, the notes would take a triumphal tone. *M out for the evening! Will come to you at seven.* It never occurred to me to rebuff any of her plans or invitations. On the contrary, my social diary was even emptier than it had been before, permanently cleared for Lydia. When we did meet, perhaps twice a week, it wasn't always for sex. We spent hours talking. She was intelligent, much too intelligent to be wasting time working in a library. I said as much several times, but she claimed she liked it. It went against the grain to think of her whiling away the hours behind that desk, when she should have been with me.

When I think of the summer that followed, it's as a series of picture-perfect snapshots, all blurring into one. Lydia on her back in the churchyard, singing with her eyes closed. Her hair, just glimpsed through the darkness in the tower at the top of the library, deserted in the summer holidays, where she waited for me. The two of us trailing our feet in the river, sharing a bottle of wine on a rare Saturday afternoon together. We were happy, as happy as we could be in the circumstances. I never got used to not having her full time, but I accepted it. Sometimes I felt guilty. I had kept up my friendship with Martin, as much out of habit as anything else. The sight of his friendly, earnest face occasionally set off a pang of nausea in me as I thought of how little he knew. I spent very little time with the two of them together, partly because it was simply too hard for me to keep my feelings to myself around Lydia, and partly because it was painful in some nebulous, craven way to see Martin taking such pride in her. He seemed to find every move she made endlessly fascinating. I would catch him looking at her intently in the course of some prosaic task like peeling an orange, and I could tell that he was marvelling at the way her fingers flexed and worked at its skin. He was quick to join in her laughter, even if he plainly did not understand the joke. He praised her dress sense, her skill at cooking, her sensitivity, to me on numerous occasions. It took all I had to smile and nod, and not to shout that he knew nothing, and that his beautiful, talented wife was spending her time away from him fucking the closest thing he had to a friend. Sometimes I thought I hated him. Other times I wished that I had met Lydia first, and that the three of us could have been friends.

Rarely, I wished that I had never met her at all. Once, towards the end of the summer, we were arguing, the same old argument that we always had. I wanted to see her the next night, and she said that it was impossible. I was always chasing her in those days. We were standing facing each other in my flat, both brimming with sour indignation. The conversation was to all intents and purposes over, but I wanted to give a final twist of the knife.

'It would be better if we had never started this,' I said. Her head jerked up sharply and I saw the blood drain from her face.

'You don't mean that,' she said.

'Maybe I do,' I shot back, unable to stop goading her now that I had got a reaction. 'It's not going anywhere, is it? Where could it go? Sometimes I think it's pointless.' I couldn't go on. She had slumped to the floor, knees drawn up to her chin, as if shielding herself against my words.

'Well, we can stop it, if you like,' she said, so quietly that I could barely hear her. The words hung in the air between us, and for a moment I thought, yes, this thing has run its course.

Leave it now, and maybe you can paper over the cracks and it'll be as if it was never there. I knew I was fooling myself. In another moment I was at her side, putting my arms around her shaking shoulders.

'I know this is hard for you,' she said, her voice muffled by my embrace. 'It's hard for me, too. I don't know what to do.'

It was the first hint she had given that there was a choice to be made. Naïvely, I had thought that this precarious middle ground could continue. Now I saw that she had gone farther, and that in the not so distant future there were two possible paths calling her—Martin or me. The knowledge frightened me. I couldn't see how the affair between us could end, but nor could I imagine her standing in front of Martin, peaceable, unsuspecting Martin, and saying that she wanted a divorce.

'I'm sorry,' I said then, moving to face her. 'I was frustrated, that's all. You know I want to be with you. And if you're thinking that you need to make a choice, I want you to know that I'm ready to give you whatever you want. If you want us to go away, start a life somewhere new, we can do it. I'll get a new job, we'll buy a place, I'll do whatever it takes. It's all I want, you know that.' I was talking fast now, words tumbling out one over the other. 'I can't imagine being without you. I won't be without you. You're right, we have to do something, I can't carry on like this.'

We didn't talk any more about it that night. I knew, though, that the conversation had started off a chain of thoughts and possibilities in her, and that they daunted her. In early September, when we had returned to school, I saw her a few times around the campus, walking with her arms crossed in front of her, so lost in her thoughts that she looked through me blankly. I think she would have come to a decision soon after of her own accord, although even now I'm still not sure what it would have been. In the event, without even meaning to, I pushed her to make the choice before she was truly ready.

We were curled up together in the library tower; it was the Tuesday lunch hour, which we always contrived to spend together. It had been one of our best times, when we seemed to be perfectly in synch, laughing and finishing each other's sentences like a couple of much longer standing. I remember that it was raining lightly outside, the raindrops making a faint tattoo of noise on the skylight above us. Lydia was lying back in my arms, smiling up at me. I wanted to prolong the mood, and fatally I snatched at something that suddenly struck me as amusing.

'You know, something funny happened earlier today,' I said, and felt her squirm in delighted anticipation. 'I was expecting a bulletin from the head of department, but I couldn't be bothered to go and check my pigeonhole.'

'So lazy,' she said, and swiped her hand up to playfully tap my face. I caught it and bit it, making her squeal in outrage.

'So anyway,' I continued, 'I asked Martin to go and check it for me. But when he was halfway there, I suddenly remembered that you might have left a note, and that he might recognise your writing. I had to sprint over to get there before him and pretend I had had a sudden spurt of energy—' I was suddenly aware that Lydia had stiffened in my arms. She pulled away, staring incredulously at me. Already I realised my mistake, but it was too late to undo it.

'How could you be so stupid?' she whispered.

'Look, I'm sorry,' I said hurriedly. 'I shouldn't have told you. Listen, it was fine—he didn't suspect anything. He thought it was funny.'

She carried on as if she hadn't heard me, talking to herself. 'How could I never have thought about anyone else seeing those notes?' she said. 'I put them in a public place where anyone could find them. We've been so stupid.' She stood up, dusting off her skirt. I leapt up to stop her, but she pushed me away, avoiding my eyes. 'I want to be by myself,' she said, and in another moment she was gone. I could have run after her, but I didn't want to arouse suspicion in anyone in the library downstairs. I told myself she would get over it, but I couldn't shake off the dread that was slowly trickling through my veins, the feeling that I had ruined everything.

The next day she wasn't at work. I waited at the library long past the time when I should have been teaching my first lesson. She didn't appear on Thursday either. It took until Friday for me to crack and approach Martin. I gave him some cock-and-bull story about having needed to borrow a new set of books for my sixth-form class, and having noticed that Lydia was not there. Immediately I could tell that there was something he was keeping from me. He had a smug, self-satisfied look about him, as if he were cherishing a special secret that excluded me and everyone else. I pushed him harder than I had thought my pride would allow, desperate to get to the root of Lydia's disappearance. Eventually he capitulated, with all the laughing good humour of a man who had everything he wanted. I was not to tell anyone just yet, but he and Lydia were leaving, he said. She had grown tired of London and wanted to settle down somewhere quieter, maybe start a family. At this point he blushed visibly with pleasure. She had always been impulsive, and ideally he would have liked to stay in London a little longer, but what was a man to do? The headmaster had been very understanding, and was allowing him gardening leave from the end of next week. He knew they would be happy, and he hoped that I would come and visit them, wherever they ended up. All at once he faltered, obviously realising that I was not heaping congratulations on his head. With a heart so full of panic, pain and incomprehension that I thought it was impossible that he should not see it, I shook his hand and wished him joy.

I saw Lydia once more before they left. She came to toast Martin at his leaving drinks—he had been at the school for six years, and although he had been consistently passed over for promotion, friendship and approbation, his colleagues apparently felt an urgent need to celebrate his reign. I watched her from the other side of the room, laughing and clinking glasses with all the suddenly gallant scientists flocking around her like bees round an exotic flower. She was wearing a tight black dress, her hair piled on top of her head, soft tendrils escaping and caressing her bare shoulders. I was furious with her, for looking so beautiful and happy, for leaving me. I thought that she had not seen that I was there at all, but when she and Martin turned to leave, hand in hand, she looked straight across the room at me for an instant. Her eyes were pleading, full of longing. I knew she was trying to tell me that she still loved me, but I looked back coldly, giving her no sign that I had understood, and then looked away. When I turned back she was gone.

I spent the next three years trying to get over her. I was promoted at work, and became head of department. I started tutoring the more demanding pupils one on one for an extra fee, and soon I could afford to move out of my box flat into somewhere far nicer. After those three years had passed I met Naomi, and she woke up the faintest echo of something in me that I had thought had died. We married a year later, and when I thought of Lydia, it was with the certain belief that I would never see her again. And for almost six years, I was proved right.

LOUISE
2007

Lydia cannot always trust her memories. Scenes and events from her childhood swim into her mind with disturbing frequency, but she seems to have no way of sorting truth from fiction. She used to have a favourite memory— her father kneeling down to present her with a hot pink flower, her mother clapping her hands delightedly in the background, the setting luminous and imbued with well-being. One day she switched on the television and saw the very same scene eerily played out in some old film she must have seen years before, the faces blurred into unfamiliarity, but everything else identical to the picture in her head. It was the first but not the last time that she realised that her mind had played a trick on her. The memory had felt like hers, but it belonged to someone else. And as the years go by, she loses more and more memories, not by forgetting them, but by handing them back to their rightful owners.

She doesn't know why, but she has always been this way. Her name, her age, all those everyday and automatically known things, have never seemed to be part of her in the way that they seem to be of other people. She is liable to misplace them, muddle them up in her head. So taking on her mother's name feels strange to her, and yet not strange. It is just as much bound up with her as her own, and it needs to be used. It's been hanging around unspoken for too long. She supposes that it is her mother's memory she's marking. However little Lydia remembers about her, and however unreliable it may be, she existed. That shouldn't be forgotten. Least of all by him.

Adam's flowers are starting to wilt. She has kept them in a vase by her bed for the past week, and for days they stayed in full bloom, their crimson petals so plushly perfect that she had to inspect them several times to make sure they were real. She knows that Sandra has noticed them; a sly hint was dropped at the dinner table, a jocular attempt to find out the identity of the sender, but she pretended not to understand. Now the roses are curling and browning slightly at the edges. In another day or two they will be dead, and she will have to decide whether to throw them out, or whether to swallow her pride and press them into dried-out husks, as she secretly wants to. Sitting at her dressing table, she plucks a petal off and crushes it between her fingers, the sweet scent rubbing off on to her skin. He cannot have known that roses are her favourite flowers, although she supposes it is a common enough choice.

This is not the first time she has sat like this, staring at the flowers. In fact, since she collected them from the pavement seven days ago, it has become something of a mid-morning habit. So when she hears the doorbell downstairs, Sandra's voice raised in polite enquiry, and the almost inaudible but unmistakable tones answering back, it is perhaps not as much of a coincidence as it might seem. Still, it is enough to make her start up from her chair and run to the door, heart hammering. She can hear him more clearly now—he is asking whether she is around, his voice strained and embarrassed. Mentally, she wills a message down to Sandra. *Tell him I'm out, tell him I don't live here any more.* And then finds with a guilty start that this is not what she wants at all.

Footsteps are approaching now, coming up the stairs to find her. She darts back to the dressing table and opens a book, pretends to study it. The door is pushed open and Sandra peeks around it—she never knocks, presumably clinging to the knowledge that despite the fact that she has been forced to take in a lodger, it is her house and therefore hers to do as she likes in. She's a big woman, comfortable and matronly with a peroxide bob and meticulously plastered make-up. Such is the size of her that for a moment, Lydia doesn't see Adam lurking behind in the shadows of the hall.

'You've got a visitor,' Sandra announces, beaming. 'The same visitor you've had every day for the past week, in fact. He finally tracked you down!' Behind her, Lydia sees Adam experiencing a silent agony of embarrassment and feels sorry for him. She suddenly realises that he must only be nineteen, and still has something of a teenager's gaucheness. He's several years younger than her, although of course there is no way he could know this. 'So!' Sandra prattles on, oblivious to the mortification she is causing. 'I suppose this clears up one mystery!' With a flourish, she indicates the roses, which have clearly been given an elegant vase and set in pride of place. Lydia feels her cheeks flame up, so that by the time Sandra retreats, with much innuendo about leaving them alone for a good chat, she and Adam are equally mute and self-conscious.

He recovers first, wiping a hand across his mouth and shrugging as if to slough off the temporary awkwardness. 'Tracked you down is about right,' he says. 'I've been looking for you everywhere.'

She is tempted to ask why but can't quite get the words out. Standing in her bedroom, where she has only imagined him up to now, he seems larger than life. His scuffed trainers, his big hands and his muscular body don't fit the quiet chintz of Sandra's box room.

'I've been quite busy,' she says. 'I did want to thank you for these, though.'

He dismisses the roses with a wave of the hand. 'Least I could do,' he says. The allusion to what happened in the club upsets her. She has been trying not to think about Isobel, or the lust-drunk look on Adam's face as she danced, and much less what happened after. 'Listen,' he continues, sitting down with a bump on her bed, 'I have been round a few times. Not quite as many as your interfering landlady might have suggested, obviously, but still, a few. I wanted to see you.' He pats the bed and she goes and joins him there, thinking that this at least cannot hurt.

'That's very flattering,' she says. 'But I can't imagine your girlfriend is too pleased.'

'It's not like that,' he says, a trifle too quickly. 'Isobel and I—we're friends, sometimes we have fun.'

'Have sex, you mean,' she snaps, aware that she is sounding jealous, but unable to help herself.

'Yeah, O.K.—have sex,' he agrees, shrugging his shoulders helplessly. He's trying to look contrite, but he can't entirely hide the ghost of a smirk. 'But that doesn't mean she's my girlfriend. Look, I feel really bad about going off and leaving you like that. I don't know why I did it. It was you I wanted to—' He breaks off and in her head she finishes the sentence with forbidden words, words that she has never said aloud. They make her feel hot, bewildered. She stares down at her hands.

'Would she like to be?' she asks then. 'Your girlfriend, I mean?'

Adam shrugs again and frowns, as if weighing up an entirely new concept. 'She might do,' he says. 'But she isn't. And besides, term ends in a fortnight. She'll be going home to Kent, and obviously I live here.' She doesn't like the inference, and looks at him sharply. He corrects himself with commendable swiftness. 'I mean, I don't mean . . . it wouldn't be going behind her back for us to spend some more time together. Because, like I say, there's nothing going on.'

'Mmm.' She isn't convinced, but wants to leave the subject of Isobel until she can think about it, alone. 'What makes you think I'm not going home for the holidays myself?' she demands. As soon as she asks, she sees a shift in Adam; he looks surer of himself, even a little angry, and with a flash of insight she realises that she is about to be challenged.

'This is the thing,' he says. 'After I'd been here a couple of times and you weren't in, I went over to Jesus and tried to get hold of you that way. But you're not a student there, are you?'

Lydia knows she will have to think fast, but she can't get rid of the nagging question in her mind. 'But you don't even know my surname,' she says.

'I know that,' he replies. Her comment seems to have taken away some of his anger; he leans back against the headboard, stretching his legs out across the duvet until they almost graze her own. 'I left a note in every pigeonhole with the first initial L.' The matter-of-fact tone in which he makes the admission suggests that, amazingly, it doesn't seem to embarrass him. As she takes in what he has done, she finds that she is flattered and more than a little amused. She can't help smiling.

'That was very enterprising of you,' she murmurs.

'Yes,' he snaps back, irritated again now. 'And I left my number so you could get in touch with me, and I've had crank calls from about a dozen people all week, mostly blokes taking the piss.'

She can't hold back the laughter that bubbles up in her throat, and has to clamp a hand over her mouth. To her relief he joins in, and for a few moments they abandon themselves to a mutual paroxysm of mirth, flapping their hands at each other in wheezing protest. 'I might have got your note, and just decided not to reply,' she points out when she has calmed down, wiping her eyes.

Adam shakes his head confidently. 'You would have replied,' he says, and for an instant she wonders what else was in the note besides his phone number. 'Besides, you've just given yourself away a bit there.' There is a pause; he looks slyly up at her, hands clasped behind his head, waiting for her to speak. 'So what is it with you?' he asks when she doesn't. 'You're living here with some middle-aged battleaxe, you say you're at college when you're not, and you can make yourself disappear for days on end. What are you really doing here?'

She can't blame him for the directness of the question, but it brings her back down to earth. She thinks of Nicholas, and feels sick. Adam's face looks sad now, reflective, as he takes in her silence. The winter sun streaming through the window picks out his features and, more than before, she sees Nicholas's strong brow imprinted on his, Nicholas's lips softened into Adam's. Just for a moment, the resemblance is so strong that she feels a surge of hatred for him, but almost as soon as it has come she forces herself to lock it back up in its box. It isn't fair to blame him, or to assume that all the unpleasant qualities she knows his father has have been passed on down the generations with Adam's birth, like gifts from a malevolent fairy godmother. She sighs and tucks her legs up under her chin, pulling her skirt down over her knees.

'You're right,' she says. 'I'm not at the university. I wish I was. The truth is that I had a bit of a falling out with my parents a month or so ago. I was at uni in Manchester, but I dropped out of my course—I wasn't enjoying it, I don't think it was really what I wanted to do—and they weren't happy about it. It got to the point where I just needed to get away, so I came here—I always liked Oxford, and I thought I'd be able to get a job. I still might . . . I haven't been looking very hard.' She stops for breath, marvelling at how easily the words have come, without her even having to formulate a story in her head beforehand. Adam has straightened up on the bed, his dark brown eyes serious and sympathetic.

'This falling out with your parents, is it bad?' he asks.

Lydia weighs up the possibilities. She doesn't want to be seen as a martyr, complete with a complicated family feud that she might well have to keep enhancing and adding to as the weeks go by. 'Not really,' she says carefully. 'They understood that I needed some space. They expect that I'll go back to studying eventually, and I'm sure I will. I think they think of this as more of a gap year.'

Adam nods, relieved; this is safer ground. 'I don't know why you didn't just tell me in the first place,' he says a little aggrievedly. 'Did you think I only talk to Oxford girls?'

'No, of course not,' she says hurriedly. 'But, you know, when we met . . . in the lecture theatre . . . it seemed the obvious thing to say. I know I shouldn't really have been at that lecture, but I'm . . . I'm interested in literature.' Again, Adam appears to accept this, half-truth as it is, without thinking it too strange. He visibly relaxes, obviously relieved at having solved the puzzle, and for the first time he shoots her a warm and genuine smile.

'Well, I like a woman of mystery anyway,' he says flirtatiously. 'Look, I'm due at a tutorial in half an hour, so I'm going to have to go. But do you want to meet up tomorrow? I'm having a few people round for drinks in my room in the evening, about nine probably—nothing major, but if you want to come it would be good to see you. Again.'

'Will—' she begins, and then cuts herself short. She had been going to ask whether Isobel would be there, but realises it is none of her business. 'Will you give me your number?' she covers up. 'Then perhaps I can call you tomorrow and we'll see.'

'Sure.' She watches him cross to her dressing table and jot down the number on the edge of her notebook. From behind, he looks tall and imposing, a grown man already, and it makes her feel young and, briefly, inadequate. She shakes the thought off, going to join him.

'Just one thing,' she says, putting her hand hesitantly on the sleeve of his coat. 'If I do come along tomorrow, I'd rather that nobody else knows my situation. I'd rather they thought I was at the university. It makes things easier,' she finishes lamely. She knows it sounds foolish, and can't really understand her reluctance herself for one lie to be replaced with another. Adam looks as if he might argue, then he nods.

'O.K.,' he says. 'It'll be our secret.' The words please him, it seems. He's standing very close to her, so close that his citrus-spiked aftershave prickles her nose. Very lightly, he puts one hand on the small of her back and the other to her cheek, two fleeting caresses that leave the parts he has touched tingling. Only two or three times before has she been this close to being kissed. On every occasion, the moment itself proved a letdown, a damp squib instead of an exploding rocket. She moves away from Adam and holds the door open for him. She won't risk the disappointment again.

'See you tomorrow,' she says. 'Maybe.' He nods and brushes her arm briefly as he leaves. From her vantage point in the attic room, she watches him as he steps out on to the street, strolls down it with his hands in his pockets and then, restlessly, as if he can't keep all his jolting and jumping nerves still, breaks into a brisk jog. She stays at the window until he has become little more than a bobbing shape on the horizon. Turning back into the room, she starts to remove the heads of the scarlet roses carefully one by one, discarding the dripping stems.

The next night Lydia stands in the porter's lodge at Lincoln College, shivering in her thin coat. It's raining again, and she has been sheltering in the lodge for almost a quarter of an hour. When she arrived, she sent Adam a text message: 'By the entrance to your college. I don't know where your room is— come down and meet me if you like.' She knows she should have called him, but when it came to it, she couldn't face the possibility of hearing his voice turn distant and unfriendly, regretting the invitation. Cursing herself, she hugs her arms around her chest, shifting from foot to foot. This is ridiculous, but she can't face turning round and going back out into the cold, hailing a taxi and spending another night alone with Sandra's television blaring downstairs.

Suddenly she hears a commotion across the quad. Peering into the dark, she can just make out a figure running towards her, feet pounding wetly on stone. Part of her already knows, but it's only when he passes under a solitary floodlight that she sees it is Adam. He runs into the lodge and envelops her in a sudden hug, crushing her against him. He's brought the smell of the rain with him—damp grass and the faint, musty scent of earth. In the fuzzy half-light of the lodge, Lydia looks into his eyes and feels dizzy.

'Sorry,' he gasps, panting from his exertions. 'I had some music on and didn't hear my phone, I only just got your text. Have you been waiting ages?'

'Not at all,' she lies, smiling radiantly. 'Am I late?'

'Not at all,' he says in turn. 'Come with me.'

They run back across the quad together in the dark, hand in hand, her unreliable high heels slipping and sliding along the rain-washed stone. By the time they reach the other side her hair is soaked and plastered to her scalp. Laughing, she wrings it out as she hurries up the staircase after Adam. They climb several flights of stairs, each one winding closer and tighter than the last. He has an attic room too, she thinks, and feels stupidly pleased at the note of similarity. When they near the door she hears the music thumping behind it, and the shouts and screeches of laughter tumbling over each other from what sounds like a dozen or more voices. She freezes; she isn't used to this. She had vaguely imagined a select group of Oxford students, sitting sedately around a bottle of wine and talking about literature, but this sounds more like a lunatic asylum. Adam sees her apprehension and grins, steering her towards the door.

'Don't worry, no one's that pissed yet,' he says. His words have the opposite effect of their calming intention on Lydia, who finds it hard to envisage the carnage that could come later. Numbly she allows herself to be shepherded through the door and into the bedroom. People are draped over the bed and chairs, lounging on the floor and perched on the windowsill. A couple are smoking a joint out of the window, deep in animated conversation. Others are bellowing along to the thrash metal track that is blaring from the stereo, so absorbed in it that they don't even turn round. A couple of girls shout Adam's name drunkenly, beaming red-lipsticked smiles and raising their arms to the air in delight. She recognises one of them as Carla, the Latin-looking girl in the club. As they approach Carla points at her and smiles again, her dark eyes half closing in recognition.

'Lydia,' she says. 'The disappearing woman. Where did you go last week? We were worried about you, girl.'

Lydia is strangely pleased by Carla's hectoring tone. She shrugs and laughs, mumbling something about having been too drunk to stay on.

'We all know what *that* feels like,' Carla agrees, with heavy emphasis. Judging by her flushed cheeks and her expansive hand gestures, she is already halfway there. 'Come and sit down,' she adds, motioning to her friend to make space on the bed. Lydia squashes herself into the space, and Carla pours her a generous measure from the bottle of gin she is holding.

'Thanks,' she says, taking a gulp. She doesn't like gin and winces over the taste, but she doesn't want to turn the gesture of acceptance down. When she looks up from her glass she sees that Adam has disappeared to the other side of the room, where he is slapping Carla's boyfriend Jack on the back and saying something into his ear. She doesn't mind him going, not now. Although she barely knows these girls, she wants to play out the fantasy that they are her best friends: sharing secrets, discussing boys and swapping clothes. She can't remember ever having friends like that. The few she made at school were always kept at a distance, although she can't remember now whether this distance was created by her or them. That evening, sitting with Carla, she begins to understand that, given a different set of circumstances, things might have been this way for her. As they drink and laugh together, she feels something inside her begin to unwind, like a coiled spring slowly releasing its tension. She has never known how to relax, but suddenly it feels easy.

'How long have you been with Jack?' she asks Carla after what feels like hours. The crowd has thinned out and the thrash metal music has given way to slow, sleepy ambient noise. Carla grins and rolls her eyes towards the ceiling in con-centration.

'Five—no, six months,' she says. 'Quite a long time, for me.'

'Have you . . .' She has been going to ask whether Carla has had a lot of boyfriends, but the question feels crass. 'Met his parents,' she finishes.

'God, no!' Carla gives a surprised bark of laughter. 'It's not like that. So,' her eyes sparkling slyly now, 'have you got a boyfriend, Lydia?' She shakes her head. 'Do you want one?' Carla presses.

Lydia can't help her eyes from drifting around the room, searching for Adam. He's sitting sprawled in a chair by the window, looking up at a girl perched on the windowsill, her slim legs encased in long black leather boots. As her gaze trav-els up she sees that the girl is Isobel. She's looking irritated, smoking a cigarette in short angry drags that expel the smoke violently up towards the ceiling. Her heavy eyeliner, red lips and pale skin make her look as if she's come off a film set, star-tlingly dramatic against the black backdrop of the window. As Lydia looks at her, she catches her eye. This time there is no pretence of friendliness. The girl stares at her with open hostility, her chin raised defiantly. The next moment she bends down to Adam with angry swiftness and hisses something. He looks over at Lydia, very briefly, than puts his hand on Isobel's leg placatingly. She shakes it off and snaps something at him again.

Carla has followed her gaze and sighs, putting her arm around Lydia's shoulders. 'Listen, Adam and Isobel have a complicated relationship,' she explains. 'They went out last year, but it didn't work out. I shouldn't say this, because we are friends, but she's a bit mental. He didn't want the hassle, but he's found it difficult to stop things completely. I keep telling him he should just let it go, but he's a man, and of course she's . . . '

Very beautiful, Lydia silently concurs. Even with her face twisted in anger, Isobel looks like she belongs on the front of a glossy magazine. She imagines Adam kissing the curve of the other girl's neck, and the rush of angry adrenalin that it gives her makes her catch her breath.

Carla pulls on her sleeve earnestly, demanding her attention. 'He likes you,' she says. 'It's really obvious. He's not in love with her. Maybe you just need to make a move—like, go up to him and say—'

She hears Carla's voice continuing, but the words are slipping away from her. Isobel has leapt up from the windowsill, eyes burning with fury, and stalked from the room. Adam gives a long sigh, rubbing his hand over his face. Sluggishly, he gets to his feet and follows her, swinging the door to behind him.

'Don't follow him,' Carla cuts into her thoughts. 'He'll be back.'

She wants to believe Carla, but she can't stop herself. She wriggles off the bed, finding that her legs are trembling. They feel like reeds, supporting her only by the thinnest of threads. She creeps to the door and peers through the crack, which shows her the staircase outside Adam's room. He and Isobel are standing face to face, not touching. She can't see Adam's face, but Isobel's is anguished, accusing.

'So why is she here?' Lydia hears her ask bitterly. She knows without a shadow of a doubt that they are talking about her. 'If nothing's going on, why is she here?'

Adam's voice is lower, harder to catch. 'I invited her,' she makes out, and then, 'I like her.'

'Well, I like a lot of people,' Isobel snaps back. 'I don't send them flowers.' Adam must look shocked at her words, because she tosses her head triumphantly. 'Jack saw you getting them last week,' she says. 'I thought at first . . . I thought they were for me.' Suddenly her voice breaks and without warning she bursts into tears, rivulets running down her perfect cheeks. Her whole body shakes with the effort of crying. She screws her fists into angry balls, pressing them against her eyes. It's too much, the emotion swamping Lydia and making her feel sick. She almost wants to go out there, put her arms around the girl and tell her that everything will be all right. But a secret part of her knows that it won't be all right, not in the way she wants. Adam is shifting uncomfortably, placing a nervous hand on Isobel's shoulder.

'I'm sorry,' he mutters, so quietly that Lydia can barely hear him, 'but you and me—this was over ages ago. I should have stopped it, but, you know . . . you're hard to resist.' He's trying to make her laugh, and he almost succeeds, a watery shadow of a smile passing over her face. 'If I'd known you were still taking it so seriously, I would have stopped it, I promise you.'

'I'll get over it,' she gulps finally, wiping the last of her tears away. Lydia can see that she's already regretting her outburst, and wants to claw back some composure. 'And what about her?'

Adam's shoulders lift, sink down. 'I don't know,' he says. There is a long silence; they look at each other.

'I'm going to head off,' she says at last. 'See you.' She reaches up, almost on tiptoes, and runs a hand through his hair, pulls his head down to hers. They kiss, on the mouth, for what feels like minutes. It doesn't seem like a goodbye kiss, but that is what it is, Lydia tells herself, that is what it has to be. She can't help seeing, though, that it is Isobel who breaks away first. With a flick of her blonde hair, she walks away, hips swaying, not looking back at Adam. He's still standing in the corridor, looking after her, as if frozen in stone.

Lydia slips quietly away from the door and looks back into the room. Although they have not been talking loudly enough for the others to hear, Adam and Isobel's departure seems to have had a sobering effect on the handful of students left. Coats are being slung on, bags gathered. The party mood is broken, and no one wants to outstay their welcome. She hears muttered discussions about the rest of the night—a club, a film in the JCR, or simply going to bed. She's not involved in any of them, and it's only then that she remembers that, despite how it may have seemed for a few warm, inclusive hours, these people are not her friends. Although she barely knows them, she feels desolate as they leave. Carla winks and waves, but it's obvious that she has forgotten their earlier discussion. By the time Adam returns, Lydia is sitting alone in the room, curled up on the bed.

'Wow,' he says, looking around as if he is surprised to see it so empty, although his friends must have passed him in the hall as they went. 'So . . . everyone left.' He takes in the mess they have left behind them; crushed beer cans, cigarettes stubbed out on the windowsill, empty packets of crisps and chocolates littering the floor. 'I should tidy up,' he says, without much conviction.

'I'd leave it till the morning,' she says. 'If I were you.' She finds that her words don't fit her mouth properly, her tongue struggling to form the right sounds. She's not sure how much gin she's drunk, but it feels as if it has all hit her at once, and the taste at the back of her throat is cloying and sour.

'I will,' he says, as if she has made an excellent and novel suggestion. She tries to determine how drunk he is and can't, her judgement too fogged to be of much value.

'Well, I'll be off, then,' she says, or thinks she says, just as he crosses to her and sits down next to her on the bed. She drops her head down on his shoulder, just because it is the easiest thing to do. They don't speak for a long while.

'Stay here,' he whispers. 'I want some company.'

All of a sudden, irrationally, she wishes that she was back in her own bedroom. She has been dreaming of kissing Adam all week, in fits and starts, the image bobbing to the front of her mind at the most unexpected times. Now she doesn't want to, but she doesn't not want to either. She feels confused and young, unsure how to interpret the messages tugging insistently at contradictory corners of her brain.

In the end she doesn't have to make a choice, because he doesn't kiss her. He simply pulls his T-shirt over his head, unbuckles his trousers and lies down. Lying there only in his tight black boxer shorts, his body is taut and lightly tanned, his chest dusted with a sprinkling of tawny hairs, lighter than those on his head. When she puts out a hand to touch them she can feel the heat rising off him in waves. Her fingers run tentatively over the bare skin, raking a path down to the band of his boxer shorts, then stop. He doesn't ask her to continue, just closes his eyes. In repose his face looks serene and almost babyish, long eyelashes curling delicately upwards. He looks less like his father this way. Lydia wriggles quietly out of her jumper and unbuttons her jeans, slipping out of them and casting them to the floor. She leaves her black bra on; she feels naked enough. Lazily, Adam's eyes open again and travel over her body. He puts a hand out to touch her, exploring her curves as slowly and minutely as if he is performing a medical examination. It should be the opposite of erotic, but somehow it's not. She holds her breath and her stomach hollows as his hand slips over it. Her body feels tense and taut, as if something might crack.

'No,' she says, not knowing why. The word is dragged up from somewhere deep inside her, and she can't take it back. He doesn't look hurt. He almost looks relieved, and this to her is even stranger than her own uncertainty.

She lies down beside him, and he wraps his arms around her, pulling her close against him. Still they don't kiss. She can tell from the rhythm of his breathing that he is losing his grip on everything, slipping away from her. In another five minutes he is fast asleep, snuggled into her, his head buried in the crook of her arm. She stays awake a long while, watching the rolling dark clouds outside the window shift and lighten as dawn starts to break. Despite the warmth of Adam's body curled around her, she is very cold. She thinks of her mother, of Nicholas, and it takes all her strength to push the thoughts away. Tiny hairs on her arms stand up and bristle underneath the covers. Small changes in the rhythm of his breathing, a cold draught running down the back of her neck. The whole of the universe outside, the dark and lightening sky sweeping out far beyond everything she can see. She feels her consciousness shifted brutally back and forth from the minute to the immense. And above it all, a tremulous sense of dread, that she has started something that she may not be able to finish, or that when it does finish will teach her things that she never wanted to know. Once or twice Adam says something indistinct, talking in his sleep. In her fuzzy, half-drunk state, she thinks that if only she could know what it is he is saying, it will help her unlock the key to her fears, and bends her ear intently to his mouth. She can't make out the sounds that spill from his lips. Violently, she shakes him awake. *What were you saying?* she hisses urgently. He doesn't reply, just looks up at her in sleepy-eyed confusion, blinking gently in the sharp light of the dawn.

The next morning everything is normal again, or as normal as it has ever been between them. They catch each other's eyes sheepishly as they dress, and laugh, acknowledging the strangeness of the night before. For whatever reason, it seems that an unspoken decision has been made to take things slowly. The mutual realisation takes a huge weight off Lydia, leaving her feeling light and airy. Infused with energy, she helps Adam tidy up the bedroom. What would normally be a chore becomes fun; they compete to throw empty cans and crisp packets into the open mouth of the bin-liner, cheering when they score a hit. Because of this it takes much longer than it would have done if Adam had been on his own, and it is almost midday before Lydia leaves. He walks her down to the porter's lodge, his arm around her shoulders. The rain of the previous night has cleared the air of all its oppressiveness, leaving it sharp and fresh.

'Term's over in a week or so,' he says at the gate. 'Maybe we can spend a bit more time together then.'

'That would be nice,' she replies. Out of the corner of her eye she sees a figure that could be Isobel, blonde and petite, lurking at the far end of the quad behind them. She reaches up and kisses Adam fleetingly on the lips, a chaste kiss, but enough to mark her territory. He looks surprised, but pleased, she thinks.

Lydia stops off at a café on the way back to Sandra's house for some food. She hasn't eaten for twenty-four hours, and her limbs feel shaky and tired. She orders a plate of fried food that would normally turn her stomach; bacon and eggs, sausages and mushrooms swimming in a sea of grease. When it comes she wolfs it down as if it's the most delicious thing she has ever been offered. She has almost cleared the plate when she feels her mobile vibrating in her bag, buzzing urgently against the side of her jeans. She digs it out and the luminous screen signals a voicemail alert—she must have missed the call as she was walking down the High Street. She presses the voicemail number and holds the phone close to her ear, shielding it from the buzz of noise that fills the café. She has to strain to hear, but there's no mistaking the voice.

'This is Martin Knight for Louise Knight,' it begins formally. Martin is still not accustomed to mobiles, and harbours a vague notion that any message left must be properly announced if it is to stand any chance of reaching its intended recipient. It's something they used to joke about, and for a while he stopped doing it, but the old habit has obviously crept back. Hearing his voice, ridiculously formal, brings sadness on her in a rush, and tears prickle the back of her eyes as he continues after a pause, presumably intended to allow enough time for the message to be miraculously connected.

'Louise, I wanted to leave you alone, as that's what you wanted,' he says. 'But we're . . . I'm worried about you. I don't like to think of you there, and I'm still not sure what you think you will achieve. I can't see what it's going to do for you, except maybe bring back painful memories. It was so long ago that we were there that I doubt you even remember our house. If this is about feeling closer to your mother, I don't think you will find what you're looking for. I don't . . .' His voice trails off. As he has been talking it has grown steadily quieter, sadder and somehow remote, as if halfway through the message he had begun talking to himself, not to her at all. 'Just call me,' he says finally. 'And come back soon. I love you.' There is another pause, then a soft click as he hangs up.

Lydia can't help replaying the slip he made at the start of the message in her head: the habit, never quite lost in the seventeen years that should have beaten it out of him, of saying 'we', rather than just 'I'. *I'm worried about you.* She had told him that she wanted to come to Oxford to be by herself for a while, that she needed to set things straight in her head. She had mentioned nothing about seeking out Nicholas, reasoning that what he didn't know couldn't hurt him. Now she sees that the opposite is true. It's the not knowing, the blank space where knowledge should be, which has made him pick up the phone. All of a sudden she becomes aware of the cloying stench of fried bacon and mushrooms from the plate in front of her. She doesn't want it any more; the smell is making her feel sick and she pushes the plate violently away and stands up. When she has left the café she stands aimlessly in the street for a few minutes, watching the city moving with people. She has the sense of being plucked out of the scene she is in, observing it from somewhere high above the rest. She will call Martin back later. For now, his unwitting words have sparked something off in her, and once thought of, she can't let it go. She wants to go back there, to the house where they used to live. The thought has scarcely formed when she sees a taxi winding its way down the street, the little orange light winking out at her. It's a sign. Without stopping to think further, she steps out into the road and raises her hand.

'Sixteen Grassmere Road, Kirtlington,' she says. Her father may be right when he says that she doesn't remember the house, but she remembers the address. She has always been better with words than pictures. As the taxi carries her out of the city centre towards Kirtlington, she concentrates on the few memories she thinks she has of the years that she lived there. She was born there, and she lived there until she was five years old. It was the first place she saw, whether she remembers it or not, and she has a right to go back there.

It takes almost half an hour to reach Kirtlington, but Lydia is so lost in her thoughts that she feels as if she has blinked and been instantly transported. As the taxi drives slowly through the narrow village lanes, she starts to feel the memories waking up. A corner shop, baskets of yellow and purple flowers hanging over its windows. A village green, flanked by rows of tall oak trees. Curving, uneven pavements that she thinks she used to trip on in furry laced-up boots almost twenty years ago. The streets are almost deserted, and it's like driving through a dream town, painted in unreal colours. When they take a right turn, the road sign swims to the front of her vision, and she realises that this is the street where they used to live. As the taxi trundles down the road she finds herself leaning forward, searching for the house. She is too far away to see the number painted on the wooden gate outside, but she knows. Smaller than she had imagined, it's more like a cottage, with sleepy-eyed windows set in sloping stone, and flower beds planted with ice-white winter roses flanking its walls. It doesn't match the blurred picture she has had in her head, but nonetheless it's instantly, inevitably familiar. Her heart constricts. She remembers sitting on the high front step in summer, swinging her legs and stroking their cat, stretched out purring beside her and baking in the heat. The warmth of its fur comes back to her, so strongly that her fingers start to tingle. She remembers her mother coming out to find her there on the step, looking up at her and squinting in the sun, her blonde hair sparkling around her head like a spotlight. Her long slim hand reaching out to pull her up.

'Twenty pounds,' the cab driver says, cutting into Lydia's thoughts. His voice is testy and impatient, as if it's not the first time he's asked for the fare. 'This is the place, isn't it?' With a start she realises that the taxi has stopped. She digs the money out of her bag and clambers out. Standing at the gate, she rests her elbows on the cold wood, peering in.

'Are you going in, then, or what?' she hears the driver whine, still hovering impatiently behind her.

'Just go away,' she shouts, wheeling round. It comes out

with more force than she had intended and she sees him visibly flinch as he pulls the handbrake up sharply and drags the taxi away from the kerb. Clearly in his eyes she has crossed the line from stupid to mad. She watches him turn in the road with a defiant screech of tyres and zoom away. Briefly, she wonders how she is going to get back. She hasn't thought this through, but she wants to be here.

Lydia turns back to the house again. Her head is flooding with pictures now. The kitchen was long and narrow, an old metal Aga running the width of one of its walls. Her mother followed the seasons with her cooking: the kitchen collected all the heady smells of boiling fruit in summer as she made jams from peaches, apples, plums that they collected together from the ancient tree in the back garden. The plums were ripe and shiny when they picked them, almost violet, making a soft squashing noise against each other as they were thrown into her red plastic pail. Sometimes they abandoned the collecting and just sat on the grass together, threading flowers through their stems to make bracelets and earrings which they hooked over each other's ears. Her mother had a yellow pair, made out of buttercups, which dangled like gold and mingled with her hair.

In the winter they had snowball fights with her father, boy against girls, him ducking and cowering behind the garden shed, shouting mirthfully in protest as they pelted him. Her hands were so cold that she thought they would freeze completely, turning her whole body into ice. After those fights in the garden she and her mother would sit on the squashy sofas in the living room, looking out at the snow falling darkly against the windowpane. There was a little lamp which always burnt in the corner of that room, shaped like a seashell. It got brighter and brighter the blacker it got outside, until it was the brightest thing there. Her father would come and join them, taking off his glasses and polishing them until they glinted.

Sometimes he put them on her nose and the whole world grew and shrank and shimmered before her eyes. 'Martin, take them off,' her mother would say, rolling her eyes indulgently, and smiling.

There is nothing sad about these memories. Lydia knows, because of them, and because her father has told her, that they were a happy family. They were happy, before Nicholas came.

'Can I help you?' a voice asks behind her. She swings round and sees a plump woman with a kind face, her hair done up in plaits around her head. Her hand rests on the gate, possessively. The other hand grips a pushchair. A baby, no more than a few months old, stares up at her with round solemn eyes.

'I'm sorry,' Lydia says, stepping back. 'Do you live here?'

The woman nods, a little uncertainly. 'Are you selling something, love?' she asks. 'I'm afraid we don't go in much for—'

'No,' Lydia interrupts, 'I live here too. I mean, I used to live here.' Despite her self-correction, it's the first statement that feels right. She has not expected this place still to feel so much like home.

'I see,' the woman says politely, not seeing at all. 'Well, we've been here ten years, so it must have been a long time ago.'

'It was a long time ago, yes.' A lifetime ago. She backs away from the gate. Her eyes feel hot and prickly and she can tell that tears are not too far away. She can see the woman's lips moving, a look of concern on her face, but she can't hear what she's saying. She is blocking her out. She turns and walks briskly down the street, away from the house. She doesn't stop walking until it's too late to look back and see it in the distance, too late to let her body do what it really wants to do and claw its way past the woman and her baby to the front door and shut them out somehow so that she can be alone there. She was wrong that there were no sad memories. As she walks they press in on her in a rush, so vivid that she can barely breathe

with the strength of them. A rainy winter morning that turned
so dark so fast that it was as if the sun had been blocked out.
Her father shouting without words, doubled up with grief. The
emptiness of the weeks and months afterwards, when three
had swiftly and inexplicably become two. She starts walking
faster to try to shut them out, but it doesn't work, and even
when she is sitting on the bus back to Oxford and leaving
Kirtlington behind, they come back to her, again and again and
again.

On our wedding day I vowed in front of seventy people that I would stand by Naomi until death did us part, and I meant it. I had never intended to marry, clinging to the clichéd belief that it killed the passion in a relationship, but with Naomi it seemed like the natural thing to do. She was conventional, had grown up with the equally clichéd dreams of a white dress and a lavish ceremony, and was not about to let them go. When it became evident, about four months in, that our relationship was serious, I could see the expected path stretching out ahead of me—a path that led inevitably up to a country church and a host of smiling guests. I didn't see the point in spending five or six years getting there. We planned a whirlwind wedding that pleased both our families, who presumably saw it as evidence of our desperate need to be publicly committed. Standing at the altar, I knew that I would never marry again. This was what I wanted, after all: security, legality, someone who was indisputably all mine.

Physically, Naomi was something new for me. Energetic and voluptuous, with a mass of red curly hair and a fine dusting of freckles over her pert nose and pink cheeks, she was the sort of girl who frequently got cast as a milkmaid in school plays, as she told me wryly on our first date. Once she showed me an effusive poem that an ex-boyfriend had written for her, painting her as a modern-day Nell Gwynn, and while I snorted and scoffed over the badly composed pentameter and the dubious rhymes, privately I thought that as far as imagery went, he had got her spot on. Men stared at her in bars, on the street, in crowded tube carriages. She wasn't beautiful, strictly speaking, if you broke it down objectively. Her chin was a little pronounced, her face a little too asymmetric, her teeth a little too crooked. She was sexy, though, and the knowledge that these men wanted her and envied me gave me a frisson that made me feel possessive and protective of her very early on. I was her bodyguard, constantly shielding her from a rioting barrage of lustful looks. She laughed a lot in bed, something that threw me at first. Sex had never been fun for me, exactly, but suddenly with her I saw how it was done, and how doing it that way could hold some appeal. In fact, it seemed for the first few months that everything was fun with Naomi, even prosaic chores like trailing around the supermarket or putting a wash on. This faded, of course, more quickly than I would have liked, but nevertheless, being with her made me happy.

Shortly after we married, I left the school that I had continued to teach at since my affair with Lydia. Although I never told Naomi the details, she knew that I had at one point had a relationship that had gone wrong with one of the staff. It wasn't her style to express jealousy or uncertainty, but I knew she wondered about the memories that being there might evoke for me. There were memories, of course, and I didn't like confronting them. Coming home to Naomi after work sometimes felt almost sordid, the reminders of my time with Lydia that the day had thrown up still clinging to my skin. Besides, I had had enough of the school and my indifferent middle-ranking position in it. I had also had enough of teaching. I wasn't a natural arbitrator, and being in class too often felt like a vain attempt at mediation between warring factions of pupils, with very little actual teaching to relieve the stress. I considered moving to a quieter school, but the problem ran deeper than that. I didn't want to stand up in front of a class of scornful fourteen-year-olds with little or no interest in literature any more. It wasn't what I had ever really envisaged doing, and looking back on the way I had fallen into the job, I realised that teaching had been intended as little more than a stopgap, a stopgap that had somehow endured for over a decade.

I wanted to go back to Oxford, become a tutor and lecturer. When I told Naomi my plan I expected her to laugh, but she embraced the idea with characteristic enthusiasm. She had had enough of London, she said, and would be happy to live in Oxford. Her own job in human resources was easily transferable, and besides, living somewhere quieter might have other advantages. It was an oblique reference to starting a family; she had often expressed reservations over bringing up children in London's messy sprawl. I didn't respond to it, but I didn't challenge her over it either. I didn't know what I thought about having children. It wasn't something that had ever been part of my life plan, but then I had said the same about marriage. In any case, it wasn't an immediate concern.

I renewed some old contacts, discovered an unadvertised vacancy, and persuaded a former tutor of mine, unorthodox though it was given my comparatively humble career background, to give me a trial. Perhaps it was simply fate—being in the right place at the right time—but even so, I couldn't understand why I hadn't done it years before. That was the thing about being with Naomi in those days; she always made things that had seemed fraught with difficulty clear and simple. All my reservations melted away. We found a rented house in Oxford while we searched for something more permanent. Packing up and leaving London felt like the right thing to do. I didn't think about Lydia much in these days, but I do remember feeling a sense of release as the removal van carried us up the motorway. I think it was only then that I glimpsed how much subconscious effort had gone into forcing back those memories, not allowing them to hurt me. I glanced across at Naomi, leaning out of the window of the van and waving goodbye to our old home. When she slipped back into her seat her cheeks were flushed and she was laughing, her unruly hair sliding from its clasp. Well-being flooded my veins. I loved her. We were moving away together, and I was going to a good job. I won't say that I thought, *What can possibly go wrong?*, or anything so clearly setting myself up for a fall, but nevertheless I was optimistic about the future.

For a while my optimism seemed to be justified. We settled quickly into Oxford, and I found that tutoring and lecturing satisfied all my dictatorial impulses with none of the soul-destroying grind that had worn me down in teaching. Naomi made friends quickly and introduced me to her social circle, so that we never had to deal with the isolation and uncomfortable codependence that sometimes comes with moving away. This honeymoon period lasted us through a good couple of years, and then it stopped. I couldn't put my finger on what changed. It was nothing dramatic, nothing as definite and self-explanatory as a growing tendency to argue more or the cessation of our sex life, which I had always presumed were the main culprits that sabotaged married life. It was more like a subtle, gradual cooling off, and it happened so insidiously that by the time I realised it had happened I couldn't work out how we had got from there to here. I knew that something had shifted in our relationship, perhaps for ever, but I couldn't quite put my finger on what it was. When I looked at Naomi I still felt affection, protectiveness, sometimes desire. I still loved her, too. These things don't just disappear overnight. Something was missing, though, and from the way I sometimes caught her staring at me across the table in a restaurant, as if I were momentarily a stranger, and one she didn't especially want to sit across from for the next two hours, I knew she felt it too.

One afternoon in 1988 I came home after my last tutorial to find her already there. This was unusual; I generally had a good couple of hours to myself before she returned from work.

Even more unusually, she was cooking, standing at the stove vigorously stirring a vat of some indefinable stew. I entered the kitchen cautiously, trying to gauge her mood. Seen as she was from behind, her body language gave nothing away. It was only when she spun round, hearing me, that I saw her face was radiant and excited, her eyes shining with emotion.

'Nick, I have some news,' she burst out before I could speak. 'I'm pregnant—we're going to have a baby. I was going to wait until the weekend to do the test, but I couldn't wait and I bought one at lunchtime and did it in the toilets at work. I'm sure they must all have thought I was mad when I came back in, but I just told them I needed to take the rest of the day off. I wanted to be here when you got back and cook you dinner so that we could celebrate.' She drew breath and buried her face in my shoulder. When she spoke again her voice was thick with tears, and this too was unusual. 'We need this,' she said, drawing back briefly to look me full in the face. It was her first acknowledgement that our relationship 'needed' anything. I wouldn't have put a baby at the top of the list of things that might help—if anything quite the reverse—but suddenly, standing there hugging her in the kitchen, I felt electrifyingly happy.

Naomi had an easy pregnancy. I saw as the months went on that her body was made for being pregnant, unlike those of some women, who look awkward and ungainly with the alien bump tacked on to their former frames. Her whole body responded to the change; breasts ripening and tautening, hips and belly swelling effortlessly to accommodate the new arrival. She had little or no morning sickness, which her visiting mother claimed to be a surefire sign of having a boy, and then, half an hour later, a girl. I said that I didn't care which we had, but secretly I wanted a boy. I suspected that I would be awkward with a little girl, find it difficult to play with her or delight in her probable penchant for frills and dolls. Ironically, I was pretty sure that the baby was indeed going to be a girl, but I kept my suspicions to myself. I contented myself with ministering to Naomi in the final months, cooking dinner for her as she lay in state like a vast empress on the sofa and washing and soaping her feet as she dangled them in the bath. I remember doing this the day before her due date, 17 December, and agreeing with her that babies were never on time and that we probably had at least another week to wait.

I was woken in the middle of the night by her gasping for breath, her hand clutching mine with more force than I had thought she possessed. The baby was coming, she said. For a wild moment I considered asking her how she could be sure, but I bit it back. Of course she was sure. For the first time in the pregnancy I felt a fleeting sense of being an outsider, bereft of a mother's knowledge and powerless to influence events in any way. I helped her fumble her way into a dressing gown and guided her downstairs. The drive to the hospital was eerily beautiful, trees lit up by garlanded Christmas lights, sparkling drops of ice blue and green flanking the streets as I whizzed past. I kept up a running commentary all the way, telling her that everything would be fine and it would all be over soon, but she didn't speak.

She had a dreadful labour, almost as if to punish her for the ease of the pregnancy. I spent almost twenty-four hours alternating between patrolling the dank grey hospital corridors drinking coffee and Coca-Cola to stay awake, and standing by Naomi's bedside, watching her face, tight with pain and fear. It shamed me, but I didn't want to see her like that. She was sanguine, a coper. Foolishly I had expected these traits to endure through everything she had to face. In those hours I saw them gradually stripped away, peeled back to reveal someone who was just as vulnerable as anyone else. The baby was finally born at one the following morning. Naomi was too exhausted to do anything but hold him briefly, then relinquish him to me.

I held him in the way I had been shown, and he stopped crying. He had tiny perfect features, spiky eyelashes jutting out from his face, and a fine covering of black hair.

'He looks like me,' I said, half to Naomi, half to myself. Standing there with him, all the fatherly feelings I had been secretly concerned I would never develop came on me in a rush. I realised that what I had been told was true: when it was right, loving someone was easy, like instinct. This little creature who didn't even have a name yet had broken through the freeze on my heart, a freeze that I sometimes felt Naomi was still penetrating inch by inch, so quickly that it left me bewildered. The matter of the name suddenly seemed very urgent. We had argued gently over our choice in the weeks leading up to his birth, and had reached a tactical stalemate which we had planned to resolve after the event, but now that the baby was here it seemed terribly wrong for us not to have named him. I knew Naomi favoured James, but as I looked at the baby, I knew it had to be Adam. I leaned over Naomi's bed, holding him up to her, and she smiled weakly.

'He looks like an Adam,' I said eagerly. 'Don't you think so? I think we should name him now.'

Naomi's lips parted as if she was about to speak. A ripple of exhaustion passed over her face and she nodded, lying back and closing her eyes. So Adam it was. A small part of me sometimes felt bad at the circumstances under which I had convinced her that it was the right choice, but another, larger part of me felt pride and exultation at having named our son; it made him feel more like mine. I stroked the top of his head lightly, and he started crying again, but it didn't matter. He was here. And actually, for the first few months, his presence did work on our relationship like a lucky charm. We were softer with each other, kinder. When I felt angry with Naomi I looked at Adam and saw the curve of her cheek written in his, and my anger melted away. Her body snapped quickly back to its natural shape after the birth, as if it were a piece of elastic that had been stretched and then released. Everything was as it had been, except better, much better. It was one chance meeting on one afternoon, when Adam was five months old, which changed everything. In the years that have followed I have often wondered if, given an informed choice, I would have turned down a different street that day. Everything—logic, emotion, common decency—points towards it being the best course of action, but somehow I still can't regret it. In my darkest moments that makes me feel evil, corrupted. I try to reason with myself, but it's like throwing pebbles to hold back the sea. If there is anything that has made me doubt what sort of a man I really am, it's this lack of regret.

I was running late for my first lecture of the day. Adam had kept us both up late, or early, with one of his rare but agonising night-long rants against the world. I was halfway to the English faculty when I remembered that I had to pay a cheque into the bank that morning. Cursing, I swung the car around and nosed it down the High Street, searching for a space. I found one on a yellow line that might have been a double once, but which was sufficiently worn away for me to be able to claim ignorance. I walked briskly down the street towards the bank and found it closed. Through its heavy glass door I could see a cleaner, doggedly pushing a Hoover back and forth across the carpet. A suited zombie walked infuriatingly slowly down the aisle, checking each paying station for pens and slips. I banged on the door, which brought a response about half a minute later from the bank clerk. His eyes looked at me vacantly through the glass. 'Ten minutes,' his lips said. I thought about arguing—it was dead on nine o'clock—but even I could see it was ridiculous and pointless to try to argue through a locked door.

Swerving away, I talked myself down. It was childish to be so worked up over a late opening at a bank. Pacing the street,

I decided to go and get a coffee while I waited. I passed a couple of my usual cafés, but the queues stretched out of the door and I couldn't face the waiting. On an impulse I turned down a side street. Sure enough, I could see a small café at the end of the road, and I quickened my steps, my heart lifting at the small victory. Intent as I was on my goal, he saw me before I saw him.

'Nicholas!' I heard a voice shout. It was familiar, and yet so obscurely so that I couldn't quite place it. I turned, searching for the source of the voice. When I saw him standing there, I didn't recognise him for a split second either. He was shorter than I remembered, his shoulders more stooped. The glasses were new, too, tortoiseshell rims lending an eccentric quirk to his face. He was beaming at me, moving forward to clap his hand on my back. To see him there was so strange that it was as if time had jolted backwards and transported me six years into the past.

'My God,' I said. 'Martin Knight.' I clapped him on the back in turn, giving a sharp bark of laughter. My heart was hammering in my chest with the unexpected adrenalin. 'What brings you here?'

Martin blinked excitedly behind his glasses, as if he was finding our meeting as difficult to comprehend as I was. 'We live here now, old man,' he exclaimed, and for an instant the thought flashed viciously through my head, *Who are you calling old?* I supposed he must be nearly fifty now, but he looked far older, and not of the modern world, like a character from a Dickens novel.

'So do we,' I said. 'Not far from the city centre. Are you still teaching?'

'I am, yes, a private boys' school,' Martin said eagerly. 'But "we"? Nicholas, you're married, I'm so glad.'

His remark struck me as strange; our friendship, after all, had been brief, and I doubted he had bothered much about my marital status in the intervening years. Unless, of course, he meant, *So glad that you're not still fucking my wife*, but the remark hardly would have been delivered with such innocent bonhomie if so. 'Yes, for over two years now,' I said.

Martin nodded, digesting this. 'Well, it really is extraordinarily good to see you,' he said, running a hand distractedly through what was left of his sparse grey hair. 'I always meant to keep up contact after we left, but you know how it is—life runs away with you.' In fact, Martin had sent a letter, not long after he and Lydia had left, but I had never answered it. Perhaps he was recasting history in a more diplomatic light, or possibly he had genuinely forgotten.

'And you,' I said, shaking him by the hand again. Strangely, I half meant it. Despite the old bitterness that seeing him had stirred up, I found a residual fondness for Martin and his endearing ways lurking beneath the surface. My friends these days belonged more to Naomi than to me, and it was always the women who were the more interesting partner of the couple; the men were mostly emasculated stuffed shirts with few original thoughts in their head.

'Look,' he said, digging into his pocket and bringing out a biro and a crumpled notepad. 'I'll give you our address and our number. You must get in touch and come round some time soon—bring your wife too, of course. Lydia would love to see you, I'm sure. She always liked you. Do call.'

I took the scribbled bit of paper. 'I will. I must go now, I'm running late.'

'Goodbye for now, then,' Martin said affably. I was halfway down the road when he called after me, an eager shout, as if he had just thought of something that couldn't wait. 'Nicholas! Do you have children?'

'One,' I called back, turning on my heel. 'A boy.'

'Wonderful! We have a girl!' he shouted, half hopping on the spot with glee. I smiled stiffly to mark my delight at this turn of events, then carried on up the road, faster than before. When I was back on the High Street, I had to look around me to reassure myself that everything was as it had been ten minutes before. Seeing Martin had catapulted me back in time, and left an eerie sense of unease behind it, the feeling I sometimes got when I woke in the middle of the night after a vivid dream and briefly couldn't remember where I was. As I walked back to the car, I ran back over the conversation. I realised that, subconsciously, I had not expected Martin and Lydia to stay together. Throughout our time together, she had never denied that she loved him, but it had seemed to me more like the kind of love you might bestow on a grateful pet than on someone with whom you would choose to spend the rest of your life. This at any rate was what I had wanted to believe. The discovery that she had lived through the last six years by his side made me think that perhaps I had been mistaken. Of course, she could be having other affairs, but somehow I thought not. At any rate, I would never get the opportunity to find out. I would throw away Martin's number and the chances were that I would never bump into him again—and if I did, I would do what I should have done in the first place and blank him completely. I reached for the scrap of paper, but in the instant of my fingers closing around it I changed my mind.

Why, after all, should I not see Martin again—and Lydia too, for that matter? Whatever had happened between us had happened a long time ago. I was over her, thoroughly so. I had a wife whom I loved, a child whom I adored. It might not have been safe once for me to see Lydia, but now, surely, the danger was past. She had chosen him all those years ago; she had made her bed and it seemed that she was still lying in it. It might do me good to confront the past and to confirm that our three-month liaison had been little more than a foolish mistake. And as for Martin and Lydia meeting Naomi . . . well, again, why not? Lydia was hardly likely to blurt out our past involvement over the dinner table. It would be satisfying to compare the two and to confirm that I had chosen the more suitable woman for me, the more desirable, the more stable. At that moment I conveniently forgot that it had not been a choice.

I had been driving the car on autopilot, barely registering the traffic that I was manoeuvring my way round. As I pulled into the faculty car park it seemed that I had been standing on the street with Martin just moments before. I walked swiftly to the lecture hall, greeted the students and launched into a speech that I knew by heart. All the way through, I was dimly conscious of the scrap of paper Martin had given me, rustling faintly whenever I moved against the cheque that I had forgotten to pay in, burning a hole in my top pocket. After the lecture I dug it out, just to make sure that it was still there.

That Saturday Naomi and I took Adam to the Museum of Natural History. Having read a book on early learning, Naomi thought that it was a good idea to expose him to culture as early as possible, just to get him into the swing of things. Privately I thought that at five months Adam was entirely incapable of telling a woolly mammoth from next door's cat, but I admired her persistence. Over the course of the preceding few Saturdays, we had been to an exhibition of modern sculpture, an art-house cinema screening and a choral rendition of Wagner's 'Parsifal' and he had resolutely screamed his way through all of them. That Saturday was no exception. We trundled the pushchair grimly past stuffed lynxes and fossilised ammonites, muttering apologies to the grimacing museum-goers as we went. In front of an illuminated display of volcanic minerals, Adam quietened briefly. We stood there, dumbly staring at the glittering lumps of rock, hardly able to believe our luck.

'He's going to be a mineralogist,' Naomi hissed. It was her favourite game to link anything at which Adam did not show active disgust with his future destiny.

'Over my dead body,' I said, equally quietly for fear of setting him off. I didn't care much for geology, and preferred to
think of Adam as the next Poet Laureate.

'No, it's a good career,' Naomi whispered, snorting with
laughter. 'Let the boy go his own way.' For some reason, I started laughing too, and we stood at the volcanic display, rocking
with suppressed mirth. Naomi was enchanting when she
laughed, the effort of it lighting up her eyes and reddening her
cheeks so that her pale brown freckles faded to rosy pink. I put
my arm around her shoulders, feeling a surge of affection for
my little family, and she leaned into me automatically. At that
moment Adam started up again, a siren wail that cut through
the silence of the museum like a red alert. I saw the curator
wheel around, frowning heavily, and start to walk towards us.

'Come on, for God's sake,' I murmured, 'let's leave before
we get thrown out.' Hastily, we pushed the chair along the
aisles, shushing Adam ineffectually, and escaped on to the
grassy quadrangle outside. Naomi flopped down on the grass,
stretching languorously in the sunshine, and laughed again.

'He's incorrigible, isn't he?' she exclaimed. 'You'd think he
could keep quiet for half an hour.'

'Darling, he's five months old,' I said indulgently. 'Sometimes I believe you think of him as an adult trapped in a baby's
body.'

'Maybe I do,' she said, suddenly serious. 'I mean, that's
what he is, isn't he? The person he's going to be one day has
got to be inside him somewhere. It's our job to make sure he
gets to be that person, that he gets it right.' She was frowning
up at the sun, her eyes creased into thoughtful slits.

'All a bit deep for me on a Saturday afternoon,' I said lightly.
In truth, her words unsettled me. I wasn't sure yet what kind
of role model I would turn out to be, and I didn't like the idea
of it potentially being my fault if our son went off the rails or
failed to be whatever it was that Naomi was hoping he would

be. I tickled the inside of her bare arm, hoping to jolly her back into the carefree mood we had shared a few minutes before, but she only sighed and sat up, shaking off my hand.

'I suppose we'd better be getting back,' she said. 'I have to be at Mum's by three.'

'What?' I had no recollection of her mentioning the visit, and it intensified my dissatisfaction.

Naomi sighed again, rolling her eyes in exasperation. 'I told you this two days ago,' she said. 'Mum wants to spend the afternoon with Adam and I said we'd go over there. In fact, I asked you if you wanted to come too, and you said yes.'

Now that she had mentioned it, I did vaguely remember agreeing to the trip, and the knowledge that she was right irked me even more. 'I don't remember this at all,' I lied. 'I don't want to trek down to Reading today. I've got things to prepare for Monday, and I want a relaxing day at home.'

'Fine,' she said shortly, taking hold of the pushchair and moving it away from me. 'We'll go on our own, then.' It was ridiculous of her to try to make an ally out of the uncompre-hending baby, but nonetheless I felt an irrational stab of pain at the thought of them being united against me. I shrugged, affecting not to care.

'Then I suppose I'll see you later,' I said. It was a small challenge; if she had softened I would probably have agreed to go with her. Instead she twitched her head angrily so that her curls shook from side to side, a funny little mannerism that normally made me laugh. That day it just irritated me, and I stalked off across the grass, leaving her. When I was out on the road I looked back and saw her pushing Adam off in the opposite direction, her back small and defeated. An immediate pang of regret shivered through me, and for a moment I thought about running to catch them up, but before I could decide she was hailing a bus and lifting the pushchair up out of sight.

I watched the bus move away, at a loss as to what to do next. I had overstated my preparations for Monday, and besides, I didn't feel like working. It was a bright, inviting May day, the air heavy with the scent of flowers and newly mown grass. As I strolled back towards home, I felt strangely sad, nostalgic. It took me a while to realise that it was the weather which was provoking me. This was the time of year when Lydia and I had begun our affair all those years ago. I remembered lying next to her under the sprawling cherry tree in the churchyard, drinking wine gently warmed by the spring sun. The memory caught me off guard, as did its accompanying sadness. I had thought more about Lydia in the last few days than I had done in years, sometimes fondly, sometimes with contempt. Meeting Martin had obviously been the trigger—it had unsettled me more than I had thought. I felt for my wallet, to which I had transferred the scrap of paper bearing his number. Perhaps I should call after all. I had been swinging back and forth on the decision all week, feeling one moment that I didn't care much either way, and the next that the choice was important, more important than I wanted to admit.

I was passing a phone box, and it felt like a sign. I stopped and went inside. It was baking hot, the glass reflecting and concentrating sunbeams like a greenhouse. A clutch of flies hummed in the corner, clustering around an abandoned sweet-smelling apple core. I tapped in the number and fed in some change before I could think any more about it. It rang five, six times. My heart felt light, relieved. No one was home, and I would not bother to call again. I was about to put the phone down when the ringing abruptly stopped and for a moment there was silence, but for a faint rustling noise at the other end of the line.

'Sorry about that,' a voice said. 'Hello?' It was Lydia. I opened my mouth, but nothing came out. Together, we listened to the silence. 'Hello?' she said again after a few moments, louder and more uncertain this time.

'Hello,' I answered finally. There was another silence, taut like a string pulled across the distance between us.

'Who is this?' she asked, but I knew that she already knew.

'It's Nicholas,' I said. 'Nicholas Steiner.'

'Oh!' she exclaimed, trying to sound surprised but offhand, as if I were a minor acquaintance from the dim and distant past. 'Martin said that he'd run into you the other day. What a coincidence, that you've ended up in this area too. He said you were married.' The last sentence came out like a non sequitur, following on too quickly from the rest of her little speech, and she covered it up with an embarrassed laugh. 'I'm afraid you've missed him, he's not here right now. But I'll be sure to tell him that you called, and . . .' She trailed off. I stayed silent, unsure how to respond. The heat of the phone box was making me feel dazed and soporific, the quiet buzz of the flies hypnotic and soothing. I waited. Miles away, down the line, I heard a soft sigh. 'This is strange,' she said quietly. 'I don't know what to say to you.'

I found my voice. 'It's strange for me too. I probably shouldn't have called, but when I saw Martin, it made me think about everything—about how I'm sorry that we couldn't have kept in touch.'

'It's pretty obvious why not, isn't it?' The words were sharp but her tone was sad, belying the snub I suspected she was trying to give me.

'Maybe.' I thought about it. 'I don't know. I suppose I wonder if the time has come when we can be friends.'

There was a pause; I could almost feel her turning the words over in her head, trying to knock some sense out of them the way a cat plays with a ball. 'I can't see how that's possible,' she answered finally.

'Why don't I come over?' I asked. I hadn't planned to make

the suggestion but it just spilled out of me. I didn't know myself why I was asking.

There was no pause this time. 'Definitely not,' she said. 'In fact, I'm going to have to go. I've got a lot going on here today.' For the first time I became aware of the faint background noises behind her voice; something that sounded like running footsteps, snatches of jangling, jaunty music that seemed to start and stop in unexpected places.

'What are you doing?' I asked.

'I have to go,' she said again. 'I think it would be better if you didn't call here again.' Before I could answer, there was a series of beeps and the line went dead. Glancing down at the monitor, I couldn't be entirely sure whether my money had run out or whether Lydia had hung up on me. Either way, the conversation was over. I leant back against the baking wall of the phone box and closed my eyes. For some reason the few minutes on the phone had drained me of all energy and I felt limp, wrung out like a rag. I stayed there until my head started to ache with the force of the sun on my forehead and the sweet cloying smell of the apple core was beginning to make me feel sick. I pushed the door open and stumbled out on to the street. It felt cold by contrast, and I walked quickly back to the car, knowing what I was going to do. The knowledge that Lydia was there without Martin was too much for me to ignore. I would go over there now, talk to her and set all the thoughts that had disrupted me over the past week at rest. Part of me knew it was a bad decision, but I gave myself no time to talk myself out of it, swinging the car away from the route home and out on to the A road, towards Kirtlington.

I followed the signs until I was at the outskirts of the village, then wound down my window and showed a passing couple the address that Martin had scribbled down for me. Their directions were vague and it took me another twenty minutes to find the right road, crawling around the narrow streets until

I felt that I must have covered the whole town. When I found it, I parked at the end of the road and went in search of number 16. It was a picture-pretty little cottage, with flower beds planted primly around its outskirts so that yellow-tendrilled flowers crept up towards the windows. I couldn't imagine Lydia tending those flower beds, but then I couldn't imagine her doing anything domestic; it was a side of her I had never had the chance to see. As I quietly unhinged the gate and walked up the path, I could hear echoes of the same jaunty musical sounds that I had strained to hear on the phone, and mingled among them, children shouting and laughing. For the first time I wondered whether I should turn back, but it was too late; my hand had taken on a will of its own and pressed the doorbell. I heard footsteps running lightly through the hall, and the door was flung open.

Lydia was standing in the doorway, frozen to the spot. Blonde hair a little shorter than it had once been, brushing her shoulders and layered around her face in a way that made her look modern, edgier. Free of make-up, green eyes wide and accusing in the pale oval of her face. The same slim, compact body lurking under a baggy shirt and shorts. I had once or twice over the years imagined how she might have changed. The hair aside, the answer was not at all. She still looked like the same woman I had dreamt about every night for months after she left—dreams that persisted long beyond my consciously missing her and wishing for her back—but at the same time she was different, because I was seeing her through new eyes. I looked at her and thought, she's just a woman. Still beautiful, that couldn't be denied, but just a woman like any other, made out of flesh and bone. Not the elusive angel I had thought I had lost, and yet a small, stupid part of me still wanted to hold her and make sure that she was real.

'I told you not to come,' she said, her voice dangerously calm.

'I'm sorry,' I replied, 'but I wanted to see you. I knew it wouldn't go away, so I came over, just to set things at rest . . . come full circle, if you like.' I could see that she didn't like. She could barely meet my eyes, staring furiously down instead at the red rug under her bare feet. Her toenails were delicately painted with pale pink polish.

'Well, that was a stupid thing to do,' she muttered.

'I know,' I said simply, and I did know, even then. 'But now that I'm here, can I come in?'

She hesitated, clearly agitated. 'Wait here,' she said, and hurried away through the hall, looking back as if daring me to disobey. I waited on the step, not moving a muscle, until she returned. 'Fine,' she said, as if in surrender. 'Come in.'

I followed her into a country-style kitchen, all rustic wood cupboards and tiled floors. Its wide shuttered windows looked out on to a long narrow lawn. As I followed her gaze I saw the children that I had heard outside, six or seven little girls, all playing some kind of complicated game, running and tagging each other, dancing in a circle and then breaking away again. Lydia went to the window, watching them intently, ignoring me.

'Not all yours, I presume,' I said drily, to cover up my confusion.

'It's my daughter's birthday party,' she answered flatly. 'Now perhaps you see why I didn't think it was such a good idea for you to come round.'

I swallowed, feeling like the intruder that I was. Looking around, I saw that the low oak table in the corner of the room was laden with party food—jellies in individual pots, gaudy coloured cupcakes and piles of sausage rolls. In the centre stood a large bright pink iced cake, leaning unsteadily to one side. Four pink and white candles were stuck into the mounds of icing.

I worked it out. 'You didn't waste much time.'

'I had her over a year and a half after we left London,' Lydia said, wheeling round to face me. 'I think I put it off long enough, don't you?'

'So you were putting it off?' I answered.

'No,' she said sharply. 'I didn't mean it like that.' We stood facing each other, both hurt and defensive. Again the memories from our affair flitted through my mind: I couldn't keep them out, couldn't erase the pictures of her lying naked next to me, looking into my eyes, as close as it was possible for two people to be. When she was that close, I couldn't focus on her properly, her face blurring into a fuzzy halo of light and dark. I used to trace my fingertips over her features, run them along the straight bridge of her nose and up to the arches of her eyebrows. I told her that it was like being blind, feeling her but not seeing. Sometimes she would close her eyes, and I would touch my fingers very lightly to her quivering eyeballs and her long dark lashes, committing them to a memory that was deeper and more instinctive than sight or sound. It was the texture of her skin which came to me then, so clearly that it was as if I really did feel it under my fingertips again. The thoughts made me feel guilty and irritated with myself. I hadn't come here to drown in lust-filled memories. If anything the opposite was true; I had wanted to purge her from my system once and for all, extract the tiny residual sting of poison that she had left. Looking at her, I suspected that I couldn't do it, and that I would never fully be able to understand how things had turned out as they had—why she had chosen him back then, and left me alone.

Lydia's face was sad and remote. Perhaps she was troubled by her own memories. We stayed like that for a long time, standing in silence in the kitchen and looking at each other, trying to make sense of things. It was only the sound of the back door slamming, footsteps running towards us, which made her start and look away.

'Louise?' she called. A moment later a little girl appeared in the doorway. Her dark brown hair was parted into plaits, giving her face a solemn, Pre-Raphaelite air. She was wearing a short blue pinafore dress, with buttons the shape of daisies running down the front, and a badge with 'Birthday Girl' emblazoned across it.

'Mummy, I'm bored of the game,' she said in a small voice, shooting me a puzzled look out of the corner of her eye as she sidled over to Lydia and put her hand in hers.

'Really?' Lydia exclaimed gaily. 'Oh well, never mind. We'll call the others in and then we can have some tea.'

The child glanced over at the table, saw the cake and promptly burst into floods of tears. Lydia instantly dropped to her knees and put her arms around her, ineffectually trying to shush her, but Louise appeared to be completely distraught, hiccuping for breath through her sobs.

'It's . . . it's not right,' she howled at last, stamping one button-booted foot on the floor. Lydia looked up at me, a long-suffering expression on her face. I laughed despite my awkwardness.

'Kids, eh?' I said. The child gave me a poisonous stare before returning to her agonies.

'All right, darling,' Lydia soothed, biting her lip to hold back the laughter I knew was lurking beneath her sympathetic tone. 'I'll fix the cake, I promise. Why don't you run back outside and let everyone know it's time for tea?'

Louise sniffed, rubbed her fists into her eyes and reluctantly withdrew. Lydia got to her feet, smiling ruefully.

'What will you do?' I asked.

'Get a cheesecake out of the freezer, or something, I suppose,' she said, raising her shoulders helplessly. 'She loved pink last week. I can't keep up.'

'I suppose I've got all this to come,' I said.

'Yes,' she replied, looking at me differently now. 'Martin said you had a boy.'

I nodded. 'He's only five months, so he has plenty of tantrums, but at least he can't complain in words just yet.'

Lydia's eyes were soft and bright, filled with something that could have been close to tenderness. 'I am happy for you, you know,' she said quietly, and her voice was gentle too, stripped of all the false aggression of her earlier comments. 'I thought of you often over the years and hoped that you were happy.'

'I wasn't, for a long time.' I thought about saying more, but I couldn't find the words.

'I know,' she said quickly. 'I know I hurt you, and believe me, I regret it every day. There's not a day that goes by that I don't feel bad for what I did—to both of you.'

Hearing her say that made me feel sad, and yet triumphant. The way she put it, she had suffered more than I had. I had been able to make a fresh start with Naomi, and I had forgotten her, or as much as was possible, but she had had to carry on in the same tainted relationship as if nothing had gone wrong. I tried to imagine her with Martin, lying by omission every single moment they were together, and suddenly the violence went out of my feelings. I pitied her. It made me feel superior somehow, knowing that she would have to go on living with the knowledge that she had betrayed him, and that she could never take it back.

Thinking those thoughts, the words were easy to say. 'I forgave you a long time ago,' I said, and it sounded true to my ears. 'We were younger then—we made a mistake.'

Impulsively, she crossed the room towards me and put her hands on my shoulders. 'I didn't want you to come, but I'm glad you did,' she said, and hugged me, just for an instant, before stepping away. 'And what you said on the phone about being friends—I don't know, it sounded crazy, but maybe it could work. We're both happy now, aren't we?' she asked, eyes anxiously searching my face. 'We don't regret how things have turned out?'

'Not at all,' I said. I was thinking of Adam, and the security and companionship that had always been the bedrock of my marriage. Those things I had never regretted.

'Well, then,' she said. 'Maybe we should try. I know this sounds selfish, but it would make me feel better in a way—to see you happy, to think that what we did hasn't ruined either of our lives—' She broke off. The children were running up the garden towards the kitchen, their excited chatter filtering in through the open window. 'If you don't mind, you'd better go now,' she said, and I nodded.

I was almost out of the front door when she caught up with me. 'Nicholas,' she said, a little awkwardly, 'all the same, I don't think I'll mention to Martin that you came round today. I think it would be better, if we do meet up again, that he's there too, so . . . well, as I say, I won't mention it.'

'O.K.' I could see it embarrassed her, having to hint that she would rather keep my visit quiet. It didn't matter to me. We would always have secrets between us, so one more would make no difference. I saw the same thought in her eyes and it made her hang her head and turn away from me, her cheeks suddenly flaming red. I let myself out and walked up the road towards my car, feeling oddly victorious, as if I had gained something unexpected and precious.

Naomi and Adam came back to our house several hours after I returned. Adam was in good spirits, smiling and chuckling in his pushchair, and I immediately volunteered to give him his bath. Naomi agreed warily, her mind obviously still on our earlier confrontation. I knew from past experience that she had expected to find me sullen and ungiving, mulling over the argument. It was true that I had a tendency towards sulking, but I found myself so pleased to see them both that my earlier aggravation with her melted away. I took Adam up to the bathroom and ran a warm bath, floating his favourite plastic toys on its surface. He sat in it happily enough, splashing and squealing, and I soaped his hair and kept up the burbling one-way conversation that he seemed to like to hear, even if his only response was the occasional squawk of surprise. Crouching by the bath, I watched his chubby limbs flailing and kicking in the water and felt a rush of protectiveness that fleetingly pricked tears to my eyes.

'He looks like he's enjoying that.' Naomi was standing in the doorway, leaning against the door frame in a silk dressing gown. I looked up at her, smiling.

'You know he loves his baths,' I said. 'I think it's bedtime, though, eh, Adam?' I lifted a compliant Adam out of the bath-water and laid him down on a towel to rub him dry.

'He should go down easily,' Naomi commented. 'He's had quite a hectic day. Listen, Nick, I'm sorry we argued earlier. I did think I'd told you about going to Mum's, but I might not have done, so I'm sorry I sprung it on you.'

'No, you probably did tell me.' Too intent on dusting Adam's plump, wriggling feet with talcum powder to look up, I made my voice conciliatory by way of compensation. 'I'm sorry too. Anyway, it was nice for him to have a change of scene.'

'Shall I take over?' she asked, stretching out her arms to scoop Adam up. 'I'll tuck him in, and then maybe we could get an early night ourselves.'

I watched her sashay through the hallway, still managing to look sensual and suggestive despite the burden in her arms. When she had disappeared into Adam's room I went to the kitchen and poured myself a drink. Whisky on the rocks; I downed it in a couple of gulps and poured another, carried it to the bedroom. Sitting down on the bed, I loosened my tie, feeling like a nervous schoolboy before a dance. We had made love only six times since Adam had been born; Naomi had never refused me, but I could tell that her mind had been about as far from rampant sex over the past few months as it was possible for it to be. I hadn't blamed her, far from it, but as I sat there fidgeting impatiently in the bedroom I realised how much I had been missing our physical contact. When Naomi came into the room she smiled at me, and immediately pulled the dressing gown from her body, stepping naked out of the puddle of silk on the floor towards me. She had never been shy about her body—it was one of the things I found most attractive about her. I cupped her breasts, still swollen and taut from breastfeeding, in the palms of my hands and kissed her nipples, ran my fingers lightly down over her stomach. I wanted to take things slowly, but as we kissed I couldn't resist any longer and we fell on to the bed together. I made love to her gently at first, then more roughly, unable to hold it back. I caught an exciting echo of the old Naomi in the way her fingernails raked my back, the toss of her red hair on the pillow reminding me of times that seemed so long ago that their memory came as a shock. I came quicker than I wanted, holding her tightly against me. Afterwards she rolled away from me, put her hands behind her head so that her breasts arched upwards, and I felt another stirring of desire, as quickly as the last had faded.

'I love you,' she said, staring straight into my eyes.

I told her that I loved her too. Ten minutes later I told her something else: that I had run into an old friend from my school in London, and that I wondered whether it might be an idea to invite him and his wife around for dinner some time soon. She agreed without asking any questions, telling me to name the day, and then yawned and snuggled up against me. In a few more minutes she was asleep. I stayed awake a long time, thinking over what I had done. At that moment, with my wife pressed up warmly against me, the baby monitor flickering greenly by the bed, it seemed safe.

Martin responded with characteristic effusiveness when I called to invite him and Lydia for dinner. 'I'd almost given up on you, Nicholas,' he commented when I called. 'How long is it since I saw you in town now—almost a fortnight? I thought you'd forgotten us!' From this I deduced that, true to her word, Lydia had not mentioned my visit to their home. We settled on the following Saturday. Martin hastened to tell me that they would find a babysitter for Louise—which was just as well, as at her age I could hardly have trusted her not to make some table-quietening reference over dinner to my curious presence in her kitchen the week before. I rang off feeling a mixture of guilt and resignation. I didn't want to have to lie to Martin, but it felt too complicated to explain the visit, and besides, I had implicitly promised Lydia to keep quiet.

Saturday came round so fast that I had no time to dwell on the multiple possibilities that it contained. Naomi was up early, slaving over the stove in an attempt to prepare as much of the food as possible in advance, so that when the guests arrived she could waft nonchalantly in and out of the kitchen as if she could create a sophisticated meal with little or no effort. In reality cooking had never come naturally to her, and before Adam's arrival we had eaten out more frequently than our wallets should have allowed. In the months since his birth I had manfully devoured more culinary disasters than I cared to remember, from leaden rice puddings to slimy, over-spiced curries.

'You're not doing anything too complicated, are you?' I asked as I wandered into the kitchen at about midday, and was met with a terse request to leave her alone. I tactically withdrew and spent the afternoon lazing in the garden, only returning inside an hour before the guests were due to arrive. I caught a glimpse of carnage in the kitchen as Naomi came to greet me, hurriedly slamming the door behind her. She was smiling brightly, too brightly, but her voice didn't crack as she told me that she was going upstairs to change. I thought about investigating the kitchen, but decided against it. I hoped, though, that the meal would turn out all right. If Martin's word was to be believed, Lydia was a brilliant cook, and I didn't want her to pity Naomi, or to feel smug in her superior prowess.

'I'll check on Adam,' I called up the stairs. There was no response. I spent half an hour or so aimlessly playing one of Adam's current favourite games—taking turns to clap hands and chant wordlessly louder and louder, culminating in a frenzy of battering hands and exuberant shouts from Adam. We had just begun the clapping for the fourth time when he gave a squeak of surprise, his eyes saucer wide and questioning as they stared over my shoulder, I turned to see Naomi in the doorway, wearing a dress I couldn't remember seeing before, pale green twined sinuously around her body like spring ivy. Her feet were bare and her long red curls fell over her shoulders in the way she knew I liked. She was relaxed now, confident that this was one way she could shine.

'You like it?' she asked simply, placing her hands on her hips and mock-pouting.

'Gorgeous.' I went and kissed the tip of her nose, smoothing my hands down the dress. 'In fact, why don't we pretend we don't hear when they ring the doorbell and just go to bed instead?'

'Don't push your luck,' she said, wriggling away from me. 'We did that last night, and besides, I'm damned if I'm going to waste all that food.' Although her words were stern, she was smiling, and I knew the compliment had pleased her. She had been jumpy for a couple of days about the dinner party, and I didn't think it was just because of the cookery challenge. Much as it was in her nature to scoff at such things, Naomi often displayed random flashes of intuition, and I thought that although she couldn't quite voice it to herself, she was aware of the nebulous tension attached to the Knights' visit. How much worse it would be for her if she knew the history between myself and Lydia, I reasoned. I had contemplated telling her that the colleague I had had the unsuccessful relationship with was Martin's wife—after all, it had been years before the two of us had met, and so I had nothing to be ashamed of on that score. I had come very close just the night before; imagined myself making an offhand, wry comment that would set the matter to rest but which I had nevertheless stopped short of making. Perhaps I didn't like the idea of my wife being aware that I had been a party in someone else's adultery; perhaps I had wanted to spare her the embarrassment of having to sit opposite Martin all evening knowing that he was excluded from a secret shared by everyone else at the table; perhaps I didn't want to risk making Naomi feel uncomfortable or jealous in the presence of another woman that I had slept with. There were certainly enough reasons to keep quiet. These thoughts flashed through my head as I pulled her back towards me and kissed her again, on the mouth this time, until I felt her start to respond.

'Honestly,' she murmured, 'do I have to tell you again? There!' She broke away as the doorbell rang sharply, making us both jump. 'They're early, and you haven't changed!'

'I wasn't going to,' I said, heading for the front door. A black T-shirt and jeans had seemed sufficient earlier in the day, but when I saw Martin in his starched collar and suit jacket I wondered whether I had specified that the event was black tie and subsequently forgotten about it. He was brandishing a bottle of wine and smiling broadly, glasses threatening to topple off the end of his nose. Behind him, Lydia stood in a straight sheath dress which it took me a few seconds to realise was almost exactly the same colour as Naomi's. Judging by the look on Naomi's face when I turned to introduce her, she had got there quicker than I had, but she quickly composed herself and beamed at the couple, holding out her hand.

'Lovely to meet you both,' she said. 'I'm Naomi. You must be Martin and Lydia. I hear green is very in this season, so we've obviously both got our finger on the pulse!' This was typical Naomi: she didn't believe in glossing over an awkward situation or pretending not to notice it, but preferred to take the pin straight out of the landmine.

'Yours is lovely,' said Lydia politely.

'What, this old thing?' Naomi said, and laughed. 'Anyway, come in, I'll get you some drinks, and then I must check on dinner. I'll let you reminisce about the old days with Nick—you must have a lot to catch up on.'

As Lydia crossed behind Naomi into the hallway she shot me a brief questioning glance, little more than a fractional lift of the eyebrows. I shook my head just as imperceptibly, and instantly felt displeased with myself. I had caught on to Lydia's question—*Does she know about us?*—and answered it without thinking, but I determined not to take part in any further silent communion. It felt disloyal; there was no reason for us to refer to the past any more, even wordlessly.

'This is a charming house,' Martin announced, looking around appreciatively. 'I think the decor must be Naomi's taste rather than yours, though, Nicholas—I seem to remember your bachelor pad in London being rather different!' Martin had visited my flat only once, but it had obviously made quite an impression on him. I laughed uneasily—I didn't like to think about the way I had lived before Naomi's feminine influence.

The three of us made small talk in the living room until dinner was ready, although Martin did most of the talking. Lydia was uncharacteristically quiet, sitting demurely in her pale green dress by Martin's side, a hand placed loosely on his knee. Although I tried not to look, my eye kept drifting back to it. I couldn't remember Lydia having been so tactile with her husband in the past.

'So you're still teaching, I take it?' Martin asked, enthusiastically scooping up a handful of nuts and nibbling on them. His small white teeth reminded me of a squirrel's.

'No, I actually gave up teaching when we moved here,' I said, feeling a spark of pride at the revelation. 'I lecture now, and do some one-on-one tutorials in college.'

'Really? That's great,' Lydia exclaimed. She looked genuinely happy for me. In the past I had often told her that I didn't feel at home in teaching and that I wanted a more cerebral, less mob-driven environment. I supposed this was the proof that they hadn't been empty words. 'That's great,' she repeated. 'You must find that so much more rewarding.'

'Some of us do find teaching rewarding, you know,' Martin pointed out, a little petulantly, moving his knee away from her hand. It was the first time I had ever seen him take issue with anything that Lydia said. Even more surprising was Lydia's reaction: she looked anxious, turning her huge green eyes on him placatingly and reaching out her hand to stroke his narrow shoulders.

'Well, of course, darling,' she said. 'You're a natural and very talented teacher, so it suits you perfectly.' Now it was my turn to swallow the implied insult, but I decided against drawing attention to it. Nevertheless, she seemed to realise what she had said, and looked awkward, smiling to cover her embarrassment. Luckily, it was at this moment that Naomi appeared, announcing that dinner was ready. We filed dutifully through to the dining room, where Naomi had laid the table with our best silver cutlery, cut-glass flutes and napkins folded painstakingly into the shape of swans.

'This looks delightful,' Martin said politely. 'If you might excuse me for a moment, I'll just use the bathroom.'

'Of course, of course,' Naomi said, ushering him back through the hallway. Lydia and I sat down at the table opposite each other. I tried to think of something to say, but nothing came.

'We have a little girl, you know,' Lydia announced, apropos of nothing, when Naomi returned. 'She's four.'

'Oh yes, that's right, Nicholas told me,' Naomi said enthusiastically. 'Louise, isn't it? I expect you know, we have a baby son. His name's Adam and he's in bed at the moment, but, well . . .' She rolled her eyes dramatically at the baby monitor perched on the sideboard. ' . . . you might get to meet him later, you never know.'

'Are you planning to have any more?' Lydia asked. It struck me as a strangely intimate question, but Naomi didn't seem to mind. She often surprised me in this way, galloping on to discussing bodily functions and deepest fears with random women met at parties before their husbands and I had even covered which make of car we drove.

'Well, I wouldn't rule it out, would you, Nick?' she said lightly. It didn't seem like the right time for a heart-to-heart so I simply made some grunt of acquiescence. In fact, I had not imagined having more than one child. Much as I loved Adam, he was exhausting, financially draining and still so young that the thought of tackling two young children at once frankly terrified me: I didn't know how people did it. Naomi didn't pick up on my reticence and beamed back at Lydia.

'And how about you and Martin?' she asked. 'Were you always planning on just having the one, or might Louise still have a brother or sister at some point?'

Lydia looked diffident. 'To be honest, by choice we would have had another,' she explained. 'But it proved more difficult the second time around. You know how it can be sometimes.' Footsteps outside alerted her to Martin's imminent arrival. 'I don't . . . we don't talk about it,' she added hurriedly, her eyes darting over to the opening door. Naomi nodded understandingly, busying herself with helping us all to soup.

'Lovely!' said Martin, rubbing his hands together and taking his place. 'So what are you ladies gossiping about?'

'We were just talking about Louise,' Lydia said.

'Ah, yes,' Martin said proudly. 'Extraordinarily clever young thing, if I do say so myself. I still think she might make a scientist, but Lydia seems to think she prefers stories, for some unfathomable reason.'

Naomi launched into the tale of Adam and the geology exhibition. I withdrew from the conversation, concentrating on the soup. I couldn't tie the flavour down, beyond that it was something green, but all the same, it wasn't too bad. Naomi had obviously made an effort. Unbidden, a memory swam into my mind: Lydia standing barefoot at the cooker in my old bachelor pad, cooking a cheese omelette from the dribs and drabs left in my fridge, the only time she had ever cooked for me. Me, ravenous after sex, lying naked on the scratchy red sofa, watching her. When we ate it I swore it was the most delicious thing I had ever tasted. As I thought back on it I couldn't help looking at her. She was already looking my way, her spoon arrested in the act of carrying soup to her mouth. I had the uncanny sense that she was remembering the same occasion, and a chill crept up the back of my neck and made me shudder unhappily. I looked away and scraped up the last of my soup.

'Delicious!' Martin delivered his verdict. Naomi made the usual polite demurrals, gathering up the plates and heading for the kitchen. Martin watched her go, then leant keenly forward across the table. 'Nicholas, she seems like a lovely woman,' he said earnestly. 'Truly, when you said you had married I wondered what on earth sort of woman you would have chosen. It was hard for me to imagine, you know, having known you in your bachelor days. But she's charming, and so attractive, I do congratulate you.'

'Thanks, yes, I'm very lucky,' I said automatically. I had grown used to people saying these sorts of things to me about Naomi, and had long since stopped wondering whether I was really so horrendous a catch as to justify the faint notes of surprise and admiration that always accompanied such declarations.

'You are,' Lydia agreed. She sounded sincere. 'I always thought you might be the type to starve alone in your garret.' A mischievous laugh burst out of her, the kind I remembered, making her eyes sparkle with pleasure. Naomi reappeared, having caught her last comment, and made some remark about being my saviour. I was obviously to be the fall guy of the evening. Ignoring them, I turned to Martin and asked him whether there had been any developments in the world of chemistry of late. It was a subject that he always contrived to make more interesting than it strictly should have been, and his informal lecture carried us through the main course. Naomi's chicken casserole was not as successful as the soup, carrying a peculiar aftertaste of something sweet and faintly medicinal. Martin diplomatically avoided mention of the food this time, restricting himself to a pleased-sounding grunt as he pushed his plate away.

By the time we had finished the dessert—a mediocre lemon syllabub which nevertheless went down well with the guests— we had also got through three bottles of wine. I wasn't sure who had drunk most, but from the fuzzy feeling in my head I suspected it might be me. Dusk was falling outside the long French windows, and by contrast the lights in the dining room seemed to shine brighter, cocooning us in their glow. Light from the dangling chandelier above us bounced off Martin's shiny pate, now almost entirely bald, and the thick lenses of his glasses. I could barely look at him. Next to him, Lydia was leaning back in her chair, her blonde hair spilling down over her bare shoulders. Her lips were painted pale pink, her mouth slightly open as she listened to Naomi talking. The green of her dress made her look pale, ethereal. On Naomi it had a strangely opposite effect, bringing out the relentlessly healthy bloom of her skin. I felt my wife's hand on my thigh, squeezing affectionately. I took it and held it under the table, gripping it tightly. I felt like I had to hold on to her, or I might drown.

'Oops,' she said, withdrawing her hand and standing up. The baby monitor was flashing red, emitting a faint crackly wail.

'Bring him down,' Lydia cried, pressing her hands together in anticipation.

'Better not,' said Naomi regretfully. 'We'll never get him settled again. If you want to see him, though, why don't you come up with me?'

Lydia started to her feet, obviously unable to think of anything better. A red flush swept through me: I didn't want her near Adam, but I couldn't vocalise why. Impotently, I watched the two women go, leaving me and Martin alone. I noticed that he was watching me very closely, fingertips pressed up against his thin lips.

'Nicholas, are you happy?' he asked bluntly. The words shifted me farther into unreality, echoing over and over inside my head.

'Of course I am,' I said, slowly sorting through my thoughts.

'You certainly should be,' he replied. At first I had thought that his question was somehow malicious, but looking at him again I saw only concern glinting in his small, kind eyes. 'You have a wonderful job, a wonderful wife, and I'm sure a wonderful son. But something tells me that there is something missing.'

'Well, there's always room for improvement,' I said stupidly. I gathered myself together: I was going to have to do better than that. 'I think it's in my nature to be reserved about being happy,' I clarified. 'I was a late starter, after all. Most men I knew got married at twenty-odd and settled into their careers far earlier than I did. Now that I have all those things that I didn't before, it feels precarious, I suppose. I have to keep something back.' I had convinced him, and myself. He nodded gravely, his eyes darting from side to side as he digested my words.

'You must learn to relax and enjoy it,' he offered. I felt a sharp stab of contempt at the banality of his advice. In the next breath I appreciated its truth, and felt bad.

'What about you?' I asked. 'Are you happy?'

To my surprise he didn't answer at once, but took off his glasses and polished them carefully with the edge of his sleeve. 'I'm not like you, Nicholas,' he said. His voice sounded a little slurred, and I wondered whether he had drunk as much as I had. 'I'm not handsome, or sophisticated. I'm something of a figure of fun—I know this,' he added sharply, glancing up at me. 'I'm perfectly aware that the boys laugh at me behind my back, and that my colleagues probably do too. I'm not the sort of man who was born to be happy.' He straightened up, his voice suddenly louder and clearer. 'But against the odds, I am,' he said. 'When I met Lydia I knew that she was out of my league, but I decided to ignore that, and sure enough, she did too, and we fell in love. So now, you see, Nicholas, I am actually just like you after all. I have a beautiful wife, a beautiful child and a job that I enjoy. We're the same. We're the same,' he repeated, and gave me a crooked, conspiratorial smile.

I don't know what I would have replied, but I didn't have to. Naomi and Lydia swept back into the room. They were laughing like the best of friends.

'Adam is so sweet,' Lydia told me. 'I'd forgotten what they were like at that age.'

'He went down again like a dream,' Naomi said. 'He didn't even want a feed, I think he just wanted to say hello. I think he'll be O.K. now. Nick, do you want to make some coffee? Then we can go through to the living room.'

I rose to my feet, feeling my head spin. 'Won't be a minute,'

I said. I walked through to the kitchen and shook some coffee into the cafetière, filled up the kettle and flicked its switch. I pushed the kitchen window open, breathing in the cool evening air. The only light gleamed from the top of the cooker. I stood motionless, listening to the kettle whistling, thin and high.

'I thought I'd bring these out.' Lydia was standing behind me, holding the dessert bowls. She put them down next to me, but she didn't leave.

I could smell the subtle fragrance that rose from her skin, apricots and vanilla. Her small, delicate fingers were curled tightly around the handle of a kitchen cupboard. Her knuckles were white, as if she were keeping her hands there by force. In profile, her face was radiant and familiar. The straight nose, the long curling eyelashes, the perfect lips that never should have been mine to kiss. As I looked at her, she turned to face me. Her chin was raised defiantly, but her eyes were sad. I thought, *You're so beautiful, I can't bear it.* For a fraction of a second, I had a crazy impulse to slap her across the face, for coming back into my life, for showing me without saying a word that there was a chance that everything I had built up had been a sham.

'Don't,' I said. She stepped forward, cancelling out the inches between us. She wrapped her arms around my neck, pressing her lips tentatively against mine. I didn't move. She kissed me again, harder this time. I realised that I should push her away and put my hands on her waist, but instead I felt them draw her closer against me. I kissed her back, and felt her fingernails scratch the back of my neck, her teeth bite down hard on my lower lip. I tasted blood. I could barely breathe, my breath coming in short gasps as if I were fighting for my life. I heard her gasp too, a short, almost angry exhalation, as she shook her hair out of her eyes and pressed me back against the counter. I wanted to fuck her right there in the kitchen. My fingers slid up under her dress, feeling damp silk and hot flesh.

A noise outside made us jump apart. My eyes went to the doorway, but it was empty. If I listened hard, I could hear Martin and Naomi chatting in the living room. A wave of relief and nausea swept over me; I swallowed to keep it down. Lydia picked up the tray of coffee cups. Her hands didn't shake.

'I'm sorry,' she said, looking me straight in the eye. Carefully, she carried the tray out of the kitchen. A minute passed. I filled up the cafetière, drawing in the dark, spicy aroma that curled up from its steam, and followed her into the living room.

LOUISE
2007

Lydia sits at Sandra's breakfast bar, eating the same breakfast she has eaten for the past fortnight: white toast, blackcurrant jam, strong black coffee. Sandra's cat rubs relentlessly against her legs, keeping up a strong, steady purr that soothes and relaxes her. She enjoys these times. While she is here, she can forget about Nicholas and Adam, and pretend that she is simply an ordinary daughter in an ordinary home. Sandra is busying herself with wiping the kitchen sideboard, occasionally commenting on the weather or the shopping that needs doing, as much to herself as to Lydia. The two of them have not moved much past the polite and stilted landlady and lodger relationship that they struck up when Lydia moved in, but it seems to suit them both. Since Adam's appearance at the house, Sandra has made the odd sly remark on his keenness, but not receiving much response, seems to have given up. Now she's singing, tuneless snatches of unidentifiable songs, wide hips shaking as she vigorously polishes. Lydia finishes her coffee and slips off her stool. She never knows whether to wish Sandra a good day, so oblivious does she sometimes seem to her presence. This time she decides to leave quietly, but as soon as Sandra hears the squeak of the kitchen door she wheels round.

'Lydia, come back, love,' she calls. Lydia reappears. Sandra wipes her hands on a tea towel, awkwardly approaching. 'I need to have a little talk with you,' she says.

Lydia thinks back over the past few days, wondering what

could possibly necessitate a talk. She has come back at a reasonable hour every evening, has been careful to keep her music down, had no one over to stay. 'Is there something wrong?' she asks.

'Well—' Sandra doesn't seem to know the answer to this. 'Not wrong, exactly, no, but I'm afraid you're going to have to move out.' Something about her manner has suggested that whatever the news is, there will be a lengthy build-up to it, and to hear it revealed so suddenly shocks Lydia, so that she cannot ask for details immediately. Sandra provides them in any case. 'Neil is coming back,' she announces, as if confident that Lydia will be happy for her. She knows from an ill-advised, tipsy conversation shortly after her arrival that Neil is Sandra's husband, who moved out unexpectedly and without much explanation a few months earlier. 'I knew the man would come to his senses. It was all a silly mistake, you see, and now that he's coming back, I shan't need the extra money any more. Besides, I'm sure you understand, it wouldn't be quite the thing to have you around when he comes back—nothing personal, dear!' She laughs heartily, perhaps to compensate for the lack of hilarity coming from Lydia's direction.

'But what will I do?' Lydia hears herself saying. She despises herself for showing her inadequacy so obviously, but she is genuinely at a loss.

'Well, there are plenty of other bed and breakfasts,' Sandra says brightly. 'I'm sure you'll find something, and of course, if it takes a few days . . .' She seems to be reluctant to finish the sentence, and her plump shoulders lift and fall.

'Right,' says Lydia. 'I suppose I'd better get out and start looking, then.'

Sandra looks slightly irritated, holding out her hands as if to implore Lydia to see sense. 'Don't take it like that, love,' she entreats. 'I didn't know you were planning on staying much longer anyway.'

'I don't know how long I'm staying,' Lydia says. She wants to get out of the kitchen. Cutting off Sandra's next words, she turns and leaves, slamming the door; it crashes satisfyingly, emboldeningly behind her. Snatching her coat from the stand, she leaves the house and heads for the bus stop, pulling the coat up over her head to shield her from the rain.

Twenty minutes later she stands in Lincoln's front quad and calls Adam's mobile. It takes him six or seven rings to answer, and when he does he sounds out of breath, as if he's been running—or having a passionate romp with Isobel, she thinks, trying to cut the thought out of her mind.

'Can I come up?' she asks.

'Sure.' He answers so quickly that her suspicion is laid to rest. 'I warn you, though, it's a bit chaotic up here.'

She climbs the stairs to Adam's room and finds that he is surrounded by a mountain of cardboard boxes, into which he is stuffing all his worldly possessions. From the way in which he scoops up handfuls of clothes, piling them into a box and squeezing them into tightly compressed balls, she divines that he is not the most efficient packer. She sits on the bed and watches him, swinging her legs back and forth.

'Last day of term,' he says unnecessarily after a few minutes. 'My mum's coming to pick me up in half an hour. Fuck knows how I'm going to get all this done by then.'

'Half an hour?' She looks at the carnage around them. 'Let me give you a hand.' She sets about refolding clothes and stacking essay folders into neatly regimented lines. 'You didn't tell me,' she says casually.

'What, that term was ending? I did,' he replies, but not looking at her.

'You didn't.' She keeps her voice light. Nonetheless he puts down his armful of DVDs and comes to crouch by her side, putting his arm around her shoulders.

'If I didn't, it's only because I keep forgetting you're not a student,' he says. 'I just assume everyone knows when term ends. Look, if you're worried that I wasn't going to keep in touch, of course I was. I was going to give you a call when I got back home tonight and see if you wanted to do something, actually.'

'Really?' She thinks it over. In his voice, the words sounded plausible, but when she replays them inside her head they come out as unlikely, paper-thin excuses. She wants to believe him, and so she gives him a small smile; reassured, he springs up again and resumes packing.

'So did you just come by for a chat?' he asks.

'Hmm. Not really.' In a rush, Sandra's dismissal comes flooding back. 'My landlady just threw me out. I've got to find somewhere else to live as soon as I can.' She realises that she has painted the scene in rather more dramatic colours than it deserves, but it sounds better that way and she wants to grab his attention. It works; he stops packing again and sits on his desk, arms crossed.

'Why the hell did she do that?' he asks, frowning.

Lydia raises her hands expressively. 'I don't know, something to do with her ex-husband, I think.'

'What will you do, then?' Adam's dark eyes are full of concern, and as she looks at them she is struck by a thought so obvious that she cannot believe it has not occurred to her before. For all these weeks, she has been trying to square their involvement with her desire to somehow get closer to Nicholas, seeing Adam and her nebulous feelings for him as an unwelcome and unexpected complication. Now she sees that far from hindering her purpose, he can serve it. Her encounters with Nicholas so far have equated to little more than a few abortive followings on the street and the peculiar and brief conversation in the café. Somewhere in the back of her mind she had started to accept that this was all there was to be, and that, curiosity satisfied but little else, she would return home having achieved and discovered nothing. Now she sees that Adam has been holding open a door through which she can pass at any time she likes, and although part of her shrinks back from the thought, she cannot resist pushing at that door.

'I was wondering if I could stay with you,' she says. Adam raises his eyebrows, exhaling slowly. She has caught him off guard, but he doesn't look altogether displeased.

'Right,' he muses. 'Just for a bit, yeah, till you're sorted out? I'd have to ask Mum, of course, but I've had friends to stay before, so I think she would be cool with it.'

She is tempted to ask whether Isobel has ever come to stay, but bites it back and asks the other question. 'What about your father?'

Adam gives a short bark of laughter. 'Oh, don't worry about Dad,' he says. 'He'll barely notice you're there.' The words are dismissive, but his tone is affectionate. Lydia is about to question further when Adam's mobile blares into life. He grabs it and listens. 'Already?' he says. 'Yeah. Well, almost, yeah. I'll come down.' He puts down the phone and turns to Lydia. 'Mum's early,' he says, rolling his eyes. 'Do you want to come and meet her?'

As they descend the stone staircase Lydia tries to remember Adam's mother. Although in those early years they must have met several times, Naomi seems like a background figure, slipping in and out of her mental vision. She remembers red hair, a voluptuous figure. Because of these things, she recognises the woman immediately from across the quad, but as she draws closer no extra spark of recognition comes with seeing her face. She supposes she must be in her early fifties, but her brow is smooth and only the tiniest of lines crease at the corners of her eyes. The red hair is pulled back from the nape of her neck into a curling ponytail. She is wearing a long, rather shapeless skirt that does not disguise the swell of her hips. Lydia can tell that once she had an hourglass shape, but the years have thickened her waist and stomach, giving her an air of comfortable plumpness.

'Mum, this is Lydia,' drawls Adam. Only by watching very closely does Lydia see a flash of pain pass over Naomi's face before she smiles and holds out her hand. *This is the power my mother's name has*, she thinks, *even after all this time.*

'Nice to meet you,' Naomi says. 'Are you at college together?' This last is addressed to Adam, and he looks panicked. Lydia realises that he is remembering her entreaty not to tell his friends that she does not attend the university, and is wondering whether this extends to his family. 'Yeah,' he says, shooting her a nervous glance. She smiles reassuringly; it makes very little difference to her either way. Emboldened, Adam adds a few explanatory and fictional words about how he and Lydia met.

'Lovely,' says Naomi. 'So, are you two planning on doing something this afternoon, or—?' She trails off, obviously at a loss as to why else Lydia would be there.

'Actually, Mum, I wanted to ask you something,' Adam answers. 'Why don't we go and open up the car boot and then we can meet Lydia back in the room?' He steers his mother away towards the lodge, looking back and giving Lydia a significant look. She watches them go, wondering how Naomi will react to the news of her coming to stay. Perhaps she will refuse, berating Adam for his impulsiveness and lack of prior warning. As she wanders back up to Adam's room, Lydia toys with the idea of saying that she no longer needs a place to stay; a sudden desire to return home, a helpful friend or relative. But she's gone too far to turn back now, and when Adam and Naomi return she can see by his face that everything is settled.

'That's cool about you staying for a bit,' he says offhandedly.

Naomi smiles and nods. 'It'll be nice for Adam to have someone to knock around with,' she says. 'He gets so bored in the holidays, don't you, love? I don't think his father and I are

stimulating enough company for him.' An obviously well-prac-
tised mother-son ritual follows, Naomi stretching out a hand to
ruffle Adam's hair, Adam ducking and diving to escape it.

'God, you're embarrassing,' he grunts. 'Come on, let's get
this stuff in the car.'

Naomi makes an expressive face at Lydia behind his back as
he grapples with one of the heavier boxes. She's trying to
include her, to make them co-conspirators, and Lydia can't
help but appreciate the gesture. She smiles, pointing at a pile
of papers that Adam has stuffed behind his desk in a bid to forget about packing them, and Naomi grimaces again and
laughs. Together, they follow Adam down the stairs.

'Will you come with us now?' Naomi asks brightly when the
last of the boxes is packed into the boot.

'I suppose I should go and collect my stuff.' Lydia thinks of
the box room at Sandra's house, which has never felt remotely
like home. It gives her a perverse sort of pleasure to think of
stripping her few possessions away from that room for good,
along with any obligation she feels to Sandra. 'If you wouldn't
mind, I could come to your house later on today.'

'Fine, fine,' Naomi says, waving her hand in a way that
shows she is not overly concerned with the details. 'We'll see
you later.'

'Thanks for helping to pack,' Adam adds, resting his hand
briefly on her shoulder as he moves towards the car. As he gets
in he looks back, over Naomi's head, and gives Lydia a wink.
It's a tiny gesture, but it sets off something inside her body, her
stomach lurching as if she has plunged off the edge of a cliff.
She smiles back at him, crossing her arms protectively across
her chest. She watches until the car has disappeared from
sight, and then runs for the nearest bus. If she hurries, she can
be out of Sandra's box room and in a taxi carrying her towards
Adam's home in an hour.

She hesitates on the driveway when the taxi has left, suddenly shy. The excitement that has sustained her through cramming her possessions into the holdall that is threatening to burst its seams, and the long ride out of town towards the Steiners' house, morphs into something closer to dread. Their house is far grander than she had imagined, a miniature palace standing in state in what must be an acre or more of lawn. She can barely remember their old house in which she used to play sullenly with dolls, sidelined by her parents and Adam's, but she is sure that it was far less majestic than this. The family has obviously come up in the world, buoyed up perhaps by Nicholas's growing profile as a lecturer. She knows through snippets she has read in local papers that he gives talks that go beyond the remit of drip-feeding students knowledge, and that he has gained a reputation. All the same, it surprises her that it should have converted itself into this sprawling piece of real estate.

She sidles forward, her eyes darting from window to window to check that she is not observed. Through the largest of these windows, she can see a long sofa in creamy buttercup yellow, a pure white rug thrown across the expanse of floor, a dangling crystal chandelier. Already she envisages a hastily knocked-over cup of coffee or an idly placed biro, imprinting a mortifying and indelible stain on the room's perfection. Her mind shrinks back from the thought and she bites her lip, wondering whether it is too late to turn back. Even as she considers the possibility, her feet have taken on a life of their own, leading her to the front door. Standing in the elegant porch, flanked with waxy-leaved plants bursting with red button berries, she raises her hand and presses the doorbell. Adam answers with suspicious haste, and she wonders whether he has been watching her from one of the windows after all, unseen.

'Hey,' he says, affecting nonchalance, but she sees a faint blush creeping across his cheek. 'Come in. Mum's making dinner and Dad's not back yet, so I can show you round.'

'Great,' she replies, lugging the holdall inside after her. Adam doesn't offer to carry it, but this doesn't surprise her. Men are probably seldom thoughtful in this way. 'This is an amazing house,' she ventures, as, although he presumably knows this, not to comment seems perverse. They are standing at the bottom of a huge oak staircase, winding up on to a mezzanine landing. Someone, presumably Naomi, has placed bowls of white winter roses along the table in the hallway next to them, and Lydia can see them reflected in its highly polished surface. When she follows Adam into the room that she glimpsed through the window her steps seem to echo.

'You like it?' Adam asks. She nods, although this is not precisely what she meant. 'It used to belong to my grandmother,' he explains. 'When she died, Dad took it over.'

'Ah.' So it is family money, and not a lucrative career, that has brought Nicholas here. She feels her grudging admiration turn to faint scorn.

Adam leads her through the hallway again and into a lavish country-style kitchen, where Naomi is vigorously whisking something in a bowl with her back to them. Adam rolls his eyes and leads her quietly out again, only pausing to explain when they have reached the mezzanine landing. 'I warn you, Mum is a pretty bad cook,' he says. 'You have to smile politely and say it's delicious, but it won't be.'

Lydia laughs, unsure whether to take him seriously. 'My mother is a pretty bad cook too,' she says. Even in life, this would have been slander, she thinks, remembering the stories her father has told her. Adam whisks her past a couple more rooms—bathroom, master bedroom, a closed door at which she briefly lingers.

'Dad's study,' he says. 'Avoid at all costs. He doesn't like anyone messing with his papers. Like I'd *want* to,' he adds irritably, his slip into the personal revealing an ancient grievance. Briskly, he leads Lydia to the end of the landing and flings open another oak door. His bedroom is larger and cleaner than the square box he litters with books and beer cans at college—all wooden floors, slanting ceiling and wide sash windows. His bed is a double, tucked cosily under the eaves in a way that makes it seem like a private den. They stand in front of it together. More because it is becoming too heavy than for any other reason, she puts the holdall down beside the bed. His eyes flick to it and back to hers in a question that she pretends not to understand, wanting him to make some sort of move.

He clears his throat, laughing a little embarrassedly. 'So, your sleeping arrangements,' he says. 'There are a couple of other bedrooms, so you could take either of those, if you wanted. Or we could make up a bed for you here, or, well . . .' He laughs again. With a flash of insight, she sees that his diffidence is at least partly feigned; he's looking at her with a cocky, charming smile which she reluctantly responds to.

'Let's just play it by ear, shall we,' she says wryly.

He shakes his head in mock exasperation. 'Tease,' he says softly, and she thinks that this may be the time at last, but before he can approach her they hear the front door slam downstairs, loud footsteps moving across the hall. Adam breaks away from the bed, smiling lightly. 'That'll be Dad back,' he says. 'Come and say hello.'

This is the moment she has been dreading the most. As she follows Adam back out to the mezzanine she turns over in her head the possibility of feigning non-recognition, in the hope that the encounter in the café will have slipped from Nicholas's mind. She doesn't have long to ponder. From her vantage point above, she sees him standing in a dark pressed suit, his sleek black head bent over the hall table as he sifts through the post that has been left out for him. When he hears the movement above him he looks up sharply, shading his eyes against the light.

'Adam?' he calls. Adam clatters down the stairs. Lydia

hangs back, leaning over the mezzanine rail. The two men share a tersely affectionate greeting, hands slapped on backs and general enquiries. 'Good to have you back,' Nicholas says cordially. 'I hope we'll see something of you these holidays.'

'Yeah, I'll be around,' Adam says. 'I've got someone staying—a friend. A girl.' He looks around, apparently only just noticing that Lydia has not followed him. 'Lydia!' he calls. She sees Nicholas's neck stiffen at the name, and descends the staircase slowly. When she is halfway down she stops and stares, as if struck by puzzlement. He's looking up at her, mouth slightly open in surprise, brows furrowed.

'Hello,' he says.

Adam catches the unusual note in his voice and looks between them enquiringly. She smiles, deciding to play the coincidence lightly. 'Funnily enough, your father and I had a brief conversation in a café recently,' she says, glancing at Nicholas, hoping that he will not mention her tears or the strangeness of the conversation.

'A small world indeed,' he says breezily, shaking off his bewilderment. She is reassured by the corresponding lightness of his tone. 'I had no idea you and Adam knew each other. Well, I wouldn't have, obviously, as our conversation was very brief, as you say.'

'Small town, more like,' Adam says, not seeming too put out by this revelation. 'Well, I won't bother to introduce you, then. Lydia's going to stay for a while—they kicked her out of her room in college for a conference and her parents are abroad just now.' She listens to his words in amazement; clearly this is a story he has cooked up himself over the course of the afternoon. She can't fault it, but wishes he had run it past her first.

'Fine,' Nicholas says crisply. He runs a hand through his dark hair, rubbing it against his scalp as if he has a headache. His face is a mask, impossible to read.

'I'm going for a slash,' Adam announces, perhaps deliberately crudely. 'See you back down here for dinner in a sec.' He clatters off up the staircase.

Lydia and Nicholas are left alone in the hallway. He has turned back to the post, rifling through the letters with what seems to her to be an exaggerated concentration. His shadow looms and twitches against the polished surface of the table. The silence lasts what feels like a long time; a fraction longer, she thinks, than it would have done had they been nothing more than two polite strangers thrown together.

'So,' he says, not looking at her, 'are you all right?'

She knows he is referring to her tears in the café, but cannot tell whether he is asking out of a sense of duty or something more. 'Yes, thank you,' she says. 'It was just a bad day.'

He nods, collecting and aligning his post into a neat pile now. 'Well, we're very glad to have you staying with us, Lydia.' The words, and the tone, are formal, and she is not sure whether the faint whiff of unease she catches is real or imagined. He turns to her, his face thoughtful and a little puzzled. 'You know,' he says abruptly, 'I knew someone with your name once, a long time ago.'

Lydia stares at him, not trusting herself to speak. Besides, what answer could there be? For a moment he looks at her expectantly, as if waiting for some kind of prompt; then the mood flickers and changes. 'It was a very long time ago,' he says again, almost dismissively, and yet not so; she can hear the edge in his voice, anger and regret and sadness all muddled up. He shoots a quick look in the mirror over his shoulder, and what he sees there seems to reassure him. He clears his throat, stands taller. 'I'll just go up and change, and then I expect Naomi will be serving dinner,' he says.

He nods at Lydia, giving her a small, tight smile, and heads up the staircase. She is left alone, swaying slightly with the unexpected adrenalin that has hit her, blinking back thoughts.

In that moment she wonders whether she should not have come, and looks over to the front door. She could walk out of this house and never return, but she hesitates a moment too long, and when she turns the other way instead, inward, towards the kitchen, she knows that the chance has closed up. She will stay here, now, until whenever the time comes for her to leave, and that time will be shown to her, not chosen.

Dinner is roast chicken with mashed potatoes, gravy and vegetables. The simplicity of the meal notwithstanding, Lydia can find nothing much wrong with it and her compliments to Naomi are more sincere than she had feared they would have to be. On hearing them, Adam and Nicholas share a conspiratorial grimace, Adam's exaggerated and disgusted as he pokes his fork searchingly into the food. When Naomi glances at him, he beams ecstatically and echoes Lydia's own compliments before looking slyly back at Nicholas. Lydia realises that the conceit of Naomi's cooking being appalling is a piece of father-son bonding that probably dates back years, and which is clung to despite its being out of date and inaccurate. She also sees, as the meal continues, that Naomi is fully aware of it and panders to it, making self-deprecating remarks and suggesting that perhaps they should have gone out for dinner.

Lydia feels that the situation should have made for a tense affair, but in fact the mood of the evening is decidedly relaxed. In an open-collared shirt, light grey spliced with pale pink stripes, Nicholas looks easy and approachable, his earlier formality cast aside. When Adam reels off an anecdote about his eccentric tutor's latest escapade, he throws his head back and laughs unashamedly. Lydia sees a flash of sharp white teeth, glinting in the dark cavern of his mouth. They are eating in the kitchen diner in front of a crackling log fire, and he rolls up his shirtsleeves as the room heats up, exposing strong forearms sprinkled with dark hairs. Once or twice, Naomi reaches out across the table to smooth her hand down his arm, her pink-painted fingernails affectionately scratching the skin. The bond between them is evident. Naomi looks at her husband with adoring eyes, blinking every so often as if he dazzles her. Nicholas is less demonstrative, but when he rises to help her collect the plates, Lydia sees his hand slip briefly to the wide swell of her bottom. She would not have thought that physical desire would survive much past forty, but it seems the Steiners are the living and contradictory proof.

Naomi brings out a lemon meringue pie for pudding, with a self-conscious fanfare. Adam eats his piece in two minutes and demands seconds, explaining to Lydia that it is a favourite of his. Irrationally, she feels warm and loving at the minor revelation, as if Adam's fondness for lemon meringue is somehow further evidence of his likeability. She concentrates on her own plate, scraping up the last flakes of pastry. This is hardly the time to be having tender thoughts or making doe eyes at Adam across the table. Nicholas rises and announces that he is going to make some coffee. Naomi is effusive in her praise, something that gives Lydia to understand that this is a relatively infrequent event. Watching him measure coffee granules into the cafetière, Naomi looks rapt and attentive, far more so than such an ordinary activity warrants.

'Sorry for all the family talk,' Nicholas says as he carries the cups to the table. The evening has been largely taken up with Adam's term-time stories and catching up on extended family news. 'I wouldn't want you to think that we're not interested in you.' He laughs, a quickly suppressed bark.

'Oh no,' Lydia says quickly. 'It's fine.'

'No, Nick is right,' Naomi interjects. 'Tell us a bit about yourself. Where do you usually live out of term time? Are your parents just abroad for a holiday?'

'I live in Devon,' Lydia says. She has never been to Devon but likes the idea of the place, which conjures up images of smiling locals, cream teas and long walks on the beach. 'Yes, my parents have just gone to Spain for a while. They have friends there, but I don't really know them.'

'Tell us more about your family,' Naomi urges. 'Do you have brothers or sisters?'

'A sister,' Lydia invents. She produces a ready-made family out of thin air: parents called Margaret and Keith, who left the bright lights of London a decade ago to live out a rural idyll; a sister, Helen, a couple of years younger, who is currently study-ing at art college in Bournemouth. As she talks about this cosy imaginary family, she watches Nicholas. He is leaning forward, polite and attentive, his powerful hands locked carelessly around his coffee cup. A lock of black hair threaded with sil-ver falls over his heavily lined forehead. His expression is tol-erant but a little bored. As she spins a fantasy about Margaret's talent for the piano, the thought flashes through her head that she could make his face change in a matter of seconds, just by letting slip some unmistakable detail. The power is in her hands, but she chooses not to use it, and she feels it sit tightly in her chest, growing ever more significant and precious.

'I'm knackered,' Adam announces after a while, when Lydia's family tales have dried up and they are sitting in com-fortable silence. 'What about you?'

'Hmm.' She isn't tired really, and wants to prolong the evening; there are questions about the Steiners' own lives that she would like answered. She can see, though, that Adam is shifting impatiently in his seat, eager to be off, and agrees to come with him. In any case, Naomi's arm is now linked through Nicholas's, her head resting on his shoulder, section-ing them off. 'Goodnight, then, and thank you very much for the dinner,' she says, standing up.

'That's fine,' Naomi says cheerfully, raising her head for an instant. 'See you both tomorrow. We're thinking of doing some shopping in town, if you're interested.'

Adam gives a non-committal grunt and steers Lydia out of the kitchen. 'Not if they paid me,' he murmurs as they climb the deep oak stairs. 'Mum just wanders about from shop to shop, spending forever in each one and not buying anything, and Dad stands around like a statue waiting for her, like he's never been in a shop before. Fucking embarrassing.' Adam seems to find a lot of things embarrassing, Lydia muses. She supposes it is part of being a teenager. At only three or four years his senior, she nevertheless feels far older, and besides, embarrassment is not something she has ever experienced with her father, largely because she has never brought a friend home to meet him.

In his bedroom, Adam throws himself down on the bed with a thump, groaning and stretching his arms above his head in a pantomime of exhaustion. She is about to suggest leaving him to sleep when he rolls over and holds out his hand, beckoning her to him. She lies on the bed next to him, his arm slung around her shoulder. They are so close that she can feel the emphatic thud of his heartbeat against her hand.

'So,' he starts, staring up at the ceiling, 'how much of that stuff about your family was true?' Despite the confrontational nature of the question, there's no venom in his tone, only a mild curiosity.

'A lot of it,' she lies. 'Most of it, really.'

He nods slowly, then turns his head towards her, frowning as if a thought has just struck him. 'You know, I was thinking earlier,' he says. 'About you and my dad meeting in that café. You knew he was my father, didn't you? You must have, because of that lecture where we met. So why didn't you tell him that you knew me?'

Lydia stiffens, but only briefly; this is a loophole she has not considered, but she can relatively easily talk her way out of it. 'It was only very shortly after that that I ran into him,' she says. 'I didn't really know you at all at that point, and besides, what would I have said? "Er, by the way, your son passed me a note in a lecture the other day"? It would have sounded a bit stupid, don't you think?'

Adam mulls this over for a few seconds and then gives a begrudging snort. 'Suppose,' he says. She can see that he is still a little hurt, his pride pricked by being left out of the conversation, even on the basis of such a short acquaintance.

'The world doesn't completely revolve around you, you know,' she says playfully. 'Typical only child.' Saying the words that have occasionally been levelled at her over the years by her father in moments of exasperation gives her a secret little thrill. Protected by Helen the imaginary art student, she can say them without fear of retaliation. Adam responds spiritedly, tickling her under her armpits until she squeals for him to let go, which to her disappointment he does almost at once.

'Sounds like you've got a nice family,' he says after a while, reverting to his earlier topic. 'I hope you make it up with your parents soon.'

'So I can leave you all alone and stop imposing on your hospitality?'

'No,' he says seriously, looking sharply at her. 'You know I didn't mean that.'

She shrugs as if it is not important. 'It seems like you've got a nice family too,' she says. 'Your parents seem very happy together.'

'Yeah . . .' he replies, as if embarking on a monologue, but nothing further comes. He's lying on his back, hands pillowed behind his head now, chewing his bottom lip thoughtfully.

'Aren't they happy?' she asks, knowing it seems unnatural to press the point, but unable to help herself.

'I guess they're just like any other couple,' he says. 'They have good times and bad times.' He closes his eyes. His hand fumbles with the buttons on his shirt and undoes them one by one.

'Do you want me to go?' Lydia asks. She means her voice to sound normal, but it comes out as a strangled whisper, forcing its way past the lump in her throat. He doesn't answer at first, just shrugs his way out of the shirt and casts it to the floor. Then he opens his eyes and looks directly into her own. For the first time she sees what she has been looking for in them, a lazy, predatory intent which makes her catch her breath.

'No,' he says. He puts his hand at the back of her neck, under her hair. The hand is gentle yet forceful, guiding her head towards his. She parts her lips in readiness and receives his. His mouth feels cold, almost alien. Their first kiss is chaste and tentative, his tongue kept decorously back behind his teeth. It is only after a few repeats of this that his lips begin to warm against hers. He senses the shift and increases the pressure, kissing her faster, deeper. She kisses him back, closing her eyes to shut out the rising sense of disturbance that is rippling through her body, but it won't be shut out, rising to a relentless hum that shakes her bones and makes her tremble in his arms.

'You're shivering,' he says, pulling back. His eyes are kind and curious. Looking into them again, she feels reassured.

'I'm nervous.' She feels the truth of the words, but cannot put her finger on exactly why.

'No need,' he says, stroking the back of her head softly and rhythmically, the way he might pet a cat. It feels nice and she leans her head back to push against his hand. 'We don't need to do anything else tonight. I'm just glad I've finally kissed you.'

'Have you been wanting to?' she asks.

Adam leans forward again, mumbling the words between kisses. 'Ever since—I first saw you—in the lecture hall, I've been wanting to,' he murmurs.

'Then what took you so long?' she murmurs back. She feels the lines of his brow crease against hers. He sighs, long and low.

'I don't know,' he says. 'I really don't.' They stay like that for a while, foreheads touching, arms encircling each other, caught in the heat of their bodies and the soft, low lighting of the bedroom. After a few minutes she feels his breathing change. He has fallen asleep, wrapped up in her embrace. Quietly, she disentangles her limbs from his and moves to the other side of the bed, switching off the bedside lamp.

Sleep does not come. She waits open eyed in bed, listening to the sound of his breathing. Now and again she turns her head to study him, accustomed to the darkness now. His full lips are parted sensuously, inviting touch. She can make out the dark circle of a nipple on the half of his torso that is exposed, the sheet flung carelessly over his body. She traces it with her eyes. She begins to feel fidgety and restless, not wanting to wake him, but unable to stay motionless in the bed any longer. She decides to go to the bathroom, fetch a tooth mug full of water. Careful not to disturb him, she slips out of bed, the chill of night air biting at her skin. The lights in the corridor are off. She gropes her way in the dark towards where she remembers the bathroom to be, battling the surge of vulnerability that comes with exploring unfamiliar territory. Gratefully, she sees a thin strip of light ahead, illuminating the base of one of the doors along the corridor. The master bedroom, she thinks. The bathroom is just next door. She heads towards the strip of light, and as she does so she hears voices, faint but unmistakable behind the bedroom door. She draws closer.

' . . . think their relationship is,' she hears Nicholas say.

'I don't care what their relationship is,' Naomi hisses. Her voice is taut with pain and anger. 'It's nothing to do with that. All I'm saying is that it upsets me, it still upsets me, I just wish you could understand that . . . and sympathise.'

'This isn't the girl's fault,' Nicholas says. 'You're upset over a name. After all this time . . . it's ridiculous,' she thinks she hears him say, but his voice is muffled, as if he is talking more to himself. 'You agreed she could come here,' he adds, louder. 'I wasn't even consulted, so how you can blame me—'

'I'm not *blaming you*, Nicholas,' Naomi's voice fires back, shrill and plaintive. 'I'm just trying to *share with you* the fact that this has brought back some memories that I don't enjoy revisiting . . . and yes, I know it's not this girl's fault, she just happens to share a name with someone who I really don't much like thinking about.'

'And you think I do?' he asks. He sounds angry now. There is a long silence. Lydia tries to imagine what is going on behind the door and cannot. After a few seconds she hears a few choked sobs, a few conciliatory mumbled words that she cannot catch.

She moves away from the door and tiptoes back to the bedroom, water forgotten, head buzzing. The easy affection at dinner was a front, she thinks. She doesn't feel angry at having been deceived. In a way she admires Naomi for fighting for her happiness, rolling it out for Lydia to see in an attempt to convince herself. Privately, Lydia also feels a sense of triumph. The perfect marriage does not exist after all, not here. It too has been tainted by what she has been through. She realises that not once in the overheard conversation did either of them speak her mother's name, as if they are both afraid of the spells it might cast or break between them. Lying back in Adam's bed with him tossing and turning intermittently beside her, she half expects to hear shouting carried down the corridor, the re-explosion of the argument into something uncontainable. She strains to hear, but nothing breaks the dark flat silence.

NICHOLAS
1989

In retrospect, I was never sure how I got through the rest of that dinner party. It would have been hard enough at the best of times, but with the best part of two bottles of wine sloshing the secret around my system, I had to pull every fibre of my being into line to put across some semblance of normality. Lydia and Martin stayed another hour, perhaps two. I sipped the strong coffee in the hope that it would sober me up, but all it did was make my heart race crazily. Lydia seemed incredibly relaxed, chatting animatedly with Naomi about the difficulties of finding good schooling. Martin seemed content to languish in the armchair, occasionally making the odd supportive comment as he drifted in and out of a doze, his glasses repeatedly slipping off the end of his nose and waking him with a start before he replaced them and started the whole performance over again. When the clock struck twelve I could take no more and made some facetious remark about coaches and pumpkins. Inane as it was, it had the effect of rousing Martin, who stumbled to his feet and announced that they should really be heading off.

'I suppose we should,' said Lydia, with what appeared to be genuine regret. 'The babysitter won't be pleased if we stay out much longer.'

We escorted them to the door and waved them off, amid a flurry of thanks and plans to meet again from the two women. When I embraced Lydia, kissing her briefly on the cheek, I half expected some signal from her, some kind of subtle clue as to how I was to interpret the kiss in the kitchen, but her body was wholly pliant, giving nothing away. When I released her, her pretty pink lips smiled, but her eyes looked through me. I felt the shutters going down. As I watched her swing her slim bare legs into the car and start the ignition, I thought, *Of course. She's driving, and she's drunk almost nothing.* The knowledge somehow intensified my shame.

'Well, that was a nice evening,' I heard Naomi say behind me. I closed the door and came inside. For a moment I thought that her tone was sarcastic, but one look at her radiant face told me that she was sincere.

'You liked them?' I asked.

'They're lovely.' She delivered her verdict with such firmness that I realised it would be no use trying to suggest that the guests had been a bore and that the evening should never be repeated. 'Martin is quite eccentric, of course, but such a sweet man, and he obviously adores her. You can see why—she's such fun, and she's so beautiful, isn't she?'

It wasn't a rhetorical question. 'She's quite pretty, I suppose,' I said, beginning to collect up the coffee cups and pile them on to the tray. Lydia's had a faint pink stain around its rim where her lipstick had rubbed off. My thumb grazed it as I picked it up; it felt soft and slippery on my skin.

Naomi rolled her eyes, but I could see my answer had pleased her. Not given to jealousy, she was nevertheless not immune to brief flashes of feminine insecurity. Together we carried the evening's leftovers through to the kitchen. As she bent to pick up a crumpled napkin from the floor, the strap of her dress slipped off one shoulder, fluid green silk peeling away and exposing one bare round breast. On another evening I might have gone over to her and cupped it in my hand. That night I stood motionless, unable to work out whether what I felt was desire or regret. I didn't want to touch her, for fear that I would discover that in fact I felt nothing. As I looked at her, she glanced up and smiled. She pulled the strap back into place more slowly than she might have done, and with a shiver I realised that the act of its slipping had been at least partly premeditated. She walked over to me and wrapped her arms around my neck.

'Why don't we leave the clearing up until tomorrow?' she suggested.

I laughed and disentangled myself, shaking my head. 'I hate waking up to that sort of chore,' I said. 'I'll get on with it now. Listen, you should go to bed, you've worked hard tonight and Adam will probably wake you in a couple of hours anyway. You deserve some rest.'

Naomi sagged gratefully; perhaps she had been playing seductress only out of a misguided belief that it was what I would want. 'If you're sure, I think I might take you up on that.'

I kissed her on the forehead. When she had left I stood alone in the kitchen by the open window, just as I had done earlier in the evening. It was colder now, and the night air stung my face. For a moment I thought I saw the shadow of a woman's body reflected in the windowpane, but when I turned sharply the kitchen was empty. I swayed dizzily, clutching the counter for support. My eyes felt hot and prickly. I stayed there for I don't know how long, until time had lost its meaning and it almost seemed as if I could turn it back and undo what I had done, unpick the chain of events that had led to the kiss and somehow diffuse them into something no more dangerous than a few shared words, a friendly embrace. I knew it was a fantasy. Too drunk to think further, I sat on the kitchen chair and rested my head on the table. When I woke again dawn was breaking. There was a searing pain in my head, and I still hadn't done the washing up.

A few days later I found myself sitting in a draughty school hall, listening to two bespectacled chemists pontificating about splitting the atom. Although I had no recollection of it, I had apparently agreed at the dinner party to accompany Martin to the talk, which was taking place at his current workplace and given by two of his most esteemed colleagues. Even if I had been able to follow the thread of the argument, the monotonous voices of the speakers would have made it difficult to concentrate, and as it was I had long since given up trying to attend. The audience seemed to be largely made up of bored public schoolboys loosening ties and staring out of windows, with a few chemist clones eagerly drinking in the lecture in the first two rows. Next to me, Martin nodded, rocked in his seat and made small affirmative noises at points of particular excitement. Once or twice he turned to me with eyebrows raised quizzically, and I nodded enthusiastically back, feeling that I owed him this much at least.

'Fascinating, don't you think?' he exclaimed when the chemists had left the stage after a torturously drawn-out question-and-answer session and a lacklustre round of applause. 'Of course, it is still such a new area, but I really believe we will see some new developments extremely soon.'

'Of course, I'm no expert,' I said, fighting my way past a crowd of surly sixth-form boys loitering in the aisle. I had rarely been so glad to have given up teaching. 'I certainly enjoyed it, though. I expect it's one of those areas which becomes ever more interesting the more you know—' I broke off, aware that Martin was no longer listening. His face had taken on the adoring spaniel look that was generally reserved for Lydia. He was staring at a slight, balding figure in a brown tweed suit, whom I recognised as one of the perpetrators of the talk.

'That is Professor Duncan Barnbrook,' Martin hissed. 'Our head of department, although of course his work extends far beyond the school.' Judging by the way his face lit up when Barnbrook looked our way and gave him a nod, this unprepossessing figure was obviously some kind of leading light.

'Good of you to make it, Martin,' the professor observed. Bumbling, Martin introduced me; I was acknowledged with a sombre nod. 'George and I were just about to go and have a glass or two of wine, if you'd care to join us.'

Martin fell over himself to accept the invitation, and within ten minutes we were sitting in an ancient public house, dusty wooden benches and walls covered with what looked like medals of war. Unfortunately, the conversation in the pub proved just as impenetrable as the lecture. Professor Barnbrook and his sycophantic deputy appeared to have no conception that their work might not be of supreme interest to everyone they encountered, and Martin did nothing to dispel this illusion. As I listened to Barnbrook drone on, I tried and failed to imagine Lydia sitting in my place. Did she ever accompany her husband to these scientific evenings, and if so, what could she possibly find to entertain her? Not for the first time, I wondered why she had ever married him. It was clear to me that she wasn't happy, couldn't be, if our kiss in the kitchen was anything to go by. I couldn't help turning the analysis back on myself, and wondering whether the easy logic meant that I too was unhappy at home, but I suppressed the thought. It was different for me. I had been drunk, very drunk, and she had taken advantage of me, however ridiculous that sounded. Over the past few days I had determined to reduce the incident to an ill-thought-out error of judgement. It wasn't that difficult. Already I had reformed my thoughts until they resembled something close to pity—pity for a restless housewife tied to a pleasant but pedestrian husband, searching for a cheap thrill outside the confines of her marriage.

I realised with a start that Barnbrook had turned viper-like towards me and posed me a question. 'I couldn't really say,' I said. 'This is fascinating, but it's not my area.'

The professor turned away with a contemptuous sniff and fell to polishing his glasses with a yellow silk cloth. I could feel

Martin's eyes reproachfully on me. My lack of participation seemed to set the death knell on the evening; after a few more desultory minutes, Barnbrook gathered himself to his feet and announced his departure. The other chemist fawned after him, snuffling his goodbyes to Martin and ignoring me entirely. Martin pumped them both warmly by the hand, wringing out a final few drops of praise, and waved them off, calling after them that he would see them the next day. On the basis of this, I wondered whether the situation really called for such an extravagant farewell, but I said nothing.

'Dear me, Nicholas, you must have been bored to tears,' Martin commented when the chemists were safely out of sight. He was trying to look sympathetic, but it came out as something of a rebuke.

'No, no,' I said hurriedly. 'I'm sorry if it seemed that way. I simply didn't feel I could contribute much.'

'Of course,' Martin said, visibly softening. It was one of his virtues that he could never be bad tempered for long. 'Well, in any case, I'm glad you enjoyed the talk. It makes quite a change to have someone to accompany me to this sort of thing.'

Here, then, was the answer to the question I had posed myself. 'Lydia isn't interested?' I asked.

Martin looked regretful. 'Not especially,' he admitted. 'As you know, she's more inclined towards the arts.'

'Did you never think of marrying somebody who shared your passion?' I asked. I knew it sounded blunt, and besides, one didn't 'think of marrying' anyone; life wasn't like that. But I wanted to hear what he would say, if only to convince myself that the Knights' marriage was all wrong, so that I could keep on feeling sorry for them.

To my surprise Martin laughed, rocking back and forth in his seat rather like a mirthful garden gnome. 'Good heavens, no,' he said. 'Female scientists are quite a breed apart. Besides, if I had married somebody like myself, how on earth would the house get run? Lydia manages me, and that suits me completely. And if I may be so bold, I think it suits her too.' He paused, the rocking slowing to a stop, his pinched, tweed-clad elbows coming to rest on the table between us. 'Our marriage surprises people,' he said. 'I believe I told you something to that effect last week. But it works extremely well.'

His confidence was impenetrable. He was gently smiling. I could have sworn that nothing in his words was designed to warn me off, or that he even remotely suspected that anything untoward had ever gone on between me and his wife. My first instinct had been correct: it was Lydia and Lydia alone who was unhappy in the marriage. Again, I felt sorry for her. Martin would never leave her, and she would probably go on drifting through the years, every so often having some dalliance with attractive men if they came her way. In any case, it was no longer my problem. Looking across at Martin's slightly stooped figure, as he squirrelled up a handful of peanuts and happily drained the dregs of his wine, I felt sorry for him too— the kind of sorrow you might feel for an uncomprehending circus bear dressed up in human clothes, unaware that he is being made a fool of.

I devoted myself to Adam and Naomi, applying myself to the task with a meticulousness that made me realise I had been neglecting it of late. With Adam, I reinstated the nightly bathtimes that had always been our ritual, but which had dwindled to once or twice a week over the past few months. I don't pretend to believe that, at just six months old, he consciously noticed the change, but he certainly seemed to take to it readily enough, shouting and splashing away quite happily. I read him stories too, something I had always shied away from in the past: the forced simplicity of children's books bored and irritated me and I had always maintained that until Adam was old enough to talk I might as well have been reading Dostoevsky.

Naomi thought otherwise, however, and accordingly I applied myself to the hungry caterpillar and his ilk with a new vigour. At the weekends, too, I made sure to spend plenty of time with Adam, something that was no hardship but which had all too often fallen by the wayside in favour of poring over some dusty tome or other or preparing for the next week's work. I swung him in the garden hammock, pushed him to the shops and back, encouraged him to take crayons and create offbeat modern masterpieces of artwork as soon as his chubby fingers could grasp a pen. Raising a baby was a twenty-four-hour job, I realised, something that should have been apparent long before.

With Naomi, the task was rather more complicated: I seemed to be able to read babies' minds easier than I could read women's. My initial attempts to take over some household chores were met with puzzlement and suspicion rather than delight. One day, she came downstairs to find me diligently loading the washing machine, and, hands on hips, asked what I thought I was doing. I thought the answer to be patently obvious, but no—what I was doing, apparently, was trying to steal her day from her. A naturally busy and active woman, Naomi had not adapted to giving up work without a fight. I had thought that the daily grind of housework would have aggravated her slight frustration rather than soothed it, but it emerged that shaping her day around snatches of non-baby-related pursuits was in fact a merciful respite. I gave up the chores without much of a fight; in any case, I wasn't as domesticated as she was, and had a habit of getting things wrong. It took me another week or so to work out that it was what I had always thought of as empty gestures that she wanted, rather than actions. I took to buying a weekly bunch of flowers, the odd box of chocolates. I left little notes on the bathroom mirror when I left for work. I sometimes called her from the faculty telephone at lunchtimes to check how she was getting on with Adam. All this went down

wonderfully. Before long the adult equivalents of Adam's contented gurgling and shrieks of joy were coming my way more
frequently than I could remember in years.

'You're such a good husband to me,' she said fondly to me
one night, leaning back against my chest, her bouncing red
curls flattening themselves against me. She smelt of the sham-
poo she always used—coconut oil and lemongrass, a sweet,
sharp smell that I had always found powerfully evocative. I
drank it in, kissed the top of her head and murmured some
thanks. I wondered why I felt so empty.

The truth was that my efforts with Adam had made me feel
closer to him, whereas my efforts with Naomi seemed only to
be serving to make me feel more and more detached, like an
actor playing out the part of the perfect husband. With Adam,
I gathered the rewards of my attention greedily, and every time
his face split in an open-mouthed smile or his pudgy hands
clapped in praise of me, I felt a pang of love twist in my heart.
I was glad of it, because it showed me that I wasn't dead inside,
but at the same time it made the contrast sharper. When
Naomi thanked me for my latest offering, I felt like a nodding
dog, mechanically accepting her affection. When she showered
me with kisses in bed on a Sunday morning, I pretended that I
could hear Adam stirring. My first thought was that it was guilt
at the illicit kiss which was warping my feelings, and that perhaps it would wear off with time. I had, after all, done what I
had sworn on our wedding day that I would never do, even if
it had only been a kiss and nothing more, and I was bound to
feel uncomfortable about it. As time went on, though, I was
forced to admit that there was more to it than that. I still
enjoyed being with Naomi; she made me laugh, brightened up
my days and would chat good-naturedly with me for hours
about things in which she had little or no interest. When it
came to anything more intimate, however, my thoughts were
elsewhere.

The smug superiority I had talked myself into feeling for Lydia had not lasted long. If she was unhappy, it was not her fault: she had married the wrong man, that I still firmly believed, but she had a daughter, a house, she didn't want to break up a family. What was she to do? I found myself thinking about her at the strangest times—mid-lecture in front of a gathering of a hundred students or more, on the telephone to my mother. Sometimes these thoughts were restricted to a vague flitting over her features or some long-forgotten memory. At other times, late at night, I physically ached for her. As I lay in bed, it was as if the taut curves of her body were tattooed on to the insides of my eyelids, always waiting for me when I tried to sleep. I fantasised about her and it took all my strength not to carry these fantasies over into my infrequent sexual encounters with Naomi. With a young child in the house, sex had settled into a pattern more cosy than erotic, and this seemed to be what Naomi had expected, for she never mentioned it or expressed any concern. If it hadn't have been for Lydia, I might have accepted it too and trusted that things would get back on track when Adam was a little older, but in the event I interpreted it as yet one more ominous sign that something was wrong with my marriage, and with me.

The phone call that I had been half expecting ever since the night of the dinner party came five weeks after it. When I heard her voice on the other end of the line, I had a crazy, light-headed impulse to ask what had taken her so long. I took the call in the hall. It was a hot day, and we had the back door open; in the garden, I could see Naomi basking in the sunshine with Adam in a pram at her side.

'I know I shouldn't be calling you,' she said.

'But you called anyway.'

'So it seems.' We were both quiet for a moment, listening to each other's breathing down the line.

'I've been thinking about you.' It was such an understatement that I felt a laugh rise miserably in my throat.

'Do you want to meet up?' she asked urgently, cutting to the chase quicker than I had expected. 'We need to work out what we're going to do.'

A couple of weeks earlier I might have said that I didn't understand what she meant. There was no question of doing anything, surely, only of laying our guilt to rest. Now I agreed. 'Where do you want to meet?' I asked.

'This might sound stupid, but I thought we could take a boat out on the river,' she said haltingly. 'At least then we won't run the risk of bumping into . . . anyone.'

By 'anyone' it was clear she meant our respective spouses, and I felt a brief flash of irritation; say what you mean, I thought, since we're doing this. At the same time, I half appreciated her sensitivity at not saying Naomi's name. 'Now?' I asked.

'If you can get away.' She sighed, causing the line to hum and vibrate. 'I don't like this secrecy, but . . .'

'I don't think this is the sort of conversation we can have in my back garden,' I said drily. 'I'll see you at St James's Dock in about half an hour.'

I rang off feeling a curious mix of despair and excitement. Speaking to Lydia had woken something up inside me, and it was a sad kind of relief not to have to let it lie dormant any more. She had been thinking about me, too, and she had called me first. I went through to the garden, where Naomi was now singing a lullaby to Adam, sprawled out on the grass with her full skirt gathered around her thighs. The sun shone on her red hair, setting it ablaze with light. Together they made a picture-perfect vignette of family life. The only thing missing was me. I swallowed the lump in my throat and stepped on to the lawn to join them.

'Darling, I'm going to have to pop out for a couple of hours,' I said. 'I've got to go down to the faculty.'

Naomi rolled over and squinted up at me. 'On a Saturday?' she asked in disbelief.

'I know, I know, I'm sorry,' I said. 'I've just realised I left some papers there which I really need to look over before Monday, and I don't want to bring them back here now and spoil any more of the weekend. I'll just go down, have a look through them and make some notes, and then come back. You're all right here, aren't you?'

'I *suppose* so,' she said dramatically, flinging her arms up before flopping back to her prone position. 'No, it's O.K., off you go. I'll probably still be here when you get back.'

I crossed over to the pram and pushed it back and forth gently. Adam was half asleep, eyes drooping in sleepy slits. He blinked up at me, his face screwing up in recognition. I touched his cheek with a fingertip, feeling uneasy. For a stupid moment I thought about taking him with me; he would probably enjoy rowing on the river. 'Don't let him overheat,' I said. Naomi made a vague noise of reassurance, not looking up. As far as she was concerned I was clearly already gone. Heart thumping, I turned and strode back across the lawn, grabbed my wallet from the kitchen table and left the house before I could give myself time to change my mind.

There was a long queue at the river, the hot June day bringing out hordes of families and teenage couples. The air was sticky with the scent of ice creams melting in the heat. I scanned the morass of bored children shifting from foot to foot, overexcited students splashing each other by the bank. It was a full minute before I caught sight of Lydia, standing near the front of the queue in a white linen dress, her blonde hair tied decorously up in a ponytail. I hurried towards her.

'I thought you weren't coming,' she said. Instantly I could tell she was on edge, her body quivering with adrenalin, green eyes intent and bright.

'What would you have done?'

She laughed despite herself. 'Got on and rowed around by myself, I suppose,' she said. 'How have you been?'

We passed the next few minutes in polite small talk until we reached the front of the queue. Chatting about my recent lectures and my plans for the rest of the weekend, I found myself wondering how we would ever break through this cordial barrier. It was difficult to imagine that the woman in front of me was the same person who had kissed me so fervently in the kitchen a few weeks before. She seemed self-contained, holding herself back from me, her slim body enclosed in its white wrapper, precious and untouchable.

She reached out for a hand to help steady her as she climbed into the boat. Her legs were lightly tanned, brushing against mine as she settled down opposite me. Neither of us spoke a word as we rowed away from the bank, out towards the farthest curve of the river. Her face was taut with concentration in the sun, watching her oar cut evenly through the sparkling water with every stroke. Guided by her, I let her steer us away from the river's central line, towards the large willow tree that hung over the water. The boat came to rest in the shallows underneath the tree, hiding us from view of the bank. She looked around her, as if to satisfy herself that she had chosen the right spot. In the pale greenish light that the tree cast down on us, she looked vulnerable and ethereal, as if she might vanish at any moment. I didn't want to speak, and for a few minutes we just sat there watching the river.

'I thought about saying that what happened at your dinner party was a mistake,' she began at last. 'I thought it would help to clear the air and then we could just go on as before. The problem is, it wasn't a mistake, was it?' She didn't look at me as she asked the question, winding a long drooping stem of willow intently around her finger.

'Not really,' I said. In reality I wasn't as convinced as she was that the kiss hadn't been a mistake, if a mistake meant something inadvisable which could well lead to unnecessary complications. Somehow, though, sitting across from her, I couldn't be as rational as I had hoped.

'I've been faithful to Martin since we moved here,' she said without further preamble, looking at me sharply, as if she thought I wouldn't believe her. 'Even when he told me he had bumped into you, the thought never crossed my mind that we would get involved again.'

'Never?' I felt absurdly hurt.

'Well . . .' She spread her hands out hopelessly. 'Only in the way that a dream might cross your mind, nothing that I ever would have thought of putting into practice.'

'So are we?' I asked. 'Involved, I mean?' The word sounded silly and juvenile to my ears, something a blushing schoolgirl might apply to her latest beau, but I couldn't think of a better one.

'I don't know,' she said. 'I think I want us to be.'

This was clearly the moment where I was supposed to announce that so did I, and we would fall into a rapturous embrace. I couldn't get the words past the lump in my throat. I felt pulled painfully in two directions, unsure which way to turn. If I managed not to look at her, I felt I would be able to say that I didn't want to see her again, not ever, and stick to it, but the instant I glanced at her again the sight of her seemed to make the words impossible to say. Her bright blonde head, the subtle swell of her breasts under the linen dress, her bare feet with carefully painted nails, all so achingly familiar and precious that I couldn't tear my eyes away. I felt the same sensation that had assaulted me the very first time I had seen her—that sense of homecoming, that whether I liked it or not, this was where I was meant to be.

My silence had lasted too long. She looked flushed, embarrassed, as if she was about to cry. 'I don't like this situation any more than you do,' she said, 'but I have to point out, you didn't seem so moral about adultery six years ago. In fact, you chased me, Nicholas. What's the difference?'

Because this time, it's immoral for *me*, I almost said, but didn't. I didn't point out the obvious, that it was fairly easy to be relaxed about committing adultery when you weren't the one committing it. 'It's not that,' I said instead. 'Last time, I was ready to give you everything it was in my power to give. I wanted a life with you—but you didn't want that, did you? You left, with him. I never understood why you did it, and to be honest I still don't. What would be the point of starting it up again, just so that you could leave me again once things got too much? Can you tell me that? What would be the point?' I realised I was shouting. I hadn't known how angry I was, or how long these words had been building up inside me. Lydia was crying now, wiping the tears away with the back of her hand. I couldn't resist a final twist of the knife. 'You're nothing but a prick-tease,' I said, and heard her gasp, as if I had struck her. As soon as I had said the words I wanted them back.

She took a few minutes to compose herself, breathing deeply and wiping away the last of her tears. 'I'm not going to pretend that didn't hurt, but I expect I deserved it,' she said. 'Listen, Nicholas, I want to make this absolutely clear to you. I loved my husband when I married him, but falling in love with you was something entirely different. I wasn't prepared for it, and frankly I didn't enjoy it, because I hated what I was doing to both of you. I decided to try and make my marriage work because I thought I owed it to Martin, and since we have had Louise things have been better, a lot better. I thought that the feelings I had for you had long since died, or at least faded away. When I thought about you, the colour seemed to have gone out of my memories—it all felt so long ago that I never thought those feelings could come back. But since I've been seeing you again, I've realised that it wasn't a question of them coming back—they never really went away in the first place, I just pushed them underground until they didn't feel part of me any more. I don't want to start an affair with you now because I enjoy the secrecy, or find deceiving my husband exciting—far from it. What I want is to find out, for both of us to find out, whether being together in the long term is something that might be worth all the pain that it would cause, and unfortunately, that means that the secrecy is unavoidable. If you know that you don't want this, you should tell me now, because then I can start trying to get over you.'

She fell silent, looking at me levelly, her chin raised slightly in what could have been pride or defiance. The length and fluency of her speech had the unmistakable air of something well thought out and rehearsed in advance, but nevertheless hearing her deliver it was like hearing my own thoughts played out loud. I couldn't stop myself; I crouched forward across the boat and pulled her into my arms. She was shaking under my touch, her hands searching for mine, grasping them tightly. I kissed her eyelids, her cheek, her lips, the base of her neck, not caring who saw. In between kisses I told her that I was sorry and that I loved her, I loved her, and I couldn't bear it if she left me again. It wasn't what I had planned, but somehow that felt unimportant. Even as I kissed her I felt a sliding sense of inevitability, the falling back into a familiar pattern that I might find impossible to break a second time, but I didn't care. When we finally pulled apart she was half laughing, half crying, her face lit up by love like that of a teenager half her age.

'Let's get this boat back and go to a hotel,' she said, and what happened after that felt strange and familiar and comforting and dangerous and right and wrong, all at once.

Although I had said on the boat that I loved her, the next few weeks felt like falling in love with Lydia all over again. When I thought about her, I got an itchy, restless feeling that made me want to do something, anything but sit around.

When I was with her, I kept on noticing new and incredible things about her—the way she interlaced her fingers when she concentrated, the slightly husky, dreamy quality of her voice when she first woke up, the way she lay on her back and counted stars out of skylight windows when she couldn't sleep. When I wasn't with her, I wanted to talk about her all the time, because everything reminded me of her, and the urge to do this, even with Naomi, was so strong that it took all my willpower to fight it. We spent the night together whenever we could, inventing family visits and overnight conferences, but more often than not our meetings were restricted to the odd snatched hour here and there. In this respect nothing had changed in the intervening years since our last affair—if anything, making arrangements had got harder rather than easier. It was frustrating, but I put up with it.

Occasionally, Lydia and Naomi went out for the afternoon together: against all the odds their friendship seemed to have flourished. I never asked exactly what they did, but judging by the drop in the balance of our joint account after these jaunts, shopping seemed to feature heavily. The first time they went out together, I spent the afternoon in an intense state of panic, unable to relax. I paced from room to room, holding a grizzling Adam tightly in my arms and murmuring words of reassurance as much to myself as to him. I imagined Lydia breaking down, sobbing out her guilt to Naomi over the coffee cups, swearing that she would never see me again. Even in the height of my panic I knew that it was singularly unlikely—Lydia was far more adept than I was at separating the various components of her life and shutting off her morals. In my less generous moments, I remembered that she had had more practice.

Still, when I heard the key turn in the lock at the end of the afternoon I had never felt so sick. The two women came in beaming and chattering, dispelling my fears instantly, and I felt an elation far beyond reason, so great that I almost looked forward to their next outing together—simply for the relief that hit me when I realised that nothing had been revealed, nothing had been suspected, and I was safe.

Once, Lydia and I rented a room on the other side of the city and spent the day there. It was mid-July and the heat was so stifling that as soon as we arrived she stripped off down to her underwear, bright white lace clinging to her hot skin. She sat in the window seat, looking out from our third-floor vantage point, legs folded decorously underneath her despite her near-nudity. We ate raspberries out of the punnet; the blood-red juice stained my fingers and I rubbed it off on her skin, a hazy red smudge lingering below the curve of her breast. As we had done many times before, we talked for an hour or so before making love. It was our unspoken fantasy that we were something more than furtive lovers; just an ordinary married couple who had all the time in the world. We talked about the future—castles in the air, nothing more—her as a brilliant and celebrated painter, me as the uncontested authorial voice of my generation. It was a game we liked playing. Somehow it felt too dangerous to talk about a future that we might reasonably attain; after that afternoon on the river, Lydia had never since made reference to any long-term plans between us. I pretended that I went along with this on sufferance, but deep down it suited me. I loved her—sometimes I felt that I would die for her, but at other times, when I was away from her and back in my comfortable domestic bliss with Naomi and Adam, I found it hard to believe that I would ever leave my family. It was an uncomfortable tug of war that I tried to avoid considering too deeply.

'I wish I had met you ten years ago,' Lydia said suddenly that afternoon. She didn't look at me as she said it, instead frowning out over the apple orchard spread beneath us, eyes narrowed in the brightness of the sun. It was the first hint she had given me that if the choice had been a fair one, Martin and me in front of her as equal eager suitors, the tide might have turned in my favour. Somehow, as soon as she said it, the mood changed, as if a black cloud had come down over us. There was something intensely unfair about what she was implying, something I couldn't even articulate, but it stung the back of my throat and made me want to cry.

'What good is it saying that now?' I said. She turned to me, pushing her shining blonde hair back from her face, sweeping it behind her ears so that I could see her expression more clearly. She looked troubled, as if she was considering my question and not finding the answer she wanted.

'I don't know,' she said finally. 'It is some good, surely.'

I thought about it for a while. 'If you mean that it's some good to know that in some parallel universe we might be together, without either of us being married to other people, then . . .' I had been gearing up to say that it was no help at all, but as I spoke the words I was flooded with an unexpected well-being. 'Yes, it is some good,' I said abruptly, surprised at myself. 'At least I know we could have been happy together.'

'Aren't we happy together now?' she asked.

'While we are together, yes,' I said, 'but more often than not we aren't.'

She moved her head half impatiently, half tenderly. 'I don't want to think about that now,' she said. She swung her legs down from the window ledge and slipped off, bare feet sinking into the fluffy cream carpet. She unhooked her bra from the back, slipped out of her pants and pressed herself appealingly up against me, sparking all my senses into action. I took her to bed as I had done so many times before and covered her with kisses, and it took me a few minutes to work out that there was something different. I had never consciously registered Lydia's wedding ring during sex before, but I registered its absence, the unbroken smoothness of her fingers running over my skin. I took her left hand and drew it up to the light. The finger was bare, a slight pale ring mark signalling itself against her lightly tanned skin.

'You've taken it off,' I whispered into her ear. 'Your wedding ring.'

Her body twisted in my arms so that she was looking straight up at me, her green eyes hypnotic and intense. 'I'm not married, Nicholas,' she said. It didn't feel like a game. Inside her, I felt myself constrict and tense. 'I belong to you,' she said clearly, spacing out each word as if she was anxious for me not to miss it. In the back of my mind I knew that this was nothing but another fantasy, but it felt so real that it took no effort at all to believe it, because she did belong to me, she was mine, and I was hers. We stayed too long at the hotel that afternoon, and leaving her at the end of the day was even worse than usual. Watching the taxi carrying her away in the opposite direction when we had got the bus back to town, I felt as if the subtle threads connecting us were being painfully stretched, not broken but tightened until it was almost unbearable.

The rest of that summer passed much in the same way as the summer of six years before, and as the days turned colder I felt myself waiting for some turn in Lydia's affections, some decision as before that would cut her off from me for good. The change came, but not in the way that I expected. As autumn came she seemed to become clingier, more dependent on me than she had ever been before. Although I didn't like to admit it, I had always been the lover in our relationship, she the loved. I didn't doubt that she loved me, but my feelings had always seemed to overshadow hers; I felt them to be stronger, more passionate, more certain. In the autumn, so subtly that I couldn't put my finger on how it had happened, that changed. Now she was the one calling our house frequently and barely managing to disguise the impatience and tension in her voice on the rare occasions when Naomi answered, so that my wife once asked me worriedly whether I thought that Lydia and Martin might be having problems. Now Lydia was the one watching sorrowfully after me as I left after our covert assignations, eyes brimming with tears at the thought of us being apart for another few days or more.

Sometimes she would fly into a rage with me, asking whether Naomi and I still slept together. Experimentally, I tried different answers at different times, but nothing seemed to please her. If I said that we didn't, she accused me of lying; if I said that we did, she winced as if I had hit her, and asked whether she was not enough for me. Her moods exasperated me, but I always tried my best to placate her, holding her in my arms until her sobbing stopped, telling her that I loved her and only her. Somewhere along the line these protestations started feeling marginally less true; nothing to really give me pause for thought or consider ending the affair, but all the same it surprised me, used as I was to hankering after her so completely that it physically hurt. As the months passed I realised that she wasn't as perfect as I had once thought, far from it, and in a bizarre way this made me feel closer to her, but more complacent. I secretly enjoyed the new feeling of power that this knowledge gave me, wrong though it felt to think that way.

Once or twice Lydia brought up what she had said in the boat on the river—that the ultimate purpose of this affair was to determine whether we could be together in the long term, and that she felt that I had forgotten that. On these occasions I found that if I challenged her and asked her whether she herself had decided whether she should leave Martin, she rapidly changed her tune, as if she was almost afraid of the question. She cited Louise as her major reason for not wanting to make too hasty a decision, demanding to know whether I thought that she could disrupt her child's fate at a moment's notice without being absolutely sure that the end justified the means. Of course, I could throw that argument right back at her, young and uncomprehending though Adam was, and so we were locked back into our vicious circle. At these times, harrowing and exhausting as they were, I wondered whether it was really worth all the effort. And then, the next time we met, she would be so enchanting, intuitively understanding exactly what I wanted, that I felt we were bound together so irrevocably that I couldn't see a way to ever disentangle myself from her.

In quiet moments on my own, I wondered how this would all end. Various scenarios flashed through my mind. Lydia and myself finally making the painful break from our families and setting off to a new life together with the children in some rural idyll. One or other of us deciding that the affair should end, messily breaking the ties and pushing it underground. A mutual decision between us to forget our plans and make a success of things with Martin and Naomi, remaining friends, or perhaps cutting contact altogether. Somehow none of these solutions felt right, or even plausible, and I spent many hours turning over the possibilities in my head and worrying about how they could ever come to pass. Of course, as it turned out, I need not have wasted my time. By the time six months had passed it was all over, and Lydia was dead.

LOUISE
2007

There is more than one way to kill someone. Some murderers are brash and unapologetic about what they do: holding a gun and pulling a trigger, fastening hands tightly around a throat. These murderers can't escape their crimes, because they are right there in front of them; it takes a certain kind of man, or woman, to stand and watch someone die. Others are less brave. Slipping poison into a waiting cup of coffee, for instance, is no less a murder than the drama of blowing brains out across a whitewashed wall, but perhaps it lacks the same conviction. Lydia has no experience of killing anyone, but she imagines that the less hands-on the crime is, the easier it is to smother your conscience and convince yourself that really, in some alternative reality, you have done nothing wrong after all.

The man who killed her mother is more divorced from his crime than most. He didn't stand in front of his victim with a gun, or beat her to death with his bare hands, or even hire someone else to do his dirty work for him. If he had ever stood up in a court of law and been accused of her death, he would never have been convicted. It doesn't mean he's not responsible. He might still be here, rather than locked up in prison, but Lydia knows that he is responsible. If you hurt someone so much that their life no longer seems worth living, then their blood is on your hands. If she thinks about it that way, it feels like a simple, unquestionable truth, striking her straight in the heart.

In the morning Naomi puts croissants in the oven and then piles them high on the breakfast table and surrounds them with little china pots containing jewel-like pools of jam: ruby, topaz, amber. A dish of golden butter sits in the centre of the pots, a sprig of holly at its side. It strikes Lydia as a lot of effort to go to for an ordinary family breakfast. At first she suspects that the extra attention to detail is for her, but when she sees the nonchalance with which Nicholas and Adam sit down and devour their breakfast, she readjusts her ideas. This is obviously how Naomi likes to do things. All the same, she makes a couple of desultory comments to the effect that she hopes no special effort has been made on her behalf, and Naomi smiles and repudiates the charge gaily. The argument with Nicholas seems to have been settled overnight. He is not overly talkative, but seems content, spooning cherry jam on to his croissant and eating absent-mindedly, one eye on the newspaper spread out across the table.

'So who's for some Christmas shopping this morning, then?' Naomi asks, eyes darting hopefully around the table. Nicholas gives no outward sign of having heard, while Adam slouches in his seat, an exaggerated pantomime of a gargoyle in distress, and exhales heavily.

'I'll do it next week,' he says. 'You get better bargains then anyway.' With a shock Lydia realises that Christmas is less than a fortnight away. Now that she thinks about it, she remembers seeing rows of rather sad-looking decorations slung down the High Street, bristling with artificial sprigs of pine, but they haven't really registered with her. She thinks of her father, and feels a pang of guilt. Perhaps she will go home for Christmas after all.

'Well, I don't know about you, Lydia, but I'm not a fan of leaving it to the last minute,' Naomi says heartily. Lydia realises she is being recruited for the shopping trip, and finds that she doesn't mind—in a way it will be a relief to get away from Adam and Nicholas for a while.

'I'll come with you,' she says, shooting a glance at Adam to see whether he minds. He doesn't seem to; in fact he seems amused, half choking on the remnants of his croissant.

'Good luck,' he snorts.

Naomi looks at him reproachfully. 'Someone might not be getting any birthday or Christmas presents this year,' she says ominously.

'When is your birthday?' Lydia asks.

Adam shifts in his seat, obviously preferring to keep this information to himself. 'Day after tomorrow,' he mumbles eventually. 'I don't want a fuss over it. I usually get some mates together, but everyone's buggered off home early this year.'

'Perhaps they didn't want to buy you anything,' Nicholas interjects from his paper drily. Adam nods placidly, seeming to accept this. Lydia feels a rush of sympathy—unwarranted, since Adam doesn't appear to be upset about the cancellation of his birthday plans at all. She must buy him something, but when she runs through the usual possibilities—socks, chocolates, bath things, DVDs—she is daunted by the potential significance of the choice. Perhaps Naomi can help, she thinks, glancing furtively at her. She isn't intimidating like some of the mothers Lydia has known in the past. In fact, she seems more like a friend, someone on a level with her.

They leave Adam and Nicholas ensconced in front of the television, half watching an old repeat of some American sitcom. Naomi puts the radio on as she drives into town, and so conversation is kept to a minimum, the odd exchanged comment on one of the songs or the stupidity of some other driver on the road. Once they are in town, Lydia wonders whether they will go their separate ways and meet back at the car later, but Naomi seems to have everything worked out. She whisks Lydia around the market, through the department stores and the little boutiques, collecting presents as they go with the efficiency of a sergeant major and suggesting possible ideas for the imaginary

Margaret, Keith and Helen. To her own surprise, Lydia finds herself contradicting Naomi when a bottle of pink-packaged scent is picked out for Helen; Helen is more of a tomboy, she explains. She is enjoying the fantasy, and even although she knows it is ridiculous, buys presents for both her imagined sister and mother, despite having no one to give them to.

Two hours later, they retire to a market café and order huge Christmas-spiced mugs of hot chocolate and toasted sandwiches. The whirlwind procession round the shops seems to have invigorated Naomi, whose cheeks are flushed apple red and whose russet curls seem to have a life of their own, bouncing crazily whenever she moves her head.

'Now, I know we haven't got Adam's birthday present yet,' she says, 'but I have a few ideas, if you can bear to go round a bit more after lunch.' She looks to Lydia for confirmation and nods, satisfied. 'He isn't that difficult to buy for, actually,' she adds. 'He likes gadgets and gizmos, mostly—useless things. You know what men are like.'

'Does he really not want any fuss for his birthday?' Lydia asks.

'He'd be disappointed if I didn't make any,' says Naomi confidently. 'We'll bake a cake, maybe take him out to dinner in the evening. You too, of course.' She pauses, as if struck by a thought, and when she speaks again her voice is lower, more diffident. 'Your parents will be back for Christmas, won't they?' she asks.

Lydia hesitates. 'I think so,' she says. This is obviously the wrong thing to say—Naomi's eyebrows fly up dramatically. 'I mean, yes,' she rectifies hurriedly, 'they will, but we're just not sure where we're going to spend Christmas yet.' Dimly in the distance, she sees some awkward decisions and explanations to be made approaching, but pushes them away from her; she'll deal with her next move when she has to.

Naomi misinterprets her troubled expression. 'I hope you

don't think I'm trying to get rid of you,' she exclaims. 'It's nice to have another girl around the place—I feel at something of a disadvantage normally.' She laughs, but Lydia catches the hint of something more serious lurking beneath.

'It's very kind of you to let me stay,' she says, meaning it.

'Honestly,' Naomi says earnestly. 'It's fine—better than fine.'

For a moment Lydia thinks she might be about to cry. She smiles, swallowing down the lump in her throat. Naomi is so nice, she thinks, and feels a sudden stab of anger. It's obvious that Nicholas doesn't deserve her. How can she bear to stay with him, knowing that he has been unfaithful to her with another woman? Naomi is not beautiful as her mother was, but she is attractive, cheerful and full of energy, surely the perfect wife and mother. As they sit in the café, Lydia tries to imagine how they must appear to passers-by: just another mother and daughter, perhaps, having lunch together as they have done so many times before. So this is what it is like. She feels angry again, but this time the resentment is towards her own mother. *I could have been here with you instead*, she thinks bitterly. It's a familiar but rarely acknowledged feeling, and she is so used to dampening it down that it passes in seconds.

'Shall we?' says Naomi brightly, standing up. Lydia follows her through the sparkling stalls decked with fairy lights, breathing in the heady scent of mulled wine. For the rest of the day, she will make believe that this is her life.

Lydia wraps up Adam's present in pale blue tissue and silver wrapping paper. Working on Naomi's declaration that he likes useless things, she has bought him a gadget for his desk, a complicated arrangement of ball bearings and pivots that swings dizzily round and round in different directions when given the slightest push. She imagines him sitting in front of an abortive essay, distracting himself with its hypnotic spiralling and swaying. It isn't the sort of thing that she would have bought anyone else—there is only her father to buy for, and he would have looked up in blank incomprehension on unwrapping a present for which there was no clear or feasible use. Anyway, if Adam reacts in the same way, she has the receipt. She finishes smoothing down the corners of the parcel and ties a navy ribbon around it tightly in a bow. Downstairs she can hear the sounds of Naomi and Adam decorating the Christmas tree, lugged in from the rain that afternoon. They always decorate it on his birthday, Naomi has explained, seeming to take comfort in the unchanging nature of the ritual.

Lydia goes to the mirror and looks at herself critically. She is wearing a dark red dress that falls just above the knee, gathered tightly around the waist with a black belt. Her dark brown hair is pinned up on her head in a precarious arrangement, but now that she looks at it she doesn't like the effect. She runs her fingers through her hair, disentangling the pins and letting it fall over her shoulders. Perhaps she should put on some more make-up. She looks askance at herself from a distance, as if trying to catch herself unawares through a stranger's eyes. What she sees seems to be missing something, but whatever it is she has no time to fix it. Adam is calling up the stairs, telling her that they will be leaving soon. She hurries down to join him, clutching the present.

'Nice!' Adam wolf-whistles appreciatively and she is grateful for his uncomplicated praise. He kisses her swiftly on the lips, and over his shoulder she sees Naomi and Nicholas exchange a look—of confirmation, perhaps, or of surprise.

'Yes, you look lovely,' says Naomi. She looks attractive herself in a turquoise dress that billows out from the waist, disguising the heaviness of her hips, and a long pendant that sways gently between her breasts when she moves. Lydia catches Nicholas watching it. He is wearing a suit, a white shirt open at the neck, his black-and-silver hair drawn severely back and revealing cheekbones so sharp and acute that they might have been carved out of stone. His dark eyes glitter like jet. He looks dangerous, she thinks, and shivers, but in another moment he smiles at her, and the cruelty drops from his face like a mask.

'Better get going,' he says lightly. 'The table's booked for eight.'

Dinner is at an expensive Indian restaurant on the outskirts of Oxford, a purple velvet-draped boudoir crammed with candlelit private booths. When she steps inside, Lydia is hit by the scents of incense and curry spices, jostling each other brashly for prominence, so strong that they temporarily close off every other sense to her. The food is so hot that she can barely taste it. Peering down at her plate, candlelight flickering intermittently across the darkness, she wonders what she is eating. Nicholas ordered for all of them with ruthless efficiency in a tone that brooked no denial, establishing only her lack of allergies as the basis for making his decisions. She tries her best to eat, but each mouthful burns the back of her throat, and the water she gulps to try to assuage the sensation only seems to clarify it, setting every tastebud on fire. Opposite her, Adam stares, his eyes travelling lazily over her face, her bare shoulders, her breasts. She looks back at him, but never for more than a second at a time. She can tell there is something different in these looks. With a light shiver, she realises that it is likely they will sleep together that night. She tries to imagine it, and cannot hold on to the concept, her mind shutting down on images that come to her unbidden.

Plates are removed and replaced by discreet linen-suited Indians, bowing their sleek heads gravely whenever Nicholas makes another unintelligible request. Finally, amid a burst of music and clapping, a large white dessert is brought to the table, studded with flickering candles. Lydia joins in the chorus of 'Happy Birthday', even although Adam looks mortified and blows the candles out as quickly as he can. The sombre waiters linger until it is clear they are no longer needed, then melt back into the shadows.

'I suppose a toast is traditional,' Nicholas declares as he divvies up the dessert into bowls. Lydia takes her first mouthful; it is strange, perfumed, with the consistency of blancmange, but mercifully cool after what has come before. 'Twenty is an important age,' he continues, grasping his champagne glass. 'A time when one makes the transition from boy to man. All I can really say to you, Adam, is that you seem to be doing it with ease . . . coping with your studies, popular with your friends—and with the ladies. Those Steiner genes coming through,' he says slyly, glancing swiftly at Lydia as if for some sort of confirmation. He clears his throat, then motions around the table for glasses to be raised. 'To Adam. Our only son. Our only child.' On the last few words his face and voice change. He immediately busies himself with drinking, but Lydia has seen the sadness that has swept over him. For a second he looks like an old man, not intimidating or frightening or anyone who could be a figure of hate. She doesn't like seeing him like this: it doesn't fit with what she thinks of him. Laughing and trading comments over their desserts, Naomi and Adam don't seem to have noticed the sudden shift in mood, or perhaps they simply don't want to. For Lydia, Nicholas's sudden gloom is oppressive, and she is thankful when the dessert bowls have been cleared and he has paid the bill and risen to collect the coats.

On the way home he seems to be recovered, singing along to the radio in a harsh baritone as he drives. She sees, though, that when they enter the house he makes straight for the drinks cabinet, having drunk only one glass of champagne at dinner, and pours himself a large measure of whisky. He stands swilling the liquid around the ice cubes in the bottom of his glass, watching it. She knows she should thank him for the dinner, but he is wearing his introspection around him like an electric force-field, designed to repel anyone who comes too close. As she lingers, his eyes flick over to her. She sees them drop swiftly, reflexively, down to her stockinged legs, and she wants to turn away, but feels frozen to the spot. The way he is looking at her is as if he has realised for the first time that she is female. After a few seconds, he looks back into his drink.

Lydia rouses herself, mumbles a thank-you and retreats before she has time to tell whether he acknowledges it or not. Naomi is lying on the long cream sofa in the front room, eyes closed, humming a tune.

'Goodnight,' Lydia says, hesitating at the door.

'See you tomorrow, dear,' Naomi says, not opening her eyes.

'Yes.' Lydia lingers, half wanting Naomi to say something more, to delay her from going upstairs. She feels suddenly shy of Adam, and guilty, as if slipping in between the crisply ironed sheets with him, his parents just rooms away, is somehow something of a slight or a betrayal. She waits a few more heart-beats in the doorway, but Naomi does not stir.

Lydia is still clutching Adam's present. She hurries up the stairs and finds him in the bedroom, unlacing his shoes labori-ously. She holds it out to him.

'Happy birthday,' she says.

Adam looks up, his face splitting into a pleased smile. 'You didn't have to get me anything,' he says, taking it.

'It's nothing much.' Suddenly she feels embarrassed about the present and wonders what possessed her to choose it. Adam tears the wrapping paper apart, his fingers puncturing the tissue with disregard. She thinks of the way her father unwraps presents—slowly, methodically, folding the paper up to be stockpiled neatly in a cupboard and reused the next year.

'Cool,' says Adam, as he examines the gadget. 'No, really,' he adds, looking up sharply, as if she has made some denial. 'I like this sort of stuff. I could put it on my desk.'

'That's what I thought.' She thinks he may be being polite, but he starts to assemble the gadget's various parts, fitting spokes into sockets, sliding ball-bearings along the long silver struts as if on an abacus. He frowns with concentration, head bent over his task, not speaking until it is done.

'There.' He goes to the desk in the corner of the room and places the gadget next to his laptop, turns back and smiles. As he comes towards her again he switches off the light. For a moment they are in total darkness until his fingers find the switch of the bedside lamp. The soft reddish glow does not give out much light, cocooning them in a pocket of semi-visibility. Adam sits very close to her on the bed, his hand stroking her hair back from her face. She sees him looking at her again, the way he did across the table earlier, a slow, lustful assessment of everything he sees.

'This is a nice dress,' he says, and even his voice is different. She is reminded of what Nicholas said—making the transition from boy to man. She almost prefers Adam when he is childish and petulant. This confident, sexy stranger intimidates her; she doesn't know what she might do in his presence. She feels her heart beat harder as he touches the material of her dress. 'I liked the present you got me too,' he says, 'but on balance, I think I like this wrapping paper better.'

'You might not like what's inside,' she says, trying to joke.

He shakes his head, serious. 'I already know I like that,' he says. He kisses her, drawing her in towards him, and she feels her leg come up to hook around his waist, almost as if it has a will of its own. His hand runs up it quickly, stroking the curve of her hip. She can feel the other hand at the back of her dress, locating the zip and tugging it down. His fingers stroke the bare curve of her back until they come up against the strap of her bra, nimbly working at the catch and releasing it with unexpected expertise. He pushes the clothes away from her and they settle into a pool at her feet. His fingers hook over the top of her pants, tugging them slowly down over her thighs. She feels herself move to accommodate his movements, letting him sweep them down over her knees, her ankles, allowing them to drop. She feels like a plastic doll as he arranges her on the bed, staring intently at her body, and then touching, kissing, in so many places that she loses track of what she is feeling and where.

He is still fully clothed. She tugs at his shirt collar. 'Take this off,' she says. He does so, and just for a second she catches sight of the eager teenager again in the way his fingers fumble at the buttons, temporarily losing their easy control. It reassures her and she smiles. 'And the rest,' she says. When he is naked she finds that she can look at him with the same curiosity with which he studies her. They lie next to each other, their bodies moulding together in a way that surprises her; there is a strange natural fit between them, with no awkward angles.

He is kissing her harder now, his hands travelling searchingly over her, finding their way between her legs. 'Do you want me to use something?' he whispers in her ear. She nods, not sure whether the answer will please him, but he swiftly reaches across and takes a small silver packet from the bedside table. He has planned this, she thinks, or maybe he has always kept them there, for Isobel or others. She pushes the thought away, closing her eyes tightly, wrapping her arms around his neck. She hears the thin sharp rip of paper and foil, feels Adam draw away from her for a moment. She keeps her eyes closed, screwing them tighter against the first moment's pain. Against her will, tears spring up and push their way out past her lashes.

'Lydia,' he whispers, 'look at me.' She opens her eyes and sees him above her, his face full of concern. 'Are you O.K.?' he asks. She nods. 'I didn't realise,' he whispers. 'I didn't . . . you're sure about this?' She nods again. As the pain fades she feels a wild sense of release sweeping up to cover her, her blood thrumming through her veins and making her shake.

She moves with him, bringing her mouth up to his neck, kissing, biting. This is instinctive; there is no need for words, thoughts, looks. She hears his breathing quicken against her ear, his arms holding her more tightly against him. 'Oh God,' she thinks she hears him say, and in another moment he moves so violently inside her that she cries out, twisting her fists in his hair, her body damp with sweat. The sensation rocks her from top to toe. When he is still, her body is still buzzing, as if poised to flee or fight. She feels his hand stroking the curve of her cheek, and turns so that he can cup her face in his palm. A moment later she meets his eyes, and feels as if she is seeing him for the first time.

He opens his mouth as if he might speak. 'Lydia, I—' he begins. She knows that he is about to say he loves her, and shakes her head; she doesn't want to hear it, not sure whether it is really true. 'O.K.,' he says, smiling. 'But thank you.'

They lie together, bathed by the fuzzy red light. As always, he falls asleep first. She watches his chest rise and fall. She can feel a sharp, sore sensation between her legs, nagging for attention, but she doesn't want to move. As she lies there the strange familiar dread pierces her contentment; a strange sense of déjà vu, eerie and unexpected, like a skeleton grinning from the darkness of the closet. She shivers, wanting someone's arms around her, wanting someone to tell her that everything will be all right. She presses her face up against Adam's chest and hugs him to her, not knowing why she is shaking.

Nicholas leaves the house early the next morning. Lying in bed, Lydia hears the swift, decisive slam of the front door downstairs, then footsteps crunching across the driveway, too brisk and heavy to be Naomi's. She glances at the bedside clock, which reads 7.15. Adam rarely wakes before nine, and she doesn't want to disturb him. He's curled up next to her, his hand brought up to his mouth in a fist, curly eyelashes fluttering gently in sleep. He looks wholly innocent, too young to be the man who pinned her down and made love to her last night with such energy and passion. Lydia rolls on to her side, stretching her limbs languorously across his. After her sleep, she feels newly purged and serene, paradoxically virginal.

'Are you going to wake up?' she asks quietly, smiling to herself as Adam stirs and shakes his head faintly, as if warding off an insect. 'Or should I leave you to it?' There is no response, only a deep sigh that seems to shake his whole body. Lydia quietly pulls away and climbs out of bed, dressing quickly in the half-light of dawn breaking through the curtains. She blows a kiss at the sleeping Adam as she leaves the bedroom, feeling sophisticated and adult. She has never been this close to a man before.

Once on the landing she notices that the door to the master bedroom is ajar. Softly, she crosses the hallway and listens outside. She can hear the slow, even sound of breathing; so Naomi too is asleep. She turns away and wanders back down the corridor. The house is silent, watchful, waiting for her to make a move. Even as her mind rebels from the thought, she knows what she is going to do. Softly, she pads down the corridor, counting the doors as she goes. The third door from the end is shut, as it always is. Although she knows that Nicholas is not there, her breath catches in her throat as she turns the handle, imagining his head raised coolly from his desk as she sidles in, dark eyes raking her accusingly. But as she knows it will be, the study is empty. Its little window is propped open, blowing a sharp cold wind through the room. Shivering, she goes and closes it, then looks around her.

The heavy dark oak desk stands like an altar in the centre, covered with folders and loose sheets of paper. She had expected everything to be ordered neatly, with killer precision. It comes as a shock to see the chaos of paper spilling over the desk, leaving no inch of space uncovered. She does not approach the desk at first, prowling around the room and examining the paintings on the walls. One abstract print, black and blue concentric circles sucking her eyes into an abyss. A dark landscape punctuated with bare spiked trees. A stark, brash portrait of a woman's face, her lips raw and parted. The pictures depress her and she turns away. On the mantelpiece stands a photograph: Nicholas with Naomi and a young Adam, probably no more than ten years old. They are all smiling, a catalogue family, the colours of the photograph unnaturally bright and perfect, as if they have been airbrushed. She looks at the photograph for a long time. Nicholas does not belong in this picture, doesn't deserve to be there. The bile rises in her throat and for an instant she screws her eyes tight shut.

She moves back to the desk and sits down. Nicholas's chair is dark wood, extravagantly carved, its arms curling into her body like those on a torturer's seat. The wood feels smooth and cold, with no sense of his presence remaining. She starts to sift through the papers scattered across the desk, careful not to disturb their alignment. Half hidden under a timetable of lectures she finds a small notebook. Across the open page Nicholas has scrawled a heading—'Christmas Memorial Lecture'. She dimly remembers someone mentioning this the previous night: a prestigious alumni event, at which Nicholas is the guest speaker of honour. Glancing back at the timetable, she sees that the lecture is due to take place the following evening; this, then, is the reason for Nicholas's recent distraction and his long periods in the study and out of the house. She tries to make sense of the scrawled notes in the notebook, but can decipher little: only the odd name—Derrida, Barthes, Foucault—with what must be some shorthand memory-jogging notes beside them. Each name is punctuated by a black full stop, as if Nicholas's pen has jabbed emphatically through the paper.

Lydia feels impatient; she isn't interested in Nicholas's work, or only from a very detached standpoint, as the student that she might have been. Restlessly, she ripples her hand across the piles of paper. She doesn't know why she has come here or what she hopes to find. Glancing down, she sees three deep drawers built into the side of the desk, and on impulse drops to her knees beside them. The first two drawers are full of stationery, blank printing paper, bundles of biros bound tightly with elastic bands. The bottom drawer is locked. She tugs ineffectually at the handle, willing it to open. It is only when she pulls away from it impatiently that she sees the glint of the key underneath the desk, glimmering at the corner of her vision. She swoops on it and fits it into the lock. It turns with difficulty, as if the lock has not been used for some time, and when she lets go of the key her fingers are coated with fine dust.

She sorts through the drawer's contents. More of the same: labels, pens, stacks of envelopes and notepaper. She almost shuts it up again, but something makes her look further, overturning everything she finds. When her fingers close around the packet of photographs she feels a premonitory shiver run right through the length of her body. Slowly, she opens the flap, on her knees beside the drawer. She pulls out the photographs inside, no more than five or six, protected by a thin layer of tissue paper. Her mother's face stares up at her across the years. She looks no more than thirty. In the first photograph she is lying on her back, limbs sprawled on the bed of an unfamiliar room. She wears a white sundress, clinging to the lines of her body. She looks as if she is about to speak, her beautiful lips half parted in a teasing smile. It seems that it would take only a tiny shift in time for her to stir and leap up from the printed surface, out of the past and into the present.

Lydia looks through the photographs one by one. In two of them, her mother looks sad, reflective, almost as if she does not know that her picture is being taken. In another, she seems happy, caught in the act of pouring a glass of wine, smiling into the camera, green eyes fixed hypnotically on the man behind the lens. The last photograph is the worst. Nicholas is holding the camera out at arm's length, his other arm wrapped around her bare shoulders. The picture is slightly blurred, as if his arm has shaken with laughter as he presses the button to take the photograph. His eyes burn straight out from the print, but her mother is not looking at the camera. She's looking at him, and there is love written all over her face, as plainly as if she could talk. The print is creased at the corners, its colours slightly worn away, as if it has been handled over and over, many times.

Lydia stuffs the photographs back into their packet. Her hands shake as she shoves it back underneath the piles of envelopes and locks the drawer. She gets to her feet. She doesn't want to be here any more. The whole room is tainted, stained with memories that he has no right to. When she catches sight of the family photograph on the mantelpiece again, she has a sudden wild desire to take it and rip it across the centre, leave the pieces scattered on the floor and let him know that she understands, that she knows that the dirty little secrets he keeps locked in his desk have made it into nothing but a sham. She has to fight to calm the impulse, pressing her fist tightly against her chest and feeling it heave and fall. This is too much to let go. Naomi and Adam do not need a man like this. They would be better off alone. In that moment, breathing deeply and swaying slightly against the strength of her anger, she wishes that she could make him disappear. As she wheels around and leaves the study behind, she feels a righteous rage rising inside her, and it feels so pure that she knows it cannot, must not be wrong or ignored.

Naomi is peeling apples, sitting at the kitchen table, her red hair tied up in a tight bun against the nape of her neck. She runs the knife carefully underneath the apple's skin, letting the peel curl away in a taut, unbroken spiral. Her concentration is so intense that it is several minutes before she notices Lydia standing in the doorway.

'Hello there,' she says when she does, smiling, but not raising her eyes from the half-peeled apple in her hands. 'Come in—I'll be with you in a minute. I just want to get this done.'

Lydia comes and sits opposite her. She watches Naomi delicately circle the knife closer and closer to the apple's stem until the peel drops away in a single piece, perfectly shorn from the glistening fruit. Naomi gives a pleased murmur of satisfaction.

'What are you cooking?' asks Lydia.

'Oh, just an apple crumble,' Naomi replies. 'Silly really, I'll be cutting them up into pieces anyway. I just like peeling them like that.'

'You do a lot of cooking,' Lydia observes. From what her father has told her, she knows that her own mother did the same, but still she finds it surprising how much time Naomi spends in the kitchen, tending to her adult brood like a 1950s housewife.

Naomi shrugs and laughs. 'I need the practice,' she says.

'I don't think so.' The compliment sounds stiffer than she intended it, and, embarrassed, Lydia grabs another knife from the table. 'I'll do one, if you like.'

'Sure.' Naomi hands over an apple. As Lydia peels, she feels the other woman's eyes on her, kind and curious. 'So,' she says after a while, her voice pregnant with teasing significance, 'it seems that things are going well between you and Adam.'

Lydia feels her cheeks flame up. For a crazy moment she thinks that Naomi has somehow divined the difference in her, that her non-virginity is shining out from her face like a beacon. She looks quickly across at her, but of course the comment is innocent. 'I suppose so, yes,' she says cautiously. This isn't the train of conversation that she wants to follow; she needs to take back the initiative. 'We're just taking things as they come,' she says more confidently.

'Well, that's very sensible,' Naomi agrees. 'I only wish I'd been as measured at your age. Or at any age, really.' She laughs again.

'You rushed into things too quickly?'

'Well . . .' Naomi rocks her head from side to side, weighing up her words. 'Not exactly, no, not in practical terms, but I suppose in emotional ones. Even with Nicholas, I fell madly in love after a few days—not that I told him that, obviously! And I was in my thirties then, so I think I would have learnt some caution by that point if I was ever going to.' Her words strike Lydia as intimate, but Naomi spills them out as lightheartedly as if she is chatting about the weather. For Lydia, the confession serves only to set the seal on her convictions. Love at first sight is something close to madness, surely not something on which to base a lifetime relationship. It is almost as if Nicholas has put a spell on her. This whole relationship is a mistake, she thinks savagely. If it had not been, Nicholas never would have strayed elsewhere, into her own family. Agitated, her hand slips and the knife she is holding skids against the tip of her finger. Blood seeps out on to the apple's pale green flesh, muddying into a dirty brown, and she winces.

'Oh no!' Naomi exclaims. She leaps up and tears off a sheet of kitchen roll, running it briefly under the tap. 'Here,' she says, crossing over to Lydia and dabbing the wet tissue at her bleeding finger; it stings and she bites her lip, not trusting herself to speak. Naomi binds the tissue tightly around her finger, and suddenly a memory flashes painfully into Lydia's mind: her mother, bathing her grazed knee after a fall outside on the garden path, cleaning grit and dirt carefully away from the skin.

Naomi has pulled up a chair next to her, her face full of concern. 'Lydia,' she says slowly, her voice faltering slightly over the name, 'you know, if there's something bothering you, you can talk to me about it. Forgive me if I'm talking out of turn, but I get the sense that you're not quite happy, and if there's anything I can do . . .'

She trails off, and in the pause that follows it becomes suddenly clear to Lydia what she must do, how she can make Naomi see what has to be seen. She takes a deep breath, sorting out her thoughts in her head. She doesn't want to get this wrong. 'There is something,' she says quietly. Naomi nods, prompting her encouragingly with her eyes. 'There's something I haven't been completely honest with you about. It's my parents. When I said they were on holiday . . . they have gone away together, but it's less of a holiday than a kind of last-ditch attempt to . . . well, to save their marriage, I suppose.'

From the way that Naomi's shoulders instantly relax, and the fleeting look of relief that passes over her face before she settles her features into an appropriate display of concern, Lydia can see that she had been bracing herself for a different sort of revelation. With a flash of insight, she thinks, *She thought I was pregnant.* The thought feels so incongruous that she almost wants to smile.

'I'm very sorry to hear that,' Naomi says, clasping her hands in front of her. 'I don't want to pry, but—'

'My father has been having an affair,' Lydia cuts in. She sees Naomi's face tighten, and feels bad, but there is no going back now. 'It's been going on for some time. I think he regrets it, but that's not much use now, is it.' She doesn't have to fake the bitterness in her voice.

Naomi doesn't reply at first, frowning intently down at her clasped hands. When she does speak, she sounds almost dispassionate. 'Not really,' she says, 'but it is something. If he is sincere, they may be able to work through it.'

Lydia makes a sceptical face. 'I can't see it,' she says.

'No, believe me,' Naomi says, her voice gathering in zeal,

'it is possible. It might not be easy, but they might even find that it—'

'—makes them stronger?' Lydia cuts in, again brutally. 'I doubt it.' She takes a moment to compose herself, thinking about exactly what she wants to say. 'I don't think she should forgive him,' she says, more slowly. 'If she does, then yes, they may be able to rebuild things, and perhaps it will seem as if they are just as good, or even better than before, but in reality they won't be, will they? He has done something that can't ever be changed or taken back, and he isn't a teenager—unless you walk around with your eyes closed, you know that fucking someone else is going to hurt your wife so much that there's the chance she might never recover.' The obscenity slips from her lips cleanly and easily, although she cannot remember ever having said it before. It hangs on the table between them. 'Who takes that sort of risk, and expects to get away with it?' Lydia continues. 'I think that he wanted to get caught, even if he can't admit it. I know that people get over it. I know that they move on. But I think it's a cowardly way out of walking away—out of doing what seems on the surface to be harder. The funny thing is, I'm not so sure that it's harder at all.'

She can see that Naomi has withdrawn from her, off into some private place which she cannot reach. Her blue eyes look suspiciously bright and liquid, her full lips pressed tightly together as if there is a danger of them betraying her, spilling out her secrets. Lydia knows that her words are nothing that Naomi must not have said to herself dozens, perhaps hundreds, of times. Instinctively, though, she knows that there is something different about hearing somebody else give voice to your thoughts. It shapes them, makes them ugly and concrete. She doesn't want to hurt Naomi, she tells herself, but it is better to be hurt than to stay for the rest of your life with a man who doesn't really love you. That is as clear as clear. Emboldened by the thought, she glances at Naomi again. She can picture the memories that are running through her mind, so clearly that she wants to take her hands and tell her that she understands the pain she is going through—understands it because it is part of her too.

'You know, nor am I,' Naomi says, and it is so long since she last spoke that Lydia has to search back through her memory to understand what she is agreeing with.

Suddenly there is a noise from the doorway. Adam is standing there, barefoot, his hair ruffled, lazy, dark eyes narrowed happily and sleepily. 'Looks like you guys beat me,' he says. 'What you making?'

The switch of mood is so instant that it throws Lydia off base for a second. As she watches Naomi bustle cheerfully back and forth, galvanised by Adam's presence into chopping up the apples and vigorously assembling the crumble, Lydia realises that she is so used to covering over her own feelings that it comes almost without effort. There is no room in her life for sadness. But Lydia knows now that it is there—beneath the surface, but only minutes deep, and painfully easily scratched into life.

Lydia stays up late that evening, watching old black-and-white films with Adam and Naomi. As the night draws on, she finds it harder to concentrate on the plot of the last film, and simply lets the monochrome images flicker across her vision, lulling her into relaxation. Naomi has lit a fire in the grate, and its steady crackle and spark are strangely soothing. Upstairs, Nicholas has barricaded himself in his study, and in his absence Lydia feels as if he is barely in the house at all. The picture feels complete: herself, legs stretched out across Adam's lap, Naomi curled up in the armchair opposite. Now that she thinks she is unobserved, Naomi looks distracted and unhappy, and Lydia averts her eyes. She doesn't want to think that she has caused this sadness, but she doesn't regret it. For the moment, it is easier not to think about it at all.

As a sudden swell of music rises and the credits roll jerkily across the screen, Adam gets to his feet, stretching and yawning in a rather too exaggerated pantomime of fatigue. 'I'm going to bed,' he announces, and shoots Lydia a look that leaves her in no doubt that she should follow soon after. A quick anticipatory shiver runs through her, excitement and desire bubbling unexpectedly up from within. She watches him leave the room; lightly muscled shoulders under his blue shirt, lean, strong legs in tight dark jeans. It is less than five minutes before she can wait no longer, and rises from the sofa, rubbing her eyes as a nod to tiredness.

'Goodnight,' she says to Naomi. She has to say it twice before Naomi looks up.

''Night,' she replies, making the effort to smile. It drops from her face as soon as it has come, her mouth springing back into sad, worried lines as if pulled by elastic. 'Sleep well.'

Lydia hurries up the stairs, but as she reaches the landing, the brief flare of anticipation she has felt flickers and fades. She remembers the previous night with Adam: his body hotly against hers, his hands searching and urgent, and something tells her that it might be better in the imagining than in the re-enacting. Suddenly she is torn, wanting and yet not wanting. Briefly paralysed, she lingers on the landing. The door to Nicholas's study is slightly ajar, and she sees her shadow fall across the bright gap of light. She knows that it will shift and darken the quality of the light within, but she does not move.

'Naomi?' His voice rings sharply out from behind the door. She hesitates for a second. It would be easiest to move quietly away, but all at once she wants perversely to do the opposite. She goes quickly to the door, pushing it open another inch.

'It's not Naomi,' she says. 'It's only me.'

Nicholas is sitting at his desk, surrounded by piles of paper, lit by the green light of the desk-lamp. He blinks at her as she stands in the doorway. He looks exhausted, vague and distracted, almost as if he does not recognise her. 'Lydia,' he says finally. 'Was there something you wanted?'

And yes, she realises, there is something she wants. Something she has been wanting ever since she first saw him. Wordlessly, she steps forward into the room.

'If you're coming in,' he says, 'shut the door.' There is nothing of the request about his voice; it is an order, softly spoken but unmistakable, and she complies. As she approaches him, she notices that he has not shaved that day. He is normally entirely clean shaven, mercilessly so, the curves of his face smooth like granite. Now she sees the fine black hairs beginning to prickle his jawline, fighting their way to break the surface of his skin. They make him look Mediterranean, earthy. For a second, because she cannot help imagining it, she thinks of the sharpness of his stubble rubbing against soft female skin. She half shakes her head.

He is looking at her too, his gaze coolly interested—roaming her body curiously as if he has never seen it before. His eyes keep slipping away, and she sees that there is a green glass bottle at his feet, half hidden underneath the desk. The tumbler on his desk is full of what she had taken to be water, but now she wonders.

'Sit down,' he says. There is a slight slur to his voice, but it doesn't reek of drunkenness; rather that he is simply very tired. When she does so, he doesn't say anything else for a while. He looks meditatively around the room, at his computer screen, at the photographs on the mantelpiece, at Lydia herself, all with the same dispassionate, distracted stare. 'It's been a long night,' he says eventually.

'Have you been working on your lecture?' she asks, because she wants to delay the other question that is nagging to be asked. She knows that the lecture is due to take place the fol-

182 · REBECCA CONNELL

lowing day, but beyond the few words that she has seen scrawled on his notepad, she knows little else. She doesn't want to provoke a conversation on it, and is relieved when he merely nods, and rubs a hand over his face as if to signal the end of the topic.

'Lydia,' he says again, and sighs. She feels an uncomfortable shiver run lightly down the back of her neck; sensing, perhaps, something of what he is thinking.

'The other woman,' she says. The words are dragged out of her, irretrievably, forcing her to continue, and as she lets them fall she feels a strange sense of release at the knowledge that at last she is facing him head-on. 'The other woman you knew, with my name. Did you care for her very much?'

He looks at her for a long moment, measuring her question. For a second, she thinks he will order her out of the room, revert to the safety of his position as host and head of the house. But the lure of the question, the memories it provokes, is too strong. He takes a sip from his tumbler, and slowly nods. 'I did,' he says. 'In fact, I sometimes wonder if she was the only woman I've ever really loved.'

Lydia draws a sharp breath, for strangely, whatever she has expected to hear, it is not this. For Nicholas to be sitting across from her, saying these unthinkable words, is so surreal that her mind will not latch on to it. A flare of anger shoots through her—for herself, for Naomi—and she opts for the safer victim. 'I doubt Naomi would be pleased to hear you say that,' she says.

'On the contrary,' Nicholas fires back. 'It's no slight to my wife. Love is different when you're young. I expect you know that for yourself by now. I believe that it's only possible to fall in love once, don't you? To think otherwise makes no logical sense. Why would anyone put themselves in such a position twice?' He is smiling wolfishly, retreating into intellectual argument.

'What position?' Lydia asks, forcing the words out behind the dryness in her throat.

'A position of danger,' Nicholas says, a little impatiently. 'Of vulnerability.' He sighs, setting down his glass with a crash. 'Perhaps you are at the other extreme—too young to understand.'

Lydia makes some noise of agreement. In that moment she hates him so much that she cannot stand to look at him, and instead she finds herself focusing intently on the greenly glowing lamp at his side, until her eyes blur and she sees spots, like the aftermath of a camera flash.

When Nicholas speaks again his voice is calmer, melancholy. 'Lydia died some time ago,' he says. 'Part of me was glad. The situation—it was complex, and untenable. But even so, there isn't a day that goes by when I don't think of her, and when I don't regret what happened. I really believe I will never get over it.' His voice is a peculiar mix of detachment and devastation.

With a great effort, Lydia drags her eyes away from the lamp and looks at him. He is watching her intently, obviously expecting her to speak. She sees his face, stern and sad, through the light that still swims behind her eyes. She regrets having come, having tried to unlock this door. There is nothing behind it that can excuse him or that can lessen the pain. She wants to end the conversation, and she chooses a platitude that strikes her as safe, anodyne, final. 'I suppose,' she says, in a voice that doesn't sound like her own at all, 'that losing a lover is always hard.'

He makes a curious sound—something between a laugh and a sob of pain. 'That wasn't all I lost,' he says. And then, before she has the chance to speak, or to close her ears against what she somehow knows she will not want to hear, he tells her something else.

NICHOLAS
1989

We had a quiet family Christmas that year. Previously, our proximity to Naomi's parents had meant that we spent most of the festive season sitting in their living room, clutching warm glasses of sherry and stale mince pies. I rarely enjoyed these occasions, dampened down as the atmosphere was by the heavy fug of overindulgence, but had always seen them as no less inevitable than the bright star rising in the east. When Naomi announced that she had delayed the familial celebrations until January, I was astonished and confused. It transpired that she felt that we should celebrate Adam's first Christmas—technically his second, I pointed out, although even I could appreciate that as a week-old baby Adam had been totally oblivious to the event—together, on our own, as a family. I was glad of her decision. For one thing, it meant that Christmas could become all about Adam, and I could pour all my effort into somehow making it special for him without being distracted by the guilt and regret that sometimes made itself manifest to me on special occasions. Besides, it gave me an excuse not to see Lydia for a few days. I needed to get away from her, needed to think and see for myself what a life without her might be like. I hoped that the break might push me in one direction or the other—show me either that I could live without her or that I couldn't, and make the decision for me as to what the hell I was going to do.

In the end, Adam didn't much enjoy his first real Christmas, because he was ill. Nothing serious, as it turned out—just one of those eye-watering coughs that seem so alarming in babies at the time. It was enough to leave him red eyed and grizzling all the way through the day, turning his face unhappily away from the painstakingly wrapped presents and beating his fists feebly on my chest in impotent exasperation. We had called the doctor out two days before, and knew that with medicine the cough would soon pass, but all the same it was distressing to see our son in such obvious misery. I caught his tiny balled-up fists and held them in my hands; they fitted neatly and snugly into my palm. Naomi and I bathed him, got the medicine down his throat with little short of force, and finally put him to bed at almost nine o'clock. After that neither of us felt much like playing charades. We sat on the sofa together and watched the Christmas edition of a soap we never normally followed: beatings and passion and hideous revelations over the half-carved turkey. Naomi fell asleep on my shoulder before the end, gently snoring into my neck. I sat with my arm around her, looking around at the tinsel strung across the lounge and the colourful fairy lights winking out at me from the tree in pride of place in front of the fireplace. I wasn't sure what I felt.

Adam remained tired and fractious for another three or four days, and we threw ourselves into caring for him and making the festive season as pleasant as possible despite his illness. When, after half an hour of making a sturdy toy pony dance lumberingly across his bedspread until my hand hurt, I finally received a wan smile, I felt inordinately proud and self-congratulatory. I felt I was succeeding with Adam, forming a bond with him that would stand us in good stead in later life. At times like this, when I got to spend so much more time with him than normal, I felt happy and reassured. Naomi and I had created him together, after all, and surely that fact alone meant that we had something worth saving. Over the course of that Christmas I almost forgot that Lydia existed, or if not forgot, at least tactically pushed her to the back of my mind. It wasn't always easy. On Boxing Day a song came on the radio that always reminded me of her: it had been playing once when we shared an evening in a hotel and we had lain side by side and listened to it in companionable silence, fresh from making love. The memory came to me so vividly that I had to catch my breath and turn the radio off before Naomi came downstairs.

For a few minutes afterwards I tried to imagine what she was doing, how her own family Christmas with Martin and Louise was playing out. I wondered if she, too, had had the radio tuned to that particular station and stood listening to the song, her body humming with the same remembrance and longing. We had made a tactical agreement not to contact each other over Christmas—although we never said so out loud, the guilt was getting to us and I don't think either of us wanted it thrown into stark relief against the backdrop of such a cosy family time. So I resisted the urge to pick up the phone, and within half an hour I was playing Scrabble with Naomi, eating clementines and sparring lightly with her over unlikely words. I could cope with this, I thought, as we went to bed that night, my eyes wide open in the dark as I lay with my arms around her, listening to her breathing. If I kept this up, then thinking of Lydia might eventually lose its pain, just as it had before. Unlike the last time, this time I knew that I could do it—survive losing her, to all intents and purposes get over her. Lying there in bed with my wife, I almost made the decision there and then, but it felt too final to contemplate. I simply turned it over in my head, tentatively accustomed myself to it, as if I were trying on an unfamiliar suit and looking at myself in the mirror from all angles, attempting to decide whether it fitted me.

On 30 December, Naomi announced that she had invited Martin and Lydia over to our house for New Year's Eve. I was angry, and told her so. I had assumed that, in keeping with our Christmas, we would spend the evening alone with Adam, and couldn't understand why she hadn't asked me first before inviting the Knights. Naomi told me that she was sorry and that she had been thoughtless, but I could see that she didn't really understand why I was so annoyed at the prospect of two of our closest friends coming over for canapés and champagne. Of course, I couldn't explain, and felt all the more guilty for it.

'I'm just tired,' I ended up apologising, my catch-all excuse for unpredictable or erratic behaviour. 'It's been a tough week, what with Adam being ill. I'm sure it'll be fine.'

Shortly before Martin and Lydia were due to arrive, I went upstairs to the bedroom and took a slim red box from where I had hidden it at the back of the chest of drawers. Before Christmas, buying Lydia a present had seemed necessary and inevitable, and I had picked out the filigree silver necklace with instinctive knowledge that she would love it, in stark contrast to the hour I spent vacillating between choices for Naomi. Now I wasn't so sure that I should give it to her, and yet I didn't want to face the thought of throwing it away or keeping it, and what that would imply. After a few minutes I slipped the box back in its place at the rear of the drawer without opening it. It was a decision that didn't yet have to be made. Standing there absorbed in thought, I lost track of time, but it was probably only a few minutes before the sound of the doorbell jolted me into action.

Looking down from the landing, I could see Martin in one of his trademark buttoned-up suits, his bald head gleaming up at me like a beacon as he launched forward and kissed Naomi on the cheek. The two of them were chattering, comparing notes on their Christmases. Lydia was nowhere to be seen. For a moment I thought he had come without her, and my heart lifted strangely at the thought. I hurried downstairs, ready to welcome him, but just as I reached the bottom of the staircase, Lydia appeared in the doorway. After a week without her, her beauty ambushed me all over again. She wore a short, dark blue cocktail dress that clung to her body like silk, subtly high-lighting her curves. Her blonde hair hung straight and sleek over her shoulders, framing her delicate face. I looked away from her, despair seizing up inside me so that I had to fight for breath. I didn't want to feel this way, but seeing her again I could only think that I loved her and that I wanted everyone else to disappear. Unfairly, I felt furious with Naomi. If she had not arranged this meeting, I could have prolonged the separa-tion for another week, maybe two, maybe indefinitely. Seeing Lydia again now served only to reignite my need for her, like that of an addict blindly craving his next fix.

'I'm really sorry,' she was saying, 'I'm afraid we couldn't get a babysitter.' It was only then that I saw Louise, hanging back in the doorway, pigtails flapping over her face as she stared at the ground in embarrassment. Dressed up in a red velvet pinafore and matching boots, she was blushing fit to match her outfit. 'She'll probably go to bed in about an hour or so, if she can bed down in your spare room,' Lydia continued.

'Of course, of course, that's fine,' Naomi exclaimed gaily. I couldn't help noticing how pleased she seemed to have com-pany, and for a second I wondered, with a stab of unwarrant-ed injustice, whether the past week's enforced togetherness had started to give her cabin fever.

'Hello, Louise,' I said. The child gave me a cautious smile. Over the past few months I had seen little of her, but I always wondered whether she remembered or connected me with the man in her kitchen on the day of her birthday party. The uncer-tainty made me more attentive to her than I would have been under other circumstances. 'Get any good presents?'

Louise nodded thoughtfully. 'A Wendy house,' she said qui-etly, shooting me a quick glance, as if to appraise what I thought of this. I nodded enthusiastically, forming my features into an expression of delight and amazement. Out of the cor-ner of my eye, I could see Lydia watching me, tentatively smiling. We had not acknowledged each other yet, but Naomi and Martin seemed not to notice anything amiss, still chatting animatedly. As they moved into the dining room, where Naomi had set out trays of vol-au-vents, fans of cheese straws and champagne glasses, Lydia put a hand lightly on the small of my back. It was a hesitant, almost shy gesture, and I felt that she was testing the water. I could have ignored her touch, but instead I swept my own hand gently along the back of her neck as we followed them through. At my touch she turned and gave me a radiant smile. Relief was written all over her face. I realised then that she, too, had used the week apart as a test, to see whether she could manage without me. From what I could see, she had missed me more than I had missed her, and the knowledge doused me with heady remorse.

It seemed like minutes rather than hours before we were lined up in front of the television, champagne glasses held aloft, watching fireworks exploding over the Thames. As we cheered and clinked glasses, I felt strange and choked up. Somehow I knew that this would be the last New Year's Eve that all four of us would be together this way; whatever happened over the next few weeks would tear the quartet apart, so thoroughly that it could never be put back together again. I kissed Naomi on the mouth, Lydia on the cheek, shook Martin by the hand, and all of a sudden it felt desperately wrong, mixed up. I turned away to hide my agitation, glancing at the baby monitor. Faint staccato dots were leaping on its surface: the festivities had woken Adam up.

'Oh dear,' said Naomi, following my gaze. 'Shall I go and check on him?' She had drunk more than usual, and her words were happy and slurred.

'No, I'll go,' I said. 'You stay here and get everyone some coffees, or more champagne, if they fancy it.' She agreed with alacrity, clearly not feeling up to the task of soothing a possibly fractious Adam. I climbed the dark staircase to his room, peeked inside. Adam's wide eyes stared up at me for an instant, then drooped again. I stood watching him for a minute or two, but he had dropped back into sleep as easily as he had been roused from it, his small chest heaving and falling deeply under the coverlet. Gently, I stroked the hair, as dark as my own, back from his forehead, then quietly backed out of the room. Instinct made me remain on the landing, listening, waiting. Sure enough, I soon heard the light tread of footsteps up the stairs. Lydia came towards me through the shadows, pressing a finger to her lips. I took her by the hand and led her down the corridor to my bedroom, closed the door behind us.

'We don't have long,' she said quietly. 'I said I was going to check on Louise.'

She made as if to draw me towards her, but I moved away and went to the chest of drawers, sliding open the drawer where I had hidden the necklace. My hands were shaking as I took the box from its hiding place and gave it to her. She gave me a brief, questioning look, then snapped it open. Her eyes glistened in the dark. She blinked once, twice, as if to keep tears away. Then she kissed me, deeply, more fervently than she had done in a long time, entwining her body with mine. I held her, midnight blue silk sliding through my hands, ran my fingers through her hair. I felt the tears wet on my cheek, and no longer knew whether they belonged to me or her.

'Enough,' I heard myself say. I broke away from her, swallowing down panic and indecision. I knew what I was about to say and it terrified me, but all at once I felt that I had no choice. 'This has gone on too long. I want to resolve this, one way or the other, and I want to do it soon.'

She nodded. 'I know,' she said, so softly that I could barely hear. 'But which way do you want?'

I felt a faint, obscure sting of resentment that she should make me say it. 'I want you,' I said. 'You know that.' Until a few moments earlier, I hadn't even fully realised it myself, but nevertheless I knew that I was right in what I said: she had known before me, always had, that this was the way it would go. My words seemed to have put her in the driving seat; I felt the authority of a few seconds before drain away, but I continued to stare at her steadily, not betraying myself. 'And if you feel the same, we have to tell them,' I said.

She gave a sudden shiver, a convulsion that shook her body and made her wrap her arms around herself. 'It's just not that simple,' she said unhappily. 'You know that. If I could do it, I would, but I can't. It's not losing me—he would get over that eventually, I'm sure of it—but taking Louise away from him. How can I do it, Nicholas? He's not a bad man, you know that. He doesn't deserve to lose his child.'

She had said this sort of thing several times before, and I had a stack of well-used retorts. If he could swallow his pride and agree to joint custody, Martin would still see Louise. What about my own fears about losing Adam? Was keeping her family together really more important to her than I was? The realisation came to me then, sharp and long overdue, that all of these were missing the point. What she was really doing was asking for my help. She was telling me that she had an impossible decision to make, and that she needed me to make it for her, to push her off the precipice. If I took the decision into my own hands, and told Naomi about us, there would be no going back and she wouldn't have to agonise any more. I took her face in my hands, the perfect oval cupping warmly, perfectly into my palms.

'Lydia,' I said. 'Do you really love me? Are you sure that you want us to be together?'

'Yes. Yes, I do,' she whispered. We were so close together that I felt the breath that came with the words, lightly across my lips.

'Then that's all I need to know,' I said.

'What do you mean?' she asked. I could feel her fingers

clutching convulsively at the loops of my belt, pulling and twisting them like worry beads. 'What are you going to do?'

'Nothing, tonight,' I said. 'I'll send you a message tomorrow.' I saw confusion and worry pass across her face and her lips opening to speak; I stopped her with a kiss, silencing her, sealing up her words. When I released her she glanced towards the bedroom door. We had been longer than we had intended, and she moved reluctantly away.

At the doorway to the landing she stopped, looked back at me. She didn't have to tell me to wait a minute or two before following her back down; we were all too used to this kind of unhappy subterfuge. All the same she hesitated, looking at me with eyes full of longing and sadness. 'I do love you, Nicholas,' she said, as if I had contradicted her.

'I know,' I said. I didn't say it back, not out loud; I didn't think I needed to. If I had known then that I would never say it to her again, I might have acted differently. Instead I simply watched her turn away, watched her shadow recede down the hallway until she was gone from view. I stood counting seconds in my head, thinking that when I reached a hundred I would go back downstairs, but I found that I didn't want to. I had no stomach to carry out this pretence any more. I lay down on the bed, loosening my shirt, still smelling the faintest hint of Lydia's perfume clinging to its folds, and closed my eyes.

I felt an intense weariness come over me. I wanted to sleep, but when Naomi came softly into the bedroom, later, much later, I was still conscious. I lay motionless, my face turned away, listening to her undress. She slipped in beside me, and I felt her hand on my shoulder, shaking it gently and insistently. She whispered my name. I didn't respond, lying stiff and still. A minute's pregnant pause later, she sighed and lay down, her head resting on my back. As we lay together, I truly believed that it would be the last time, and I didn't know how I felt, didn't know how to measure what I would be losing and gain-

ing. I didn't know whether I was doing the right thing, whether
it was too late to change or whether I could even if I wanted
to. I knew only that I would never be able to cut Lydia out of
my life, and knowing that made all the other thoughts,
inevitable though they were, seem entirely futile.

New Year's Day dawned dull and miserable, rain dirtying
the bedroom windowpane. I lay and listened to it falling. I had
slept for only a couple of hours, but I felt strangely energised.
My doubts of the night before had hardened into certainty.
Breaking my relationship with Naomi would be painful,
hideous even, but it was the only way out of the vicious circle.
I wanted to give her some warning, a small, stupid part of me
thinking that it would help her, and so when she woke and
rolled over, stretching her hand out to caress my shoulder, I
inched away from her. Puzzled, she touched me again, and I
felt myself flinch.

'Are you O.K., Nick?' she asked. I was silent. 'I was worried
about you last night,' she said appealingly. 'You didn't even say
goodbye to the Knights. Were you just tired, or is there something else?'

I glanced at her, forcing a small, tight smile. 'I'm fine,' I
said, the coldness of my tone belying my words. Inside, my
mind was whirring over the possibilities. I could come out
with it now, but the situation felt surreal and wrong: the two
of us in bed together, half naked, with our son asleep in the
next room. Much better to let her believe that I was angry for
some unidentifiable reason and leave her alone for the morning, so that when I returned she would be well and truly prepared for some kind of showdown. Selfishly, I didn't want
her to make things any more difficult than they had to be,
and the thought of her being affectionate, cajoling and good
tempered was almost enough to make me lose my resolve
altogether.

I got out of bed, reaching for my dressing gown. 'I'm going for a shower,' I said. I felt Naomi's eyes on me, hurt and puzzled, as I left the room. 'Happy New Year,' I thought I heard her say as I closed the door behind me. I may have been mistaken.

By the time I came back to the bedroom she was gone. I towelled off my hair and dressed in funeral clothes—black high-necked shirt, pressed black trousers. Looking at myself in the mirror, I straightened my collar. I felt a heavy sense of things coming together, sorting themselves into the solution that I had always known would come. For a moment I tried to imagine living with Lydia, our relationship stripped of all its secrecy and danger: saw us sitting cosily round the breakfast table, kissing and holding hands in public, introducing each other at parties. I had no idea whether these things would drain the passion steadily away from us, the way that I now saw they had done with me and Naomi. The idea of desiring Lydia any less than I did now, of the day coming when the sight of her naked body would prompt nothing in me beyond a mild, automatic stirring of familiarity, was so foreign to me that I saw no point in worrying about it. I brushed my hair in front of the mirror, sweeping it back from my forehead in a way that Naomi had once said made me look like a vampire. As I recalled her words I smiled, then frowned. I couldn't deny the affection I still had for her, but it wasn't enough, not any more. I switched the thought off, turning away from the mirror.

I went to Adam's room. He was still sleeping, lulled as he often was by the hypnotic mood music of the rain pattering on to the skylight above his bed. I went and sat beside him, resting my hand lightly on his outflung arm where it protruded clumsily from the bedclothes. He stirred slightly in his sleep, expelling a sigh, like an old man. The thought of not being there when he woke up every morning made me drop my head and blink. I had always scorned parents who stayed together for the sake of their children, but I suddenly realised how easily it could be done—although in reality, it was purely for my own sake that I wanted to keep Adam with me. He was far too young for a divorce to make any real impact, particularly if I still saw him regularly. I couldn't believe that Naomi would exclude me from him out of spite, and I didn't even want to entertain it as a possibility.

'It'll be all right,' I said out loud, my empty words echoing stupidly around the bedroom. 'I still love you,' I tried again. Speaking to Adam felt meaningless, a pathetic attempt to make myself feel better. I stood up, my shadow falling across his cot, feeling my heart twisted up painfully inside my chest, leaving me gasping temporarily for breath. I left the room without a backward glance and went downstairs.

Naomi was reading the paper in the lounge, her eyes glazed in that way which betrayed that she was not really reading at all. She looked up hopefully when I came in, but before she could speak the telephone rang. I crossed swiftly to it, grateful for the lifeline, and said hello into the receiver, glancing across at Naomi as I did so. She had retreated back into her paper, resigned to being patient for my attention.

'Good morning,' a voice said cheerfully, and I realised that it was Martin. 'And Happy New Year! Just calling to say thank you for last night.'

'That's fine—I'm glad you enjoyed it,' I said awkwardly. 'Sorry I disappeared without warning towards the end. I was rather tired.'

'Oh, don't worry,' Martin breezed on. 'I quite understand, it was rather a late night, after all.'

There was a pause, and I became aware that I was expected to carry on the conversation. 'So . . . what are you doing today?' I asked, at a loss for what else to say.

'Well, I've been abandoned, I'm afraid,' Martin rattled on, still relentlessly chirpy. 'Lydia has taken Louise swimming, so

I rather thought I might do a spot of DIY. We were planning to put some shelves up a good while ago, but you know how it is, these things get delayed. I'm not much good with a hammer, unfortunately, but I'm sure I'll manage. Of course, if you were at a loose end . . .' He trailed off hopefully. I saw that the call was his elaborate way of asking for company and assistance. I opened my mouth to make some excuse, but the rush of sudden affection that I felt for Martin surprised me. Even in my wildest dreams, I could not envisage any way in which our friendship could continue after he was told that I had been having an affair with his wife, no matter what the circumstances. To all intents and purposes, then, this was undoubtedly the friendship's last day, and perhaps it was fitting that we should spend it together. Martin had never been anything approaching a soulmate, but he was a decent man, and not someone whom I would have chosen to hurt. Besides, joining him for the morning would get me away from Naomi in the way I had planned, and was surely preferable to wandering around the park in the rain or sitting in some grey, depressing café.

These thoughts flashed through my head so fast that I barely hesitated before answering him. 'I'll come over, if you like,' I said. 'I could bring some tools, if you're short of anything.'

I let Martin get through his usual effusive burst of thanks and hung up. When I turned back to Naomi she was looking at me with a mixture of accusation and plaintiveness. 'You're going out?' she said unnecessarily.

'Yes,' I said. 'I'll be back in a few hours.'

'If you're going to see Martin, Adam and I could come with you?' she suggested tentatively.

'I don't think so,' I said shortly.

My words flicked the switch in her from conciliation to anger. 'Nick, I don't understand what I've done wrong,' she burst out, her face twisted with the injustice of it. 'Everything was fine last night, so why are you being like this?' She was on her feet now, gesticulating as she talked as if she would like to grab hold of me and shake some sense into me. I battled with the desire to shout that she had no idea, that everything had not been fine, not for months, or even years, and that almost every time we had slept together recently I had been thinking of Lydia and not her. I bit my lip, so hard that I tasted blood, and walked out of the house. Behind me I heard her screaming for me to come back, but I swiftly got into the car and reversed down the driveway, switching the radio on loud as I did so to block out her voice and my thoughts.

Martin answered the door to me some twenty minutes later, his hands covered in sawdust. He was wearing a beige T-shirt and ill-fitting jeans that looked several years old, and with a start I realised that I had never before seen him out of formal wear. He caught my look and laughed. 'I know,' he said. 'I'm not often in mufti. I thought it might be more appropriate, on this occasion.' He padded through to the kitchen, where he had laid out a tea tray. 'Perhaps a cup of tea before I show you my handiwork thus far,' he said.

We sat at the kitchen table, drinking tea and eating the digestives that Martin had arranged carefully on a willow-pattern plate. He talked about his plans for the coming term, the upcoming events in the chemistry department that he would have a hand in, his enthusiasm for guiding his students through the run-up to their O-levels. Looking at his animated, guileless face, I couldn't help wondering how he would cope. Perhaps he would throw himself even farther into his work, letting it absorb him so thoroughly that his colleagues would be hard pushed to see that anything was wrong. I comforted myself with the possibility, unlikely though it was, that he would find Lydia's departure to somehow be a blessing in disguise.

After we had drained the pot of tea, Martin took me through to the garage, where he seemed to have made some attempt to saw uneven blocks of wood into something resembling shelves. His success was dubious, but I smiled and made suitably impressed noises. Obviously pleased, he showed me the plans that he had drawn up for how they would be assembled and mounted. We sat down together on the garage floor.

'Perhaps if I put these brackets on,' he said doubtfully. He brandished a screwdriver and reached for the first bracket, clearly at a loss as to how to continue. I helped him hold it in place. Soon we had settled into a routine, and the shelves began to take some sort of shape.

'This is only the start, of course,' Martin pointed out after a while. 'Once these are done, I'll look at doing up the kitchen, and perhaps adding a bathroom unit as well.'

'Quite a bit of effort you're going to,' I commented. 'Are you looking to add value?'

Martin rolled his head from side to side in a yes-no motion. 'Well, perhaps eventually,' he conceded. 'But to be perfectly honest, we're not really thinking about selling the house, not for some years at least. We're quite settled here.'

I felt a lump in my throat and swallowed it down. This was no time to be getting sentimental. 'I suppose you wouldn't want to move any distance for quite a while anyway,' I said, taking refuge in practicalities. 'What with Louise only being four, she must have just started school here, and of course you wouldn't want to uproot her.'

Martin said something indistinctly, his words muffled by the screws that he was holding between his teeth as he grappled with a bracket.

'Sorry?' I said. I waited as he finished his task, laid down the screwdriver, took the screws from his mouth, wiped his hand across his lips.

'Five,' he said, smiling indulgently. 'Louise is five.'

Sometimes, the pain of discovery is made all the sharper by the random way that it hits you, a bolt from the blue. When Martin threw out those words, casually and without a second thought, that pain struck me like an unseen assailant, lurking with intent in the darkness. But that wasn't all. In that moment, I found that discovery can be even more bitter if, just as you are ambushed, you realise that you should have seen that faceless assailant all along. Should have paid more attention to the light footsteps behind you, the moving shadows out of the corner of your eye. Instead, you pushed your awareness to the back of your mind, never acknowledged it, put your instinctual knowledge down to paranoia, and strode blithely on down that street towards the danger. As I stared at Martin, happily working away again, intent on his task, I remembered. Lydia's face when I appeared at the door that day, panic stricken and wild; waiting in the doorway while she disappeared; a cake with four wonky candles stuck in its surface and a small child crying and complaining, *It's not right, it isn't right.* Perhaps, even then, I knew what was wrong, and chose not to see it.

Somehow I got to my feet and excused myself. Upstairs in the bathroom, I locked the door. I felt my legs unsteady under me, and sat down with my back to the wall. I tried to trace the lines of Louise's face in my mind. I couldn't see her, only a hotch-potch of features: dark eyes, like mine, dark plaits of hair falling either side of a serious oval face. I didn't know whether she looked like me. Bowled over by Lydia, I found it hard to see anyone else when she was in the room, and I realised that I had barely looked at her child, not really, not for more than a couple of seconds at a time. I found myself trawling back through the years. When Lydia had left me six years before, I had thought that I would never get over the pain of losing her, but I had rationalised it. She had bound herself to Martin. She had gone with what I had always thought to be her strongest claim—her marriage. Had she known, even then at what must have been little more than a few weeks into her pregnancy, that she was carrying my child? How else to explain her disappearance? I remembered the passion of that first summer, the hundreds of times that Lydia and I had made love, not always planned, not always as careful as we should have been. She had told me, not once but several times over that summer, that she was barely sleeping with Martin. A heavily regimented, once-monthly performance, barricading herself against him. Even if the odds had not pointed to the truth, her guilt confirmed it, and more and deeper than this, the sudden instinctive certainty that I felt, as if my eyes had been opened to a truth so obvious that I must have been blind not to see it.

Numbed by shock, I had felt detached and clinical as I sorted through these memories, and I was caught off guard by the sudden fury that shot through me. I thought of all the times that Lydia had held Louise up as the reason, the only reason, why she could not leave Martin, her pious declarations that she could not bear to tear a father apart from his child. I saw them for what they were. She was a coward, not wanting to face up to the reality of toppling herself off the lofty pedestal of Martin's adoration, not wanting to dirty her own name, even to a man she no longer loved. Or had she been merely playing with me all along? Waiting for me to demean myself and tell my wife that I was leaving her for another woman, only to turn around with politely raised eyebrows and dismiss me as a fantasist for some secret sick gratification of her own? Ugly possibilities tangled themselves up in my head.

I was on my feet now, my hands shaking. I snatched a vase from the sill and threw it with all my force at the wall, watching glass foam and splinter against the pale blue tiles and scatter around my feet. It wasn't enough, did nothing to quell my rage. I had been a fool—a puppy panting after his mistress. I had thought that our secrets were bound up together, that only with each other were we truly honest. Now I saw that she had been playing with fire, torn between her physical desire for me and her reputation, not caring enough to tell me the truth. I saw the family we could have had—the two of us and Louise, other children. It slipped through my hands like water. The chance to grasp it had passed me by six years ago, and I had never known.

There was a knocking at the door, soft at first, then more persistent. 'Nicholas!' Martin was calling, his voice distant and fuzzy in my head. 'Nicholas, are you all right?'

I unlocked the door and he pushed it open, his mouth forming into an O of surprise as he saw the glass shattered at my feet.

'I'm sorry,' I said, and looking at him then, my words were genuine; I had never felt more sorry for him. 'I lost my balance and the vase fell.' My words seemed to come from some way away, stiff and robotic.

'Don't worry, old chap, no problem at all,' Martin was saying, scurrying forward, then retreating again, as if at a loss what to do. 'But are you all right?'

'I'm not feeling very well,' I said. 'I'm not sure what's come over me. I think I should go home.'

'Of course, of course,' Martin exclaimed. Haltingly, he held out a hand to help me over the mess of glass. I took it and stepped shakily forward. His hand felt warm, solid, in mine. 'Please, do call me and let me know you're feeling better tomorrow,' he said anxiously as we went to the front door.

I nodded and turned to leave, but a thought struck me and I turned back. 'Do you have a piece of paper?' I asked.

Martin looked briefly quizzical, then appeared to shake the curiosity from his mind, as if it was more important that I should have what I wanted. He pointed towards a pad of notepaper next to the telephone. 'This is Lydia's,' he said, 'but I'm sure she wouldn't mind.'

'Thank you,' I said. I tore off a sheet. It was bordered with delicately drawn bluebells, picked out in cerulean against the cream notepaper. 'I'm sorry for all the drama. I'll call you soon.' I left him in the doorway, wringing his hands in nervy concern, peering after me as I glanced back, his head bobbing up and down as he tried to digest my strange behaviour.

Out on the street, I turned the corner and stopped the car. I pulled a pen from my pocket and smoothed the notepaper out on the dashboard. I wrote without pause for consideration, gripping the pen tightly to stop my fingers from shaking, letting the words flow by instinct on to the page.

> Lydia,
> There is so much to say and what I could say would never be enough. Suffice it to say that the scales have fallen from my eyes. I see you now for what you are: selfish, complacent, poisonous, evil. I only regret that it has taken me this long to end what should never have begun.
> There is no point in answering this letter. I don't want to see you, speak to you, touch you: you are dead to me. The first time I saw you, I knew that I would always love you. But sometimes over time the things we know unravel into nothing more than the things we thought we knew. This time I was wrong.
> Nicholas

I folded the paper back into my pocket, got out of the car and strode back down the street. Rain soaked through my jacket and clung coldly to my skin. It splashed over my shoes, scattering bright skeins of raindrops around me as I walked. By the time I reached the end of the street I was drenched through, my hands stiff and cold. Awkwardly, I unlatched the disused postbox. I wiped my hands on the inside of my jacket, took the folded paper out and pushed it to the back of the box, its edges just visible in the dark. I knew that Lydia checked the box routinely, even though I seldom needed to write to her any more.

Occasionally, I would send the odd love note, singing her praises like a hapless idiot. At the thought of these notes, anger flared up again, bright and sharp like a knife, making me hiss through my teeth and clench my hands.

Her face flashed into my mind, as I had seen her the night before, anxious and imploring in my bedroom doorway, asking what I was going to do. Here was her answer. It would not be the one she was expecting. I slammed the postbox shut. I tried to slam shut, just as decisively, the all-too-automatic feelings of yearning as her image swam before my eyes. She did not love me, and I would not love her. As I returned to the car and drove away from the temptation to tear up the letter, every nerve in my body nagged me back, whispering that I should forgive her, that perhaps there was a good explanation. I despised myself. I drove home slowly, carefully, not trusting myself to do otherwise. The windscreen was clogged with drives of rain, trickling too fast for the wipers to push them away, and so it didn't seem to matter so much that I was crying; it didn't seem to matter at all.

The next few hours passed with surprising normality. By the time I arrived home, I had composed myself sufficiently to face Naomi. Not having expected me home so soon, she was rattled and edgy, prepared for an argument. I embraced her and apologised, told her that I had been tired and irritable. She was wary at first, trying to probe deeper to find a reason for my earlier coldness. Again, I told her I was sorry, and this was a rare enough event for her to forgive and forget.

'I'm sorry too,' she said, her face buried in my shoulder as we stood hugging in the hallway, Adam looking on placidly and uncomprehendingly from his playpen. 'I feel like I haven't been the best wife recently. I know we haven't had as much time together since Adam.' Hearing and recognising his name, Adam let out a conversational whoop. I smiled, breaking away from Naomi to go to the playpen and take hold of his outstretched hands.

'It's inevitable,' I said, staring down at my son's beaming face. 'Things will get better. I know it.'

We spent the afternoon playing with Adam, watching television, eating toast and drinking freshly brewed coffee as the rain continued to pour down outside. Cocooned as we were in the warmth of our sitting room, the morning's events felt like a dream. I didn't want to revisit them, not yet; didn't want to think about Louise, and much less about Lydia. Automatically, I stroked Naomi's curls as she lay on the sofa, her head in my lap. The scene was eerily familiar. We had played it out dozens of times before, and would doubtless do so dozens of times again. It felt routine. It felt fine. Comfortably desensitised, I told myself that I could cope with this old way of life, the same way that I had coped before Lydia had come back into it and torn it apart. This was my destiny: a wife, a son, and whatever the future held for us. I knew that the emptiness I felt would gradually suck in on itself, growing smaller and smaller until it was barely noticeable; that the hard, dense weight in my heart would lighten into nothingness. It had to, because to think otherwise was almost unbearable.

As the film finished Naomi rolled off the sofa, sighing. 'It's almost six,' she said. 'I think I'll take him upstairs and give him his bath, read him a story. That is if you don't want to do it?'

I shook my head. I wanted to be alone. 'I think I'll just stay and watch this,' I said, channel-flicking at random. I landed on a studio talent show, all lurid colours, pumping music and inept performances. Naomi shot me a look of surprise, but didn't comment, instead gathering Adam into her arms and carrying him out of the room, softly talking to him. Alone, I switched off the television and sat staring at the blank screen. The silence seemed to push me, inviting me to think about all the things I didn't want to entertain. Was this how it would be?

I would have to surround myself with people, never giving myself a moment's peace in which I might drop my guard, relent and return to Lydia. The thought made me recoil. I pressed my hands to my temples, which were gently aching, as if all my nerves were pulled into tight, tender strings running through my head. Closing my eyes, I gently massaged the skin above my ears. Flashes of colour swam before me in the blackness. I was very tired. I had just begun to formulate the idea of going upstairs to have a nap when I sensed it. My eyes still closed, the darkness briefly took on a deeper quality, as if a shadow had fallen across the dull light streaming in from the window behind me.

I opened my eyes and looked sharply behind. In the same instant I heard an angry screech of brakes, saw the white car swing itself recklessly into the driveway. It ground to an abrupt stop, the wheels spraying fountains of dirt and gravel. I should have walked away, but I stood transfixed. Lydia leapt out of the car, slamming the door shut. Her face was wetly streaked with make-up, mascara darkly rimming her eyes. She was wearing a white dress which fell to her knees, the hem picked out in vivid red. The rain moulded the white linen to her body, lovingly clinging to its lines. As she ran, I saw her breasts rise and fall underneath the translucent fabric, almost obscene. In another ·moment she would be at the front door. The thought galvanised me into action, my body and mind wrenched unpleasantly into wakefulness. I ran to the door and stepped out into the rain, barring her from entering.

She ran at me without a word, struggling to get past, arms and legs kicking out at me. I kicked the door shut behind us and held her, forcing her away from me. Still neither of us spoke. I could hear her gasping for breath, ragged and harsh, as she flailed against me. Anger made me too rough, and she winced with pain as I dug my fingers into her arm, but she didn't retreat. Even if I carried her bodily to the car, I couldn't make her drive. Wildly, I looked around. I strode to the side of the house, dragging Lydia with me. Out of sight, we stood together, inches apart, under the huge spreading apple tree by the side wall. Its branches hung heavily, clogged by rain, sending up a heady sweet smell of dust and decay. Underneath, I could smell the faint scent of apricots, the perfume she always wore, and it made me feel light headed and sick.

'I *had* to come,' she said, almost accusingly, gulping for breath.

No, I thought, *you didn't. You do as you like; you of all people don't do anything just because someone else has made you.* Out loud, I said, 'I don't have anything left to say.'

'But I don't understand,' she half shouted, pushing back her wet hair with her hands. I could see tears starting to her eyes. 'How could you say such horrible, hurtful things? Yesterday you said you loved me, you said you were going to sort everything out. I don't understand.'

Her face was hot with passion, her breasts rising and falling beneath her white dress. The rain had picked her nipples out; I saw them, straining darkly through the cloth. I couldn't help looking, couldn't help remembering the dozens, hundreds of times that my lips had closed around them, caressed her, tasted her. Vitriol spat and sparked inside me. I thought, *You have broken this, not me*, and the thought made me grit my teeth.

'No, I'm the one who doesn't understand,' I said levelly, my voice soft and controlled. 'I don't understand why you came here, when my letter must have made it obvious that I never wanted to see you again.'

'Because I deserve an explanation!' she screamed, grabbing my sleeve, pulling me towards her.

'And that's not all I don't understand,' I continued, as if she had not spoken. 'I don't understand why you claim to love me, when it's clear that you barely know what love is. I don't understand why you have stayed for all these years in a marriage that is so clearly wrong for you. But most of all, I don't understand why, when the chance came for you to leave that marriage, to be with the person you claimed to love and to have a child with him, you chose instead to hide the fact that his child even existed, to stay with your husband and to lie to everyone who is foolish enough to love you.' The words were not rehearsed, but they poured out of me smoothly and swiftly, as if cut out by a knife.

For a few moments there was no sound but the rain falling heavily through the leaves. I hadn't been able to look at her as I spoke, but when I had finished I looked straight into her eyes and saw something I had never seen there before—fear, and guilt. She was trembling, her mouth half open in shock as she groped for words. She blinked once, twice, looked down at her feet. She was wearing pretty red shoes, smeared with mud and scuffed by her reckless struggle against me. I found myself staring at them, my eyes stupidly tracing the lines of the silly silver buckles that sat on top of them like bows on a Christmas present.

'How did you find out?' she whispered, and I realised that she had considered and discounted a denial in those few silent moments.

'Your husband gave you away,' I said, spitting out the words. 'The small matter of Louise's real age. I don't know how you ever thought you could keep up this pretence. Did you even stop to consider how this could possibly work, if we were ever together as you said you wanted us to be? If I ever spent any amount of time with our daughter at all? If I was there when her next birthday came around? How could you be so fucking stupid?' Somewhere along the line I had lost control. I was shouting at her, my hands gripping her shoulders, shaking her as she stood pliant before me, her head dropped low. 'How could you do this to me?'

She whispered something, cleared her throat. 'I don't know,' she said. 'I would have told you.'

I released her. In an instant, as quickly as it had come, my anger had drained away. I felt numb, indifferent. I looked at her and wondered what she had ever done to make me think she was worthy of all this, that she was worth all this pain. 'Just go,' I said.

My words seemed to send her into hysterics. The tears that shock had kept to a minimum spilled over her cheeks, mingling with the rain. 'Don't leave me, Nicholas,' she sobbed. 'I know I've been selfish, and stupid, I know all that. I don't know what I was thinking. Maybe . . . maybe I wasn't sure what I wanted before, but I know now. I want you.'

Despite the pain that briefly twisted my heart, I laughed. 'Well, I suppose that's what they call poetic justice,' I said. 'Because for the first time, you can't have me.'

She looked at me for a long moment, as if trying to judge my sincerity. Her face was white with shock, her green eyes glittering sharply with hurt. I saw her breasts rise and fall shakily in a sigh. When she spoke again she was calmer, and her voice was quiet, almost reflective. 'You can't escape me,' she said.

In the years to come I would wake again and again from dreams that played back those few seconds to me so exactly, so perfectly capturing the sad certainty of her voice and the ghostly look of her face and her body clad in white, that they left me shivering and sweating, gasping for breath. She spoke those words as if she somehow knew how true, in a manner that I could never have guessed at, they would turn out to be. In the unfriendly dark of those moments, I often wondered whether they were a premonition, or a threat. In that instant, though, as she stood in front of me, they enraged me. I felt my hand jerk up from my side as if pulled by some alien force. As hard as I could, I slapped her across the face. I felt my hand connect with the soft, cool flesh of her cheek as she tried to turn, a fraction too late. When she raised her head again a red rash blazed and swelled across her left cheekbone. For a moment I thought she would speak. I saw her throat convulse as she swallowed, biting back the pain.

'I—' I said. Part of me wanted to say I was sorry, but the words stuck. I wouldn't apologise to her, not now.

She turned on her heel and walked away down the path, placing her feet precisely one in front of the other, her heels clicking wetly on the gravel. Her blonde hair was plastered down her back, moulded to her white dress. Lower, the material clung to her narrow hips, the red hem branding the backs of her knees like a slash of blood. I followed her around the corner, watched her walking towards the car. As she opened the door and started the ignition I could see her hands shaking crazily, but her face was set and serene. She reversed quickly down the drive, but as she went she shot me a look. The light had gone out from behind her eyes. She looked at me as if I were a stranger, and in that moment I felt like one, to her and to myself.

I stayed for a few minutes looking at the blank space where she had been. Then I felt for the key in my jacket pocket and unlocked the front door. As I stepped inside I caught a glimpse of myself, reflected in the hallway mirror. I looked ugly and ill. I ran my fingers through my drenched hair, listening. I could just hear the gentle splash of bathwater above. That aside, the house was silent. I thought of Naomi and Adam upstairs, bound together in their innocence. Slowly, I approached the staircase. I crept up the stairs and turned left along the hallway, bypassing the bathroom. I took a towel from the radiator in our bedroom, sat on the bed and wiped my face and hands, rubbed it across my hair. I looked down and realised that I had been standing outside in my socks, which were cold and waterlogged, sticking to my skin. Carefully, I peeled them off and dried my feet, put on another pair. I didn't know what to do next. Time passed; I wasn't sure how much, perhaps twenty minutes or more. When I stood up again blood and air rushed to my head. I descended the stairs, my vision fuzzed and dreamlike. I went to sit back down in front of the television, but I couldn't do it. I went to the hallway and pulled on my shoes, let myself out again.

The rain had slowed to a faint drizzle. I started walking. I didn't know myself where I was going. When I reached the end of the drive, something told me to turn left, and I did. The road was deserted, and in the back of my mind I found myself thinking that this was strange. It was only when I turned the tautly curving bend that I saw it. A thin cordon, white striped with orange, drawn across the road ahead. I shaded a hand across my eyes as I walked closer. An ambulance, tawny lights warmly blinking in the grey haze. The white car, snarled and crushed at the side of the road against the stone wall, as if someone had picked it up and thrown it where it fell. Two men in uniform, clustered together around the car, their heads bowed.

As they heard my footsteps they turned. I saw their faces, and didn't need to see any more, but I kept walking. When I reached the cordon I stopped, and took hold of it with my hands. In the shadows through the splintered window I saw her hair tumbled out like a fountain across the wheel. I couldn't see her face. I felt a soft internal blow to the heart, a tangible thud that left my head swimming. The car, her hair, the sweep of road seemed bright and false, like colours in a dream. The two men approached, and I saw their mouths move and heard them saying something to me, but I couldn't catch the words; they splashed through my fingers like mercury and, try as I might, I couldn't hold them.

One of the men walked me home. I handed him my keys at the front door. When he opened it, Naomi was standing there. Her blue eyes were round and anxious.

'Where did you go?' she asked, addressing me but looking at the man in the yellow-striped coat by my side. 'What's going on?'

I walked through the hallway, went into the lounge and closed the door. I sat down on the sofa and rested my head against its cushioned surface. The door was not enough to keep their voices out. I heard him explaining to her: a crash, my appearance at the scene, a state of distress. I heard him describe the vehicle, read out its number plate, and her gasp of recognition. She cried out, once, in disbelief: '*No!*' I could not be sure, but I thought she was crying. I heard her say Martin's name. The man's voice dropped lower, and I couldn't make out his words, only a soft rhythmic murmur that made me feel tired, very tired.

I heard the front door close. A few minutes later, Naomi appeared in front of me. She was holding two cups of tea, one of which she extended to me, and for a moment I had the urge to laugh. She must have heard that it was good for shock. I took it and my mouth felt the cloying sweetness of the sugar I never normally took.

She sat down beside me. 'I can't believe it,' she said. Out of the corner of my eye, I saw that she was holding the thick, dark blue material of her skirt between her fingertips, pulling and twisting at it. She was shaking her head slowly back and forth, as if trying to assimilate and settle the information that was seeping through her brain. 'We only saw her last night. The ambulance man said there was no indication that another vehicle was involved. It looks like she simply lost control of the car. Was she coming to see us, do you think? It's terrible to think of it happening so close.' She shook her head again, more briskly this time, swatting thoughts away.

I realised that I should say something, but my mind was blank. She was watching me, waiting, obviously wanting to dissect the tragedy, chew it over from every angle until we could spit it out and put it behind us. I knew that my silence seemed unnatural, but I didn't care. I drained the last few drops of tea, glutinous and clogged by the sugar that had settled in the bottom of the cup.

'You must have had a dreadful shock,' Naomi said. She put her hand on my arm, tentatively, her fingers fluttering on my sleeve. 'To come across it like that.' There was a pause; no more than a few seconds, but taut with unanswered questions. 'What were you doing, anyway, walking down that way?' she asked eventually, her voice diffident and light. 'I thought you were just downstairs.'

I didn't reply. I thought she would ask again, but she didn't. She simply collected up the teacups and took them out to the kitchen. When she came back, she stroked the top of my head and said that if I wanted we could do something, get out of the house, or if I would prefer it we could stay in. Stay in, go out, stay in, go out. The words echoed in my head, singsong like a nursery rhyme, draining themselves of meaning with each repetition. We stayed in, the television set rattling cheerily in the corner of the room, the light gradually darkening until we were sitting in the gloom. At some point, I vaguely registered Naomi standing up, going to switch on a lamp. I saw her face as she sat back down. She looked pale, stunned, as if she was uncovering piece by piece a truth that she would rather had stayed hidden. We sat together, the room full of conflicting sorrow. She didn't speak to me for the rest of the evening. I knew that she had never been impulsive or irrational. She wanted to be sure that she was right before accusing me of what she now knew, and what she was realising that perhaps she had always known.

I got up early the next day, before Naomi woke, or so I assumed—I had fallen asleep on the sofa, and there was no sign of her downstairs except for an envelope, Martin's name written across the front in her handwriting. I dressed quickly, put the card in my pocket, and set out to see him. As I walked up the path to his house, my feet felt unsteady and treacherous. The cold had hardened into ice, a faint slippery sheen covering the ground. I rang the doorbell, but no answer came. I stepped back and looked at the house. Its windows were dark and motionless. I rang the bell again. When a few more moments had passed I put my hand to the door and pushed. It swung open, left on the latch. Quietly, I entered. I saw him through the hallway, sitting at the kitchen table, staring at the boiling kettle sending up a faint whine. It was the only sound. When I cleared my throat it felt as if I was shattering the air.

Martin looked up, his grey eyes vague and distracted behind glasses. 'Nicholas,' he said. 'Thank you for coming.'

I came forward into the kitchen, taking it in. Unwashed plates and coffee cups sat on the sideboard. Martin made a faint gesture with his hand, motioning me to sit down; it would take more than a family tragedy to burn out his ingrained courtesy. I sat.

'I thought I should,' I said. 'Naomi wanted to come, too, but I thought I should see you alone first. She sent you this.' I held out the card in my hand. Sadly drooping lilies in a long dark vase, a message of sympathy. Martin took it and looked at it for a long time before setting it aside.

'Thank you,' he said. I waited for him to continue, and when he did he took off his glasses and rubbed his eyes, his fists muffling his words. 'It's very peculiar, you know,' he said slowly. 'A scientist is used to the cycle of life. A scientist is also used to life's randomness, to there being no kindly regulating God. But it is very strange the way that at times like this something else takes over. All that I can think is that it seems very unfair. The concept of fairness—it has no place in science, really. But then neither, I suppose, does love,' he added. His voice was melancholy and detached.

'I suppose not,' I said.

Martin tipped his head back, placing two straight fingers neatly under his chin. It was a pose that I had seen him adopt before, usually when he was deep in thought, and it was a moment before I realised that he was simply using gravity to roll back tears into his eyes. 'Thank you for coming,' he said again. 'I'm afraid I must insist that you leave now, though.'

'Why?' I asked.

He sighed, replaced his glasses and stood up. Martin was not a tall man, but looming over me as I sat at the kitchen table, he somehow seemed imposing. 'Lydia said something to me before she left,' he said. 'I don't intend to tell you what it was. I have been thinking it over and over, though, ever since she left this house, and I have come to the conclusion that it can only mean one thing. I don't wish to dignify you with the chance to explain. I am sure that in the circumstances you will understand why our friendship has to end, and why I have to insist that you do not attempt to contact me again.'

I swallowed. I felt sick. 'Martin,' I began, standing up, stretching out a hand. He shook his head, a short clipped motion. The cold, haughty look on his face should have made his small, kindly features look ridiculous. Instead it gave him a kind of dignity so profound that I had to look away. 'I'm sorry,' I said, and turned to leave. Unexpectedly, he followed me through the hallway. As he held the front door open a flash of insight came to me. He wanted to show me out of his house, to finish things between us once and for all, to close the door and find some comfort in the meaning that the simple act reflected back to him.

I could not leave before asking a final question. 'Where is Louise?' I asked.

'My daughter is with her grandmother,' Martin said. He spoke the words confidently, and I realised that this, at least, was something he did not know, and perhaps had not thought to guess. I looked at him for a long moment. In other circumstances I might perhaps have fought for my daughter. For an instant I felt an angry righteousness thrum through my veins. She was mine by rights, my flesh and blood, and I had already been kept apart from her for too long, but as I looked at Martin, I realised my limitations. I had always thought of myself, with a mixture of contempt and pride, as more devoid of conscience than any man had a right to be. I had fucked his wife so many times and in so many different ways that they had all become muddled up in my head, and shared companionable drinks and conversations with him all the while, but somehow, I couldn't do him this final indignity. As I nodded and left, hearing the door slam behind me with bleak, crashing finality, I let her go.

I had walked the five miles to Martin's house that morning, and I would have to walk them back. I set out, already knowing what awaited me when I returned. As clearly as a video playing inside my head, I could see the shock, the tears, the recriminations, the rehabilitation that could last months or maybe years. I knew despite this that I would stay with Naomi, and she with me. At that moment, I couldn't vocalise why, but I knew it and it brought me a kind of cold comfort. As I walked back through the frozen streets, I thought how beautiful and sad the black branches of the trees looked against the greying skyline. Looking at them almost hurt me. I barely wanted to admit it, but something told me that this was how it would be from now on. There was no way to get rid of this weight in my heart. There was no way to divorce the pleasure of whatever was to come from this pain that seemed to numb my skin and narrow my veins. Lydia had been right. I couldn't escape her, and I wasn't sure if I wanted to, and this was the price that I had paid and that I would have to keep on paying, for ever, for the rest of my life.

As Nicholas speaks, emotion ripples across his face. He is not looking at Lydia, his eyes distant, as if he is seeing the past played out on a screen inside his head. He paints a picture that would have made anybody else feel sorry for him. A daughter, briefly found, then lost again, irretrievably so, by a choice that seemed closer to necessity. As he tells her of the many times since those days when he has wondered where his daughter is and what she is doing, Lydia has a sudden hysterical urge to laugh. As he tells her that in a way he is glad that he does not know his daughter, because the memories of the affair would then be too concrete, ambushing him every day, she wants to scratch her nails across his haughty reflective face and draw blood. But he sees none of this. Years of self-control over her emotions have made her face a mask. When she catches sight of herself in the mirror beyond his desk, the woman she sees staring back at her looks coolly serene, politely sympathetic, nothing more.

After what seems an eternity, his voice stops. He reaches for the green glass bottle at his feet and pours a slow, deliberate measure into the cut-crystal glass. The liquid sparkles as he raises it to his lips. When he has drunk, he sets the glass down again, so quietly that it seems they are in a soundless bubble, cocooned and apart from the world. She gets to her feet. Blood and air rush to her head.

'I should go to bed,' she says, her words cutting through the silence like knives.

He looks up, and nods. He doesn't see her for what she is, only this painted doll who means nothing to him. 'I shouldn't have said those things to you,' he says mildly. 'I expect I can count on your discretion.'

In the darkening shadows of the study, his face is lit by the green lamplight in such a way that she feels she can see his soul. She thinks that if she were to reach forward she could touch it, pull it out of him and leave him as nothing but an empty shell. 'Yes,' she says. 'You can count on me.'

She leaves the room and walks down the corridor, counting her steps in her head. She has used this strategy before, blinding her mind with numbers so as to avoid the unpleasant, vicious thoughts crowding in on her. It takes her forty-eight steps to reach the bathroom. Inside, she locks the door and touches her fingertips to her forehead. It is burning hot, a pulse humming beneath the surface of the skin like a caged bird trying to escape. The nausea overtakes her so swiftly and inevitably that she barely has time to drop to her knees. She rakes her hair back from her face and vomits into the toilet bowl, painfully, feeling her guts twisting and emptying. She leans her forehead on the cool white marble of the bowl, fighting dizziness, counting her heartbeats one by one until they have slowed into rhythm.

It feels as if a poison has been purged from somewhere deep inside. When I raise my head I realise that I'm not hiding any longer. False names, false identities . . . these things can't help now. She isn't part of me any longer, not the way she was; I've let my grip on her slip. I'm just me. I'm just Louise.

After my mother died, I didn't see my father for over two weeks. He was in no state to deal with me, so numbed and shell-shocked by the sudden violence of her vanishing that he could barely rouse himself to draw the curtains in the evening, let alone cope with a tearful five-year-old girl. This I found out later, much later. At the time, I understood his disappearance as little as I understood my mother's. When seventeen days had passed and he turned up at my grandmother's door, tired and grey and old but heart-wrenchingly familiar and loved, I ran to him and buried my face in his coat. I expected the pain to halve; only one parent lost instead of two. I soon realised that it didn't work like that.

I had always been a quiet child, but after my mother's death I became a parody of myself. I didn't want anyone else to enter our world, and I knew my father would never remarry. Finding Lydia had been a gift from the gods for him, an unexpected and unearned pearl landing in his lap. No one else would ever compare. We were on our own, then, and that was the way I wanted it too. I had watched my father carefully, and I had learnt his lesson. Love was not worth the risk. Even if the object of your love didn't end up crumpled across a steering wheel with their brains blown out against a stone wall, you could still get hurt.

I knew what Nicholas had done. A few weeks after she died, I found the letter he had sent her, pushed into the slats under their bed where I had crawled to sit in the hot dark air. I had no way of knowing whether my father had hidden it there, or whether he had not known it existed. In the thin shaft of light that filtered in under the bed, I slowly spelt out its words. Only time made sense of them. By the time I was old enough to appreciate the reality of the affair, I couldn't even contemplate the possibility of my mother being anything other—anything lesser—than what I remembered her to be. Nicholas, then, must be to blame. He had held some kind of power over her, tricked her into making a mistake, gathered her to him and then thrown her away. *I don't want to see you, speak to you, touch you: you are dead to me.* I wondered whether he had known that she would die, that his words had such power. I took the letter and hid it in my bedroom, and when we moved away a few months later, I kept it.

From then on three figures dominated me. One was my father. The second was dead; the third I never saw.

Martin I was with so much that if I closed my eyes he was still there. Round, kind, sad face. Long delicate fingers that knitted themselves together when he thought. Someone who would never leave you and who was always so close that despite his fragility it sometimes felt as if he was the only thing you could depend on.

Lydia I met only in my dreams. Blonde, smiling, unchanging, perfect, like an airbrushed photograph. Beautiful clothes and soft skin. Eyes that looked at you as if they understood you, both loving and distant at once. Someone you wanted to be close to, longed for, ached for.

Nicholas I barely remembered in reality, but I knew him. Clever, dangerous, cold. Black hair and dark eyes that made him look like the devil brought to life. A sharp, husky voice that could hypnotise women. Someone who could break things, who had the power to ruin a life and the detachment to walk away from it as if it had not mattered.

I wait outside Adam's bedroom, my hand on the door handle, delaying the moment when I have to see him again. I remember that only half an hour earlier I was desperate to be with him, to throw myself on to him and entangle my body with his, mingling sweat and skin. Already it feels like another life. I push the door open. Adam is lying on the bed, wearing nothing but a pair of black boxer shorts, hugging the tops of his thighs like slicked-on oil. I don't want to look at his body, to feel any stirring of desire, but I can't help it. Longing and revulsion fight inside my chest as I come and sit down on the edge of his bed. His hand travels lazily over the small of my back, round my waist and over my stomach, then lower, lower. I take his hand and hold it tightly, push it away.

'You O.K.?' he asks.

I shake my head. For a moment I imagine this scene rewritten; a sister coming to a brother with a problem to be shared, a companionable chat untainted by what we have done. I'm not sure that it could ever have happened. 'I'm not O.K.,' I say.

Adam scrambles to sit up. He looks apprehensive, a little boy about to be told off. 'What's up?' he says, his words tight and fearful.

I had thought it would be easier not to look at him, but strangely I feel that I need to meet his gaze. 'We can't see each other any more,' I say. 'I'm sorry, but there is no point in discussing it. It's impossible.'

'What?' he says. He frowns, his head tipped to one side, a parody of confusion. 'Why not?'

I shake my head, not trusting the words that he doesn't need to know not to spill themselves out if I speak. Adam has inched closer towards me, his hands appealingly placed on my waist. I feel the ugly chemistry buzzing between us; primal, powerful, but always with that dreadful undercurrent of resistance, of instinctive wrongness. I should have known. He is trying to kiss me, his lips searching for mine. I feel that nagging hunger waking up inside me, so recently uncovered, which will now have to be forced back underground and buried so deeply that it can never surface again. I want to scream with the unfairness of it. For a few light-headed seconds, I wonder whether this need matter. I let his mouth find mine, part my lips with his tongue, but as soon as I do so the nausea rises back up again. Our flesh, our blood, linked by a precarious bundle of genes. Linked by our father. '*No*,' I say, and push him away, so hard that he falls back against the bed.

When I dare to look at him again I expect to see hurt in his eyes, but instead he is angry. 'I knew it,' he says, his fingers tugging at his hair, wrenching it. 'I knew it. Why am I so fucking stupid?'

I am silent, watching him, unsure of what he means.

'Look,' he continues, 'she means nothing to me, Lydia, I promise you. I'll tell her not to contact me again. I should have done it ages ago, I don't know why I didn't, just some stupid fucking ego-stroking exercise, I suppose. It was just a cheap thrill, not like with us.' He gesticulates across the room, and I see he is pointing towards his mobile phone, lying on the desk next to his computer. 'I never just leave it lying around,' he says. 'It's almost like I wanted you to find out.'

Slowly, I piece together what he is saying. 'You think I looked through your phone?' I say.

'Well, yeah,' he says. 'How else would you know about it?'

I nod, slowly. 'Isobel,' I say.

'Well, yeah,' he says again. Now he looks cautious, concerned, as if he suspects he may have jumped to conclusions too quickly. 'That is why, isn't it?' he asks.

I wonder whether I should feel betrayed. The thought that he has been communicating with another woman, saying God knows what to her behind my back while telling me that he adores me and cannot believe his luck, is painful but somehow inevitable. I think: *Like father, like son.* 'Yes,' I say. 'That's why.' I am grateful that he has given me his guilt, that I don't have to feel that I am discarding him, throwing away what in other circumstances might have been the best thing that had ever happened to me.

'Well, please, let's at least discuss this,' he says eagerly. 'Anyone can make a mistake.'

'It wasn't a mistake, Adam,' I say. Detached, I register that I sound calm. Reasonable. 'I think Isobel is the one you should be with.' I see him open his mouth to interrupt, but I shake my head, raising my voice as I continue. 'I know you think that you care for me,' I say, 'but I also think that deep down you know that this is not right. You badly want it to be, I know that, but for some reason it just doesn't fit and you can't force it. You know what I mean, don't you?'

There is a long silence, and then he nods. Slumped on the bed, he looks defeated and young, all the stuffing knocked out of him. 'I really did want this to work,' he says. 'I'm not lying, I really do think you're amazing. I've never felt this way about any other girl. But—'

'It's not right,' I repeat.

'I guess not. In fact,' he says slowly, 'I suppose that me still being in contact with Isobel at all proves that, doesn't it? If everything was right with us, why would I have bothered?' He is looking at me hopefully, appealingly, obviously wanting me to pat his shoulder and tell him that he has hit the nail on the head. I want to tell him that he is wrong. That sometimes novelty and cheap thrills are the only lures that a man may need to look outside any relationship, even one where nothing seemed to be out of kilter, where everything fitted. And that if some men are more predisposed than others to this, then his bloodline must make him more predisposed than most, and that maybe he will always be looking out for the next thing, never satisfied with what he already has. But I don't. I just nod, and as I do so I see the tension drain out of his face and, cautiously, he smiles.

'I'm sorry it didn't work out,' he says, and stands up, comes towards me. He pulls me into his arms for a hug, resting his chin on the top of my head so that when he speaks again I can feel his words buzzing through me. 'I'd like to think we'll always be friends.'

'Yes,' I whisper. *And more than that*, I think, *much more*.

'Do you want to stay here tonight?' he asks, still holding me close against him. It has the ring of a proposition: one last night in Paris. Despite myself I feel a laugh bubbling up from inside me.

'I think I'd better sleep in one of the spare rooms,' I say. 'I'll take my case.'

'Hey,' he says jokingly, stepping back and raising his hands. 'You can't blame a guy for trying.'

We laugh together and then the moment passes as quickly as it came, and his face drops and everything feels sordid and sad. I snatch my case from under the desk and heave it on to my shoulder. 'I'll see you tomorrow,' I say. He nods, lips pressed together in such a way that it seems he might be trying to stop himself from crying. I don't want to be around for the moment when he loses control, if it comes. I slip out of the room and close the door quietly behind me.

In the red-painted room down the hall, I stand in front of the mirror and scrape my hair back from my ears, tie it back in a tight knot behind my head. I glance at myself from a distance, trying to see the boy that I could have been. I can't see anything of Nicholas in my face. Even when I approach the mirror and place my hands on the glass, I can't see him behind my eyes, dark and similar though they are. I know it proves nothing; I can't see Martin either. I can see him even less.

I lie down on the bed. Tomorrow, I will go home. I've been away too long, I tell myself, and I don't want to be here any more in any case, don't want to have to fight the thoughts of the unwelcome bond between us every time I see his face. But there's something I need to do first. I already know that Adam and Naomi must never know the truth. As little as Nicholas deserves them, they deserve this even less. Nicholas, though, is a different matter. I want him to know that I know who and what he is. I want him to know that, despite his physical claim, he will never be my father, and that I am choosing to be rid of him and Lydia and everything that they have done. As I lie there, I imagine confronting him, a perfect speech spilling out from my lips. I know that if we were standing face to face the words wouldn't come, just as they didn't come sitting there opposite him in the study, what now feels like a lifetime ago. I need to find another way. When the idea comes to me, it makes me gasp and put a hand to my chest. I can feel my heart tapping an unsteady tattoo against my fingers. Suddenly and clearly, I know what I have to do.

*

It is midday before I wake. I dress in white underwear and black clothes. The house is eerily silent, walls taut and tense as if they might crack. I brush my hair, seven long strokes in front of the mirror. Downstairs in the kitchen, I pour myself a tall glass of water and drink it down in one long gulp. I set the glass down on the draining board with a crash that splits the silence open. Slowly I walk through the hallway. Through the half-open lounge door I can see Naomi, stretched out on the buttercup-yellow sofa, reading. I hesitate for a moment, peering in at her. My lips part to say goodbye, so quietly that she cannot hear.

Carrying my case, I step out on to the driveway. Snow has fallen overnight, too wet to settle, gathering in greyish piles of slush along the gravel path. It collects and gathers on my shoes as I walk. It is so cold that my breath seems to freeze in front of my eyes, misting and fizzing into the air. I wait on the road for twenty minutes before the bus comes. My fingers are stiff and stupid as I fumble for my purse and feed the coins through the glass. On the upper deck the bus is clammy and humid, windows steamed up from the inside. I lean my head against the wet glass and watch indistinct shapes smearing across the windowpane as the bus carries me into the city. I get off when everybody else does and find myself on the High Street. Hundreds of shoppers jostle past me, bags full of Christmas presents and Christmas food. My own shopping list is short and cheap. I walk down to Boots and buy everything that I need. I think I see recognition and alarm in the eyes of the man behind the counter when I hand him my credit card, but of course it's all in my head, and I give him a painted smile as he hands me my bag.

Back out on the street I pause. I'm not sure where to go. Eventually I head back in the direction I have come. When no more than ten minutes have passed, the tall, Gothic structure of a college looms in front of me. I'm not even sure which one it is, but it doesn't matter. The porter doesn't look up when I pass through the lodge; to him I'm just another tourist. It takes me a while to find what I'm after. A stone staircase, leading down into a dark basement. I walk down the narrow stairs: four toilet cubicles with steel doors, one rusty shower, a row of scuffed metal washbasins. I go into the shower cubicle and lock the door.

I cast my clothes to the floor. My blue fingers search in my plastic bag and tear at the packet of bleach. The shower head sends out a reluctant trickle, quickening as I turn the handle. Cold water dampens my long dark hair and my breath hisses in sharply as it lashes at my body like a whip. I rub the dye over my scalp, drawing each handful of my hair through my fingers right to the tip. I can feel it burning at the roots, sparking and crackling like electricity. Naked, I sit back against the steel wall and wait. The hands of my watch crawl round. When the time comes I rip open the second packet of dye. A girl smiles out at me from the cover, blonde and beautiful, long hair whipping around her face in a way that reminds me of memories that I barely knew I had. I tip my head back and rake the dye through my hair.

When I have towelled it dry I pull my white underwear back on. I turn to my case. Under the lining the dress lies pressed and folded. White linen, straight and short, a slash of red silk running all along the hem. They wanted to bury her in it. Martin told me. He kept it for me. Seventeen years ago he washed and pressed it, wringing out the violence that clung to it, but as I raise it to my face I think I can still smell her in its folds. I had thought of it as a talisman, nothing more, the only thing I had left of her. It has not been worn since she died. I pull the zip all the way down and step into the dress. It moulds to my body as if it was made for me, white linen clinging to my hips and breasts like water as I zip myself inside. Red silk settles across my knees like a supple line of blood. Red shoes, arched and delicate, silver buckles perched on top like bows on a Christmas present. They fit my feet like Cinderella's glass slipper.

I stand up and go to the mirror, scissors in my hand. Framed by the curtain of white-blonde hair, the face doesn't look like mine. I comb the hair over my eyes with my fingers, hold it in front of my face and cut. I snip her fringe out across my forehead. Pale hair falls like ash into the basin below. When I step back, her outline bounces back at me.

I fetch the make-up I have bought and line it up on the ledge in front of me. I coax her out from under my skin. Blusher to define my cheekbones, make them crueller and sharper. Pale pink lipstick, plumping my lips and setting them in a new light, provocative and possessing. Light grey shadow to hollow out the socket of my eyes, cradle them like jewels in the paleness of my face. Emerald powder dusted across my lids, calling out the green that lurks around the pupils and making it shine.

When I step back again, my vision fails me for a moment and I can see nothing but bright shapes, bobbing crazily against the mirror. When they clear, they leave me light-headed and shaking. She is staring into my eyes. I have brought her back from the dead. But she doesn't feel like a mother. What she fills the room with feels close to evil.

I leave my possessions behind in the dark basement. When I step back into the outside world, the cold sinks its teeth into me and shakes me from head to toe. I'm shivering as I walk, ignoring the curious glances that flit across me as I go. Curiosity is not all that's in them. I see the lust in the men's eyes, the way their heads whip round and stare at me, the way their throats rise and fall as they swallow. This power feels corrupting, compelling. My hips sway under the thin dress. Under my feet, slush and ice slide against the heels of her red shoes, making me feel as if I am walking a tightrope. I can feel my cheeks burning, blood rushing hectically under the skin like fever.

When I reach the faculty they have already started to arrive. Tall men in dark suits, women in well-cut dresses and high-heeled shoes. I slip into the throng. Glasses of wine are lined up along a long table at the side of the waiting room, lines of white and red twinkling like fairy lights against a green tablecloth. I stretch out my hand and take a glass of white wine. It is sour, cold and sharp, prickling the back of my throat. Out of the corner of my eye I can see them again: men, talking to their wives but looking at me. I toss my long white-blonde hair back from my face and see a dozen of them following its curve and sweep with their eyes. All of them want me. They want to take my body and use it, suck the life out of it, just like him.

The heavy oak doors swing open. The crowd starts to pour through into the lecture hall. I follow. A man at the door is taking tickets, but I slip past him, manoeuvring quickly and lightly into the hall. I take my seat halfway back, at the aisle, next to a man of sixty or more. From behind his glasses, I can see his eyes roving furtively, darting back and forth from my legs to my breasts to my face and back again. I stare straight ahead and wait.

Nicholas strides on to the stage to a swell of applause. Gravely, he inclines his head. Like a conductor, he raises his black-clad arms to quiet the crowd. He goes to the microphone and starts to speak, and his voice rings out, harsh and cutting, across the full length of the hall. His knowledge is etched on his face. As he speaks his hands slash and grasp the air. His dark eyes burn into the crowd, seeing everyone, seeing no one. He has them all in the palm of his hand. I let him talk for fifteen minutes, perhaps more. He has settled into his rightful authority, pacing his speech, confident and brooking no denial. From time to time he pauses, searching around the room as if daring to find a man who will disagree with him, but the audience stays rapt and silent.

The rhythm of his words rolls around in my head. I rise to my feet and stand alone. The people around me start to mutter, nudge each other, frowning and whispering. I step into the aisle and walk towards him. My heels click on the wooden floor. Slowly, like a man in a dream, he turns. His voice grinds, falters and stops. Blood drains from his face. He grips the lectern for support, his lips parting with words that he does not know how to say. He looks as if he has seen a ghost. I walk closer, never taking my eyes off him, hypnotic, powerful.

He has forgotten the murmuring crowd. *Who are you?* he whispers.

NICHOLAS
2007

When I see her, I do not stop to think about the impossibility of her being there, or the strangeness of her sudden appearance through the crowd. The thoughts that pulse through me are deeper, dragged up from somewhere far beyond reason or rationality. She has come back to me. My words dry up in my throat. The speech that I have run through internally for weeks, honing and polishing every word, slips from my mind. I search for the next line. Briefly I glance down at the notes propped on the lectern in front of me. I see the scrawled words, but they might as well be written in hieroglyphics. Darkly curved symbols dance meaninglessly in front of my eyes. I feel my gaze dragged back to her, my heart beating in such a way that my whole body feels rocked with shock, and something close to fear.

As she comes closer I see that of course she is not Lydia at all, and yet she is. She has Lydia's clothes, Lydia's body, Lydia's hair, Lydia's high, sharp cheekbones. But she is someone I don't know.

'Who are you?' I whisper, and hear the words swept up by the microphone before me, whipping and echoing round the hall. I step away from the lectern. At first I can't help seeing the sea of faces seated before me, all with the selfsame expression: puzzled, uncomprehending, bordering on indignant. For a moment I hesitate, look back, but the impossibility of carrying on with the lecture, or of making any attempt to explain, is stronger than any other sensation. I mumble something, clear my throat, say it louder, to everyone, to no one. *You must excuse me.* And then I take her by the arm. My fingers close around solid flesh and bone, and I am half surprised. I lead her up the aisle away from them all, walking faster and faster until I can hear her high-heeled shoes clacking to keep up with my pace. As I let the oak door slam behind us, I can hear the murmurs of discontent explode into an outraged babble, but I close my ears to the throng and stride down the corridor. I lead her into a small, musty lecture room, heavy green curtains drawn across its windows shutting out the light. I back a chair up against the door, barring them from coming in and her from going out. And then I look at her again.

She is trembling, her perfectly painted lips parting to violently draw in air. I take her by the shoulders and stare at her. Under the white-blonde hair, the make-up and the white dress, I can see the other Lydia, the one I had met only as my son's lover, the one that I had thought I barely knew. Now I can see I never knew her at all. Facts and instincts fit together in my head. Names jumble, all mixed up. Lydia, Louise, Lydia, Louise. My daughter.

'I didn't know,' she says, so softly that I can barely catch her words. She is staring right back into my eyes, her own unblinking and fringed with dark lashes, the sweep of emerald across her lids coaxing out the green of her irises beneath the dark brown pools that I know now must be just like mine. Her tone is not plaintive. It's accusing, bitter. When she tosses her hair back from her face and lifts her chin, I see her mother's mannerism, queasily brought to life.

'Nor did I,' I say, and although we are talking at cross-purposes, we are both aware that the knowledge we both have and the gaps in that knowledge match up, fit us together, whether we want it or not.

She takes a short, sharp breath, as if unsure how to continue. I can feel my legs shaking beneath me, but I force myself to keep standing there, my hands on her shoulders. 'I've always blamed you,' she says. As she speaks she shrugs off my hands and steps backwards, the small of her back pressed into the chair against the door.

I don't need to ask her what for. There are so many things that she doesn't know and couldn't understand, but all the same I can't tell her that she is wrong and that I am blameless. I have always known that Lydia's death would not have happened without me in her life. I have always known that I tainted things, my love working like an unlucky charm, steering both of us towards disaster. I feel myself nodding mechanically, but even as I do I feel the inequality of my burden.

'It isn't the full story,' I say.

'I know that now.' She pauses. 'She should have told you about me. She should have told us both,' she says. She sounds reflective, almost cold. I wonder whether she too is imagining the family that she might have had, and whether she too is unable to tell if it would have been a happy one, and whether it might have been worth the pain of its inception.

'I know you don't want me,' she says, and then frowns a little, the line that deepens between her brows so strangely and suddenly familiar that I shiver. 'I know you never did,' she amends, as if for clarification.

'It's not that simple,' I say, and mean it.

She shakes her head. 'You have your family already,' she says. 'There's no space.'

In my heart I know she is right. The past two decades have bound me to my wife and son so tightly that the bonds feel impossible to unpick, even if I wanted to. Unwanted, a picture flashes into my head: Naomi's face, twisted with pain and dismay, if I were ever to take this trembling girl to her and explain who she is, ask her to accept her. We have spent years rubbing at the dark stain that shadows our relationship. In the past few, it seemed that it had all but disappeared, and the thought of reopening those wounds makes me feel dizzy and sick. I can't contemplate facing her, or facing Adam. And at the thought of Adam, something deeper stirs, something as yet nameless. Pictures I do not want to fit together with words. His hand on Louise's back, his lips touching hers, and more than this; the images flashing at me with sudden shock, my mind closing down from what they mean. I look at her. For a moment the thought darts through my mind, so quickly that I have no time to stifle it: she's just a woman—beautiful, desirable, dangerous. The knowledge half frightens me. Without wanting to, I wince and blink, turning my face away to hide the sudden smart of tears. When I look back Louise is nodding, as if I have confirmed her words.

'You have to understand something,' I say nevertheless, and suddenly it feels desperately important that she know this. 'However hideous things were at the end, I loved your mother. I loved her so much that I couldn't imagine my life without her, and if she was still alive, I think we would have found a way to be together in the end, despite everything.' I have never voiced these thoughts before, even to myself, but they pour out of me with such readiness that I know they have been lurking beneath the surface all along, and I can't stop them, even though I know that they may hurt her. 'I don't mean to imply that she never loved Martin,' I say, 'because she did, I know she did, but the relationship between us was different. I can't begin to make you understand—' I break off, all too aware of the truth of these words. 'However wrong it was, I loved her,' I say again. 'I still love her.'

Louise is staring down at her feet, at the red shoes with their silly silver buckles. 'But not me,' she says.

I swallow. Sudden sharp injustice pierces my chest, makes it hard to breathe. 'God,' I say. 'I never had the chance.'

She raises her eyes to mine, tips her head a little to one side, puzzled, thoughtful. All at once I want to step forward and take her in my arms, enfold her, protect her, but my limbs feel frozen. It's impossible. But she opens her mouth to speak again, and takes a step towards me, and I see her eyes glaze over, her hand go to her forehead, and she crumples to the ground, and suddenly it's possible after all.

I go and kneel beside her, gather her unconscious body against me and hold her tightly. I examine her, put my hand to her forehead and find it burning hot. I look around, unsure of what to do. The room is totally silent, watching me. Kneeling by Louise's side, for the first time in my life, I almost feel like praying.

Only a couple of minutes pass before I see her eyelids flicker, as if dreams are running hectically under their surface. Her lashes peel apart. She sighs, a long, slow sigh that seems to exhaust her. 'My father,' she says.

My heart thuds faster with the exhilarating shock of the words. 'Yes,' I say.

Her face creases. 'No,' she says, and I realise how stupid I have been. 'We have to call Martin. We have to call my father.'

We wait for Martin in a tiny shop-soiled café at the station. I have bought Louise a cup of coffee, and every now and then she takes a sip and then reverts to her huddled position, her hands clasped around the cup, my black coat around her shivering shoulders. I don't know what she said to him. Whatever it was, it was enough for him to say that he would be on the next available train. I want to ask, but the words stick in my throat. We have barely spoken since we left the café, but every now and then she looks at me from under curiously veiled eyelids, as if she is searching my face for something. Once, she half smiles, and I smile back, but as soon as she sees my response the smile drops from her own face and she looks away.

'I'm glad you came,' I say at last. I'm not sure whether it's wholly true, but part of me does feel glad. For so long now she's been a spectre at the back of my mind, stuck in time at five years old, still the grave, pigtailed little girl in her buttoned boots. Seeing her now, my heart already aches with her loss, but at least I have another picture to add to my memories.

She half shrugs, acknowledging me. 'I'll never forget this,' she says, and although she has not said that she is glad too, her words somehow seem closer to how I feel than my own.

'Louise,' I say. I want to say that I wish things had been different and that she could be a part of my life, I a part of hers. As I struggle to frame the words, her mobile lights up on the table in front of us, buzzing impatiently. She snatches it and listens.

'I'm still in the café,' she says. 'You just turn right.' When she puts the phone down her face is flushed and almost fearful. 'He's here,' she says.

I barely have time to prepare myself for the sight of Martin before he appears in the doorway. Silhouetted against the greying skyline as he flings the door open, he is taller than I remembered. As he comes closer I see that his face is strangely unchanged. Somehow, now that he is in his mid-sixties, it fits him in a way that it never did before. It is as if all his life he has been growing awkwardly towards this age, and now that he has reached it, he looks right, dignified and serene.

He crosses to Louise, with the short, quick steps that I remember, and embraces her. I watch her lean her head against his neck, bury her face against him. Her shoulders shake briefly, as if convulsed by a burst of tears. He smooths the hair back from her face, his eyes wide and shocked at its colour. Quietly, he speaks to her, words that I cannot hear, and she answers.

Minutes later he turns to me. 'Nicholas,' he says, and inclines his head. There is restraint in his look, but he has not lost the politeness of decades before. 'It's been a long time.'

Too long, I want to say, but I don't want to risk a denial.

Instead I simply nod. Martin looks back and forth between us, one delicate hand betraying his calm, scratching at the back of his neck uncertainly. His eyes prompt Louise.

'I went to a lecture Nicholas was giving,' she says. 'I was curious to see him after all this time. Afterwards, I felt ill, and I fainted. He helped me. He had no idea who I was. When I explained, he insisted on waiting with me while you came, and bought me a drink.' The lies pour out of her fluently, her voice mellow and sweet. She has her mother's knack for fabrication, and mine. I see Martin nodding, accepting her story, turning to me with some awkwardness.

'Well, I suppose I must thank you for that,' he says, 'but I think I should take Louise home now.'

At his cue she shifts and approaches me. 'Goodbye,' she says. I see a sadness flit across her eyes, elusive but unmistakable. I try to smile, and for just an instant she takes my hand and presses it. When she releases me, I feel her touch still burning into my palm. They go to the door together. I see Martin stop and speak to her again. She nods, and steps outside, out of my sight, away from me, and that's it. She's vanished, and at once, far quicker and with a bleaker finality than I could have imagined, it feels as if she was never there.

Martin is still lingering at the doorway. Sharply, he looks back into the café to where I am standing. He steps back inside, comes quickly to stand in front of me. I can see the wrinkles etched into his face, bathed in the harsh fluorescence of the strip lights above us. The tortoiseshell glasses that he always wore have been replaced with a more sober pair, black rimmed and delicate. They give him the air of a preacher, someone both sanctified and irreproachable.

He clears his throat. 'Nicholas,' he says. 'I also wanted to thank you for something else.'

The surprise of it forces a sharp, embarrassed laugh out of me. 'What on earth for?' I ask.

He is silent for a long time. I can hear the strip lights humming above our heads, the background bustle of plates being served and customers chatting. 'For my daughter,' he says at last. 'For Louise.'

Looking at him then, I realise that he is very far from the fool I once thought he was, walking around with his eyes closed and his head in the air. He knows, and although I have no way of telling whether the realisation has come to him over many years of thought and painful discovery, or whether the sight of us together a few moments before has picked up some faint and telling resemblance that even I myself can barely see, I realise that he knows as well as I do that this truth is inescapable. It can never be unknown. I want to say that I am sorry. I want to try to explain. All the years of lying; the betrayal of a friendship that should never have happened; the failure to do him the justice of the truth many years before. I open my mouth to speak, but he shakes his head. There are some secrets that do not need to be told. Looking steadily at me, he holds out his hand, and I take it.

ACKNOWLEDGEMENTS

My lovely agent, Hannah Westland, Peter Straus, and everyone else at Rogers, Coleridge & White; Clare Reihill, Mark Richards and everyone at Fourth Estate; Dr Chris Greenhalgh; Charlotte Duckworth and the Ms B girls.

About the Author

Rebecca Connell graduated from Oxford University in 2001. She writes about youth culture and lifestyle for numerous magazines. *The Art of Losing* is her first novel. She lives in London.

FIC
CON

PA

6-15

DISCARDED

Newfoundland Area Public Library

Newfoundland, PA 18445 (570) 676-4518